TALES OF MOONLIGHT AND RAIN

Translations from the Asian Classics

市井ノ隠素位玄
才未隆己之志頽然泳
芳散倖乃義蘭恵
意哇出乎千華委絕
至眠丙子春題
世狗原生肖像
百二老童子

TALES

OF

MOONLIGHT

AND

RAIN

Ueda Akinari

A Study and Translation by
ANTHONY H. CHAMBERS

COLUMBIA UNIVERSITY PRESS
NEW YORK

Columbia University Press

Publishers Since 1893

New York   Chichester, West Sussex

Copyright © 2007 Columbia University Press

All rights reserved

Library of Congress Cataloging-in-Publication Data

Ueda, Akinari, 1734–1809.

[Ugetsu monogatari. English]

Tales of moonlight and rain : a study and translation by Anthony H. Chambers.

p. cm. — (Translations from the Asian classics)

Includes bibliographical references.

ISBN 978-0-231-13912-0 (cloth : alk. paper)

ISBN 978-0-231-13913-7 (pbk. : alk. paper)

ISBN 978-0-231-51124-7 (electronic)

I. Chambers, Anthony H. (Anthony Hood)

II. Title.   III. Series.

PL794.8.U3413   2006

895.6'33—dc22   2006015127

Printed in the United States of America

c 10 9 8 7 6 5 4
p 10 9 8 7 6 5 4

Frontispiece: Tosa Hidenobu, portrait of Ueda Akinari (1786).
(Tenri Central Library, Nara)

CONTENTS

ACKNOWLEDGMENTS

Haruo Shirane provided the initial spark by asking me to translate three stories from Ueda Akinari's *Tales of Moonlight and Rain* for his *Early Modern Japanese Literature: An Anthology, 1600–1900*, and then suggesting that I translate the whole collection. Deborah Losse, Lawrence E. Marceau, and Donald Richie deserve special thanks for their encouragement and suggestions. The College of Liberal Arts and Sciences at Arizona State University provided time for the work by giving me a year's sabbatical. Even with time, the study and translation would have been impossible without the pathbreaking work of earlier scholars and the compilers of the marvelous reference works we all depend on. Thanks go also to my incomparable circle of friends and colleagues, who sustain me emotionally and intellectually.

Michael Ashby read the first draft and made countless perceptive comments. I am also indebted to Jennifer Crewe, Anne McCoy, Irene Pavitt, and the rest of the staff at Columbia University Press. The anonymous readers recruited by the press offered encouragement, pointed out errors, and provided valuable advice. Any problems that remain are, of course, my own responsibility.

The translation is dedicated to all my teachers, especially, Ch'en Shou-yi, who introduced me to the study of East Asia; Makoto Ueda, who introduced me to Akinari; Robert H. Brower, who tutored me in Japanese court poetry; and Edward G. Seidensticker, my principal mentor over the years.

TALES OF MOONLIGHT AND RAIN

INTRODUCTION

Tales of Moonlight and Rain (*Ugetsu monogatari*), nine stories by Ueda Akinari (1734–1809) published in Osaka and Kyoto in 1776, is the most celebrated example in Japan of the literature of the strange and marvelous. It is far more, however, than an engrossing collection of ghost stories. Japanese scholars regard it, along with *Genji monogatari* (*The Tale of Genji*, early eleventh century) and the stories of Ihara Saikaku (late seventeenth century), as among the finest works of fiction in the canon of traditional Japanese literature. The reasons for this esteem have to do primarily with Akinari's elegant prose—a model of literary Japanese enriched by Chinese borrowings—and with his subtle exploration of the psychology of men and women at the extremes of experience, where they come into contact with the strange and anomalous: ghosts, fiends, dreams, and other manifestations of the world beyond logic and common sense.

Tales of Moonlight and Rain exerted a powerful influence in the twentieth century. Many novelists—including Izumi Kyōka (1873–1939), Tanizaki Jun'ichirō (1886–1965), Akutagawa Ryūnosuke (1892–1927), Ishikawa Jun (1899–1987), Enchi Fumiko (1905–1986), and Mishima Yukio

(1925–1970)—were avid readers of the collection. Two of the tales inspired Mizoguchi Kenji's cinematic masterpiece *Ugetsu monogatari* (1953; known to Western viewers as *Ugetsu*), which is widely regarded as "one of the greatest of all films."[1] Deeply rooted in its eighteenth-century cultural context, *Tales of Moonlight and Rain* is nonetheless a work of timeless significance and fascination.

The Early Modern Period in Japan

In 1603 Japan began to settle into a long era of relative calm and prosperity after a century of disastrous civil war (Warring States period [Sengoku jidai], 1467–1568) and nearly forty years of gradual pacification and unification (Azuchi–Momoyama period) under the successive warlord-unifiers Oda Nobunaga (1534–1582), Toyotomi Hideyoshi (1536–1598), and Tokugawa Ieyasu (1542–1616). The Tokugawa shogunate—the military regime established by Ieyasu—governed Japan for 265 years, an era that is commonly referred to as the Edo period, after the site of the shogun's capital, or the Tokugawa period. The emperor and the court continued to hold ultimate, though symbolic, authority in Kyoto during these years, but real power was wielded by the Tokugawa bureaucracy until it collapsed in 1868 and the Meiji emperor moved from Kyoto to Edo, which was then renamed Tokyo.

Cultural historians refer to the years from 1603 to 1868 as the early modern period and have divided it into three parts on the basis of cultural and political developments: early (1603–1715), middle (1716–1800), and late (1801–1868).[2] The first blossoming of early modern literature came toward the end of the seventeenth century, particularly with the work of three major figures: the fiction writer Ihara Saikaku (1642–1693), the poet Matsuo Bashō (1644–1694), and the dramatist Chikamatsu Monzaemon (1653–1724).

The period we are most concerned with here, the eighteenth century, can be regarded as the time when Tokugawa culture reached its high point.[3] The stability of the country under Tokugawa rule (among other factors) made possible a flourishing of artistic activity by and for commoners, who previously had enjoyed only limited access to high culture.[4] The man now recognized as the outstanding Japanese author of fiction in the eighteenth century was such a commoner, Ueda Akinari. By the time he began writing, a good education was no longer the monopoly of the court aristocracy, the samurai class, and the clergy: literacy rates were comparable to those in Europe,[5] and education had spread to large numbers of affluent residents of the great cities of Kyoto, Osaka, and Edo.[6] As a commoner, Akinari wrote primarily for an audience of other well-educated urban residents.

About the Author

Ueda Senjirō was born in 1734 in Osaka, then the commercial center of Japan.[7] Akinari, the name by which he is known, is a pen name that he began to use in the early 1770s. His mother, Matsuo Osaki, was the granddaughter of a peasant from Yamato Province who had gone to Osaka to become a merchant; the identity of his father is not known. In his fourth year, he was adopted by a prosperous merchant named Ueda Mosuke. Surviving a severe bout of smallpox that left several of his fingers malformed, the young Akinari had a comfortable childhood and received a good education, possibly at the Kaitokudō, one of the most prominent of the new schools chartered by the government to provide "an appropriately practical Confucian education" to the children of the merchant and artisan classes.[8] The curriculum would have included the Confucian canon—the Four Books (*Lun yü* [*Analects*] of Confucius, *Da xue* [*The Great Learning*], *Zhong yong* [*The Doctrine of the Mean*], and *Mengzi* [*Mencius*]) and the Five Classics (*I jing* [*The Book of Changes*], *Shu jing* [*The Book of Documents*], *Shi jing* [*The Book of Songs*], *Li ji* [*The Book of Rites*], and *Chun qiu* [*Spring and Autumn Annals*])—and Japanese classics, especially *waka* (thirty-one-syllable court poems), *Ise monogatari* (*Tales of Ise*, ca. 947), and *The Tale of Genji*.

Akinari's earliest surviving literary efforts are *haikai* verses included in several collections published in 1753 and 1755. Although composing haikai (playful, humorous) poetry, an outgrowth of *renga* (linked verse), began as an amusing pastime, it had evolved into a serious pursuit by the eighteenth century. Akinari continued to write haikai throughout his life—even if he did not take it as seriously as did some of his contemporaries[9]—and the pursuit brought him into contact with important literary figures in Osaka and Kyoto, including the painter and haikai poet Yosa Buson (1716–1783), and with proponents of *kokugaku* (National Learning or Nativist Study), which emphasized the philological study of ancient Japanese literature.[10]

Akinari never made his living as a writer, however. He married Ueyama Tama in 1760; they enjoyed a happy marriage but had no children. Akinari's adoptive father died in 1761, leaving to Akinari the family business and the responsibility for supporting himself, his new bride, and his adoptive mother, to whom he was devoted. They lost their business and all their belongings to a fire in 1771, after which Akinari turned to the study of medicine, probably under Tsuga Teishō (ca. 1718–ca. 1794), one of many intellectuals of the time who combined scholarship, writing, and medicine. Akinari worked as a physician in Osaka until 1787, when he retired from medicine and occupied himself with scholarship, teaching, and writing. How he supported his family during these years is unclear; he may have lived on accumulated savings, and he may have earned some money from teaching Japanese classics.

Along with his friend Buson and his sometime mentor Takebe Ayatari (1719–1774), Akinari was a classic example of

the eighteenth-century *bunjin*—a nonconformist, indepen-
dent artist, typically a painter and writer, who, though not
a member of the aristocracy, devoted himself or herself to
high culture, stood aloof from commercial or political profit,
and felt disdain for the "vulgarity" of contemporary society.[11]
What the bunjin of the mid-Edo period shared was "avoiding
the 'vulgar' (*zoku*) and placing themselves on heights beyond
the reach of the 'vulgar.'"[12] The bunjin ideal was inspired in
part by the Chinese *wen-jen* (written with the same characters as *bunjin*, signifying a person of letters) of earlier times,
and one aspect of the eighteenth-century bunjin's avoidance
of vulgarity involved the study of Chinese culture, including
vernacular Chinese fiction. This was true of Akinari.

Akinari's first works of fiction, however, owe little to Chinese models and much to the *ukiyo zōshi* (books of the floating
world) tradition of the late seventeenth and early eighteenth
centuries, with its typically lighthearted, satirical treatment
of the foibles of ordinary people. Akinari produced two collections of stories in this genre, *Shodō kikimimi sekenzaru*
(*A Worldly Monkey Who Hears About Everything*, 1766) and
Seken tekake katagi (*Characters of Worldly Mistresses*, 1767),
which turned out to be the last significant ukiyo zōshi.[13] Akinari quickly turned his attention to other interests.

One of these was National Learning. Akinari had begun a
serious study of the Japanese classics, especially waka, before
1760. A few years later, he studied with Ayatari and then with
Katō Umaki (1721–1777), a disciple of the great nativist scholar
Kamo no Mabuchi (1697–1769). This led him to abandon
the ukiyo zōshi tradition in favor of writing fiction that is far
richer and more serious, as well as treatises on such classics
as *Tales of Ise*; the *Man'yōshū* (*Collection of Myriad Leaves*, ca.
759), the oldest anthology of Japanese poetry; and the *Kokinshū* (*Collection of Ancient and Modern Poems*, 905), the first
imperially commissioned anthology of waka. His studies also
embroiled him in a famous scholarly debate, which continued over a number of years and on various subjects, with the

most noted of the National Learning scholars, Motoori Norinaga (1730–1801)—a confrontation that Blake Morgan Young
has characterized as "a clash between the rustic's blind faith
and the urbanite's critical scepticism," Norinaga, who lived
in Ise, being the rustic.[14] Their disagreements ranged from
phonology to mythology. Norinaga's arguments depended on
his absolutely literal reading of ancient Japanese compendia
of myth and history, while Akinari insisted on a more inter-
pretative, empirical approach.[15]

Akinari's studies of ancient Japanese literature merged
with bunjin ideals, especially the avoidance of vulgarity and
the fascination with Chinese fiction, to shape the solemn
beauty of his masterpiece, *Tales of Moonlight and Rain*. The
nine stories in this collection frequently allude to, quote
from, and borrow words and phrases from Japanese classics
and Chinese fiction and rise above zoku—even though most
of the characters in the stories are commoners—to achieve
the aesthetic ideal of *ga* (elegance, refinement), which had
been associated with Kyoto court culture.[16] No one doubts
Akinari's authorship of *Moonlight and Rain*, but he signed
the work with a pen name and never acknowledged that he
had written it. Although the collection is the principal basis
for his fame, he probably would have preferred to be remembered for his waka, his studies in National Learning, and his
expertise in a form of tea ceremony.

As a scholar, Akinari distinguished himself through edit-
ing and publishing works by Kamo no Mabuchi and his circle. In 1773 he wrote *Ya kana shō* (or *Yasaishō*), a commentary
on the particles *ya* and *kana*, but for some reason he would
not allow it to be published until 1787, when it appeared
with a preface by Buson. *Kaseiden*, Akinari's biographi-
cal study of the great *Man'yōshū* poet Hitomaro (late seventh–early eighth centuries), apparently was written in 1781.
The astonishing *Reigotsū* (ca. 1793) was "a comprehensive
work in six sections, one each on the names of Shinto deities, the names of Japan's provinces, noted products of the

various regions, poetry, terminology, and systems of *kana* orthography," but only the kana section survives.[17] In 1794 he published *Man'yōshū kaisetsu*, a short study of the ancient anthology, and in 1800 he began a comprehensive commentary on the *Man'yōshū*, which, however, he left unfinished. *Kinsa* (1804) and *Kinsa jōgen* (1804) bring together favorite poems from the *Man'yōshū*, with Akinari's commentaries on them.

Akinari also compiled several miscellanies. Two are collections of humorous and satirical stories: *Kakizome kigen kai* (*New Year's Calligraphy and a Sea of Changing Feelings*, 1787) and *Kuse monogatari* (*Tales of Eccentricity*, 1791; published 1822), whose title parodies *Ise monogatari*. *Tsuzurabumi* (*Basket of Writings*, 1805–1806), a collection of his prose and poetry, represents the final stage of Akinari's serious literary work, as he saw it; after it was published, he threw all his manuscripts down a well. *Tandai shōshinroku* (*A Record of Daring and Prudence*) was completed in 1808.[18]

Akinari wrote waka and haikai verse throughout his adult life and was one of the most distinguished waka poets of his time. His personal collection of waka, *Aki no kumo* (*Autumn Clouds*), was completed in 1807. He also distinguished himself as an expert in *senchadō* (the Way of *sencha*), a form of tea ceremony that employs tea leaves instead of the powdered tea of the better-known *chanoyu* ceremony. *Seifū sagen* (*Trivial Words on Pure Elegance*, 1794), his treatise on senchadō, is a classic in the field. Pottery implements that Akinari made for the ceremony survive.[19]

Akinari did not abandon fiction after *Moonlight and Rain*. In 1808 and 1809, he gathered ten of his stories and essays under the title *Harusame monogatari* (*Tales of the Spring Rain*). The collection is uneven, partly because Akinari died before he could polish it to his satisfaction, and perhaps because he wrote more for his own enjoyment than for publication. The pieces in *Spring Rain* are less tightly structured than the stories in *Moonlight and Rain*, and the

element of the marvelous and strange is relatively unimport-
ant. The language is plainer, and there is much less reliance
on Chinese sources. Perhaps even more than the tales in
Moonlight and Rain, the stories and essays in *Spring Rain*
attest to Akinari's studies in National Learning, particularly
in the emphasis he placed on *naoki kokoro* (true heartedness,
sincerity, guilelessness), which he apparently held to be the
essential nature of the Japanese people. The stories in *Spring
Rain* represent Akinari's most important fiction aside from
Moonlight and Rain.[20]

In 1793 Akinari and his wife moved from Osaka to Kyoto,
where they lived in poverty near the temple Chion-in, on the
east side of the capital. His wife died in 1797. Within a few
months, Akinari, whose vision had been failing for some
time, went blind, but then regained partial vision in one eye.
He continued his writing and scholarship as he moved here
and there in Kyoto, depending on friends for support, until
his death in 1809 on the twenty-seventh day of the Sixth
Month (August 8, in the Western calendar), in his seventy-
sixth year. His grave is at the Buddhist temple Saifukuji, near
the Nanzenji monastery.

Bunjin, National Learning, and Yomihon

The result of Akinari's synthesis, in *Moonlight and Rain*, of
a bunjin orientation with the National Learning was a new
genre: the *yomihon* (books for reading).

The distinction between ga and zoku arose from ancient
Chinese poetics and was embraced by Japanese artists of the
Tokugawa period. As the painter Gion Nankai (1677–1751)
said, "*ga* is neatness, propriety, elegance; *zoku* is vulgarity."[21]
This analysis was applied to all the arts, including painting
and literature. From the Japanese point of view, elegant literary genres encompassed Chinese poetry and prose, including fiction; Japanese court poetry and linked verse; classi-

cal *monogatari*, such as *Ise* and *Genji*; and *nō* dramas.[22] The traditional ga–zoku aesthetic was modified, however, by Japanese artists in the seventeenth and eighteenth centuries from a system that distinguished clearly between the courtly and the common, into a quest for elegance in realms that had traditionally been considered vulgar. Thus Bashō urged his students to raise their minds "to an enlightened state, [and then] return to *zoku*," by which he meant "practicing *ga* while remaining in the ordinary *zoku* world of haikai."[23] In short, "Bashō raised haikai poetry, traditionally a *zoku* form, to the world of *ga*, thereby confounding the traditional distinctions of *ga* and *zoku*."[24]

The objective of finding elegance in the vulgar dovetails with one of the goals of the scholars of National Learning, the "articulation of links between the mythological past, the recorded history of the aristocratic few, and the daily lives of common folk."[25] This agenda is related, of course, to the rising wealth and influence of the urban classes—primarily merchants and artisans—in the early modern period and their desire to participate in the high culture associated with the court aristocracy. The consequent blurring of the distinction between ga and zoku can be seen clearly in *Moonlight and Rain*. As a bunjin, Akinari rejected the common, and all the elegant genres are reflected in *Moonlight and Rain*. At the same time, the peasants (zoku) in "The Reed-Choked House," for example, are remarkably well versed in waka (ga), and the inclusion of haikai (zoku) in the same context as waka and Chinese poetry (ga) in "The Owl of the Three Jewels" implicitly raises haikai to the same level of elegance. In *Moonlight and Rain*, then, peasants and haikai participate in the aristocratic tradition as Akinari lifts them—and eighteenth-century Japanese fiction—from the vulgar realm of ukiyo zōshi to the elegant sphere of court poetry and monogatari.[26]

The National Learning agenda is reflected in *Moonlight and Rain* in at least two other ways. First, the philological study of ancient Japanese texts, one of the principal activities of National Learning scholars, influenced Akinari's choice of vocabulary and phrasing so often that a reader is hard put to count the examples.[27] Indeed, the abundance of archaic words and expressions from, and allusions to, the *Kojiki* (*Record of Ancient Matters*, 712), the *Man'yōshū*, *Tales of Ise*, the *Kokinshū*, *The Tale of Genji*, and other classics is the main reason that *Moonlight and Rain* is difficult to read. The classical lexicon also serves to associate *Moonlight and Rain* with court literature. Second, in opposition to the Confucian emphasis on rationalism, scholars of National Learning insisted that many things lie beyond the ability of human beings to understand, analyze, and explain—a belief that was based on an unquestioning acceptance of Japanese mythology.[28] While Akinari rejected Norinaga's uncritical embrace of ancient mythology, he did share the National Learning scholars' propensity to "celebrate the mysterious wonders of life,"[29] which takes an especially vivid form in *Moonlight and Rain*.

In synthesizing the bunjin aesthetic and National Learning, Akinari produced a masterpiece in a new genre—the yomihon, a more serious form of literature than its predecessor, the ukiyo zōshi. The term *yomihon* comes from the genre's characteristically heavy emphasis on the written text, as opposed to oral narratives and booklets in which illustrations play a central role. The language of yomihon, including *Moonlight and Rain*, is elegant, somewhat archaic, and often full of allusions to Chinese and Japanese antecedents. In short, the emphasis is on serious reading. The first yomihon writers were Tsuga Teishō, who probably instructed Akinari in medicine, and Takebe Ayatari, one of Akinari's mentors in National Learning. Teishō's *Hanabusa sōshi* (*A Garland of Heroes*, 1749) is considered the first yomihon. Its prose style is characterized by *wakan konkō* (a blend of Japanese and Chinese) and *gazoku setchū* (a blend of elegant and vulgar). Like *Moonlight and Rain*, *A Garland of Heroes* consists of nine stories adapted from Chinese sources to Japanese settings and grouped into five books, as does its sequel, *Shigeshige yawa* (1766). It seems likely that Akinari modeled his collection on Teishō's.[30] Ayatari's *Nishiyama monogatari* (*A Tale of the Western Hills*) appeared in 1768, eight years before the publication of *Moonlight and Rain*. In contrast to Teishō's and Akinari's yomihon, *A Tale of the Western Hills* consists of ten chapters grouped into three books and concerns a contemporary scandal in the capital. The prose style of *Moonlight and Rain* combines that of *A Garland of Heroes* with the elegant, neoclassical prose of *A Tale of the Western Hills*.[31] *Tales of Moonlight and Rain* is unquestionably the finest of the early yomihon.

About *Tales of Moonlight and Rain*

COMPOSITION AND PUBLICATION

An advertisement at the end of Akinari's story collection *A Worldly Monkey Who Hears About Everything* announces the forthcoming publication of two more works by the same author: *Characters of Worldly Mistresses* and "Shokoku kaisen dayori" (Tidings from a Cargo Ship in Various Provinces).[32] *Worldly Mistresses*, published the following year, repeats the advertisement for "Tidings from a Cargo Ship," adding "Sekenzaru kōhen" (A Worldly Monkey, Part Two) to the title, and announces a forthcoming work to be called "Saigyō hanashi utamakura somefuroshiki" (Saigyō Stories: Poetic Sites Bundled in a Dyed Cloth). The context and the titles suggest that both "Tidings from a Cargo Ship" and "Saigyō Stories" were to have been ukiyo zōshi like *A Worldly Monkey* and *Worldly Mistresses*, but neither "Tidings from a Cargo Ship" nor "Saigyō Stories" was published. In their place came *Tales of Moonlight and Rain* in 1776, with a preface dated 1768, the year after the publication of *Worldly Mistresses*.

Why the preface bears the date "Meiwa 5, late spring" (the Third Month of 1768) has been the subject of considerable research and discussion, since the preface and the stories were first published eight years later. There are good reasons to think that a preface that Akinari had drafted in 1768, as part of the "Saigyō Stories" project, was followed by eight years of studying, writing, and revising before the tales in *Moonlight and Rain* reached their present form.[33] Another possibility is that Akinari used the date of 1768 so that his work would appear to be contemporaneous with *A Tale of the Western Hills*, the preface of which is dated "Meiwa 5, spring, Second Month."[34]

Moonlight and Rain belongs, of course, to a different genre—yomihon—from *A Worldly Monkey* and *Worldly Mistresses* and, presumably, their planned sequels. Nevertheless, the titles of the unpublished works contain tantalizing suggestions of connections with *Moonlight and Rain*. First, both titles—"Tidings from a Cargo Ship in Various Provinces" and "Saigyō Stories: Poetic Sites Bundled in a Dyed Cloth"—anticipate the prominence of travel in *Moonlight and Rain* (in all but the last of the nine tales) and the location of all the stories in the provinces (as opposed to the great cities). Second, "Saigyō Stories: Poetic Sites Bundled in a Dyed Cloth" anticipates *Moonlight and Rain* in two additional ways: Saigyō, the beloved poet-monk of the twelfth century, appears in the first *Moonlight and Rain* story, "Shiramine"; and "poetic sites" (*utamakura*), place-names used frequently in poetry and listed in handbooks of poetic composition, are mentioned in almost all the tales, with special prominence in "Shiramine," "The Carp of My Dreams," "The Owl of the Three Jewels," and "A Serpent's Lust." In short, "various provinces," "Saigyō," and "poetic sites" in the titles of the unpublished ukiyo zōshi are important elements in *Moonlight and Rain*. There can be little doubt that *Moonlight and Rain* grew from the germs of "Tidings from a Cargo Ship in Various Provinces" and "Saigyō Stories." The resulting yomihon is a work of far greater psychological depth, narrative sophistication, and historical and philological awareness than *A Worldly Monkey* and *Worldly Mistresses*, and it incorporates two new elements: the adaptation of Chinese stories and the strange or anomalous.

TITLE

The title *Ugetsu monogatari* (literally, "rain-moon tales") comes from the phrase "misty moon after the rains" in the preface. It alludes to the nō play *Ugetsu*, in which Saigyō appears, as he does in "Shiramine," and in which rain and the moon are central images.[35] Commentators have also pointed to a passage in "Mudan deng ji" (Peony Lantern), a story in Qu You's *Jiandeng xinhua* (*New Tales After Trimming the Lamp*, 1378), one of Akinari's principal sources for "The Kibitsu Cauldron," which suggests that mysterious beings appear on cloudy, rainy nights and in mornings with a lingering moon. In any case, educated East Asian readers would probably guess immediately that a book containing the term "rain-moon" in its title would deal with the strange and marvelous.

SOURCES

Much has been written about Akinari's use of Chinese and Japanese sources in *Moonlight and Rain*—more than sixty Chinese sources, according to Noriko T. Reider, and more than a hundred Japanese.[36] (For the titles of important sources, see the introductions to the tales.)

Akinari used his sources in several ways. For some tales— "The Chrysanthemum Vow," "The Carp of My Dreams," "The Kibitsu Cauldron," and "A Serpent's Lust"—he borrowed the story line of a Chinese work, always with signifi-

cant modifications that ease the transition to a Japanese setting. Further, many scenes and situations in the tales echo
those in Chinese or Japanese sources. Examples include the
description of Katsushirō's house when he returns from
the capital in "The Reed-Choked House," which echoes the
"Yomogiu" (The Wormwood Patch) chapter of *The Tale of
Genji*; the depiction of the temple at Yoshino in "A Serpent's
Lust," which echoes the "Wakamurasaki" (Lavender) chapter of *Genji*; and the arrival of Kaian at the village in "The
Blue Hood," which echoes chapter 5 of *Shuihu zhuan* (*Water
Margin*, fourteenth century), attributed to Shi Nai'an and Luo
Guanzhong. Akinari also borrowed words and phrases from
his Chinese sources and from the Japanese classics he stud-
ied, especially the *Kojiki*, the *Man'yōshū*, *Tales of Ise*, and *The
Tale of Genji*. Finally, he seems to have structured individual
stories along the lines of Chinese tales and in imitation of
the structure of nō plays, and the organization of the collection as a whole seems to be influenced by the nō.

Far from trying to hide his indebtedness to Chinese
and Japanese precedents, Akinari undoubtedly hoped
and expected that his readers would derive pleasure from
recognizing his sources and appreciate his ingenuity in
adapting them. The borrowings, allusions, and echoes that
fill *Moonlight and Rain* also add richness and complexity
to the tales. As with the references to earlier texts in *The
Tale of Genji* and the use of *honkadori* (allusive variation)
in Japanese court poetry, the reader's awareness of other
texts interacting with Akinari's adds resonance and depth
to the reading experience.[37] The borrowings also draw the
reader into the text and involve him or her in the creative
process, as they reward, flatter, and delight the reader who
is erudite enough to recognize them.[38] Finally, the liberal
use of Chinese and courtly Japanese sources lifts *Moonlight
and Rain*, by association, into the elegant realm of *Water
Margin* and *Genji*, the two works that Akinari mentions at
the beginning of his preface, and, in the same way, lifts

Akinari himself into the lofty company of his Chinese and Japanese predecessors.

Even when Akinari's borrowings from Chinese sources are most direct—in "The Chrysanthemum Vow," "The Carp of My Dreams," "The Kibitsu Cauldron," and "A Serpent's Lust"—he ingeniously adapted the stories to Japanese settings and enriched them with a psychological complexity that is absent in their Chinese counterparts. Again and again, the reader is struck by the wonderful aptness of the time and place in which Akinari placed his tales. By making Akana Sōemon a samurai in "The Chrysanthemum Vow," for example, he introduced the themes of samurai loyalty and honor, whereas the character who corresponds to Sōemon in the Chinese story is a merchant who simply forgets the date of his appointment.[39] In "The Carp of My Dreams," Akinari introduced the crucial theme of Buddhist compassion by placing a Buddhist monk at the center of the story and invoked a long tradition of descriptive Japanese literature and art by setting the story at Miidera. In "The Kibitsu Cauldron," he introduced Shinto elements— prophecy and the role of spirits—by connecting the characters to the Kibitsu Shrine. In "A Serpent's Lust," he imbeds the Chinese-inspired story line in the context of Japanese legends about storied places: Kumano, Yoshino, and Dōjōji. In these carefully chosen settings, Akinari's characters reveal distinctive personalities, unlike the characters in his Chinese sources. As Robert Ford Campany has pointed out, the authors of Chinese anomaly accounts were not concerned with "the 'inner' nature (*xing* 性) of intellectual and emotional disposition, nor the structure of the self's ascent toward perfection through self-cultivation, but precisely humankind's *taxonomic place* among other kinds of beings, the nature of its *relationships* to other kinds."[40] In *Moonlight and Rain*, by contrast, it is precisely the characters' inner natures—*saga*, the reading in Japanese of the character read *xing* in Chinese—that concerned Akinari, as

Uzuki Hiroshi emphasizes in his commentaries.[41] Donald Keene makes the same point: "The very fact that one can describe Katsushirō's character places him in an altogether different category from Chao or Seiroku [who correspond to Katsushirō in the Chinese and Japanese antecedents to "The Reed-Choked House"], neither of whom displays any distinctive traits."[42]

NARRATING THE STRANGE

Moonlight and Rain has been called a collection of "ghost stories,"[43] "gothic tales,"[44] and "tales of the supernatural."[45] In Japanese, they are called *kaidan*; indeed, the edition of 1776 includes the subtitle *Kinko [present and past] kaidan*. As Reider says, "Kaidan are tales of the strange and mysterious, supernatural stories often depicting the horrific and gruesome," and the word *kaidan* means "narrating the strange."[46] No one would argue with "strange and mysterious," but "supernatural" is probably an inappropriate word, since what is considered to be supernatural in one culture is regarded as merely strange—but natural—in another.[47] Belief in revenants, spirit possessions, and other phenomena that we might call "supernatural" was widespread in eighteenth-century Japan and was apparently shared by Akinari.[48] If the term "supernatural" is inappropriate, so is "fantastic," as defined by Tzvetan Todorov, because "the basis of the fantastic is . . . the ambiguity as to whether the weird event is supernatural or not,"[49] and such ambiguity is absent in Akinari's world. "Strange" and "anomalous," words that have been used in the study of Chinese stories, are more useful when discussing *Moonlight and Rain*.[50]

Strange beings abound in Japanese art, folklore, and literature. They include *kami* (Shinto deities); spirits, deities, and divine beings from other traditions, such as Buddhist and Chinese lore; spirits of humans, living or dead, that can possess other people; revenants; *oni* (demons and fiends); *tengu* (goblins); trickster animals, such *kitsune* (fox) and *tanuki* (raccoon-dog); and other animals, such as serpents, that have strange powers. All of these, except kami and trickster animals, figure prominently in *Moonlight and Rain*. The vengeful ghost of the former emperor Sutoku returns to earth as king of the tengu in "Shiramine." In "The Chrysanthemum Vow" and "The Reed-Choked House," a faithful revenant fulfills a promise. In "The Owl of the Three Jewels," vengeful ghosts return as *asura* (J. *ashura* or *shura*), violent human beings who, in Buddhist lore, are reborn as violent demons. "The Kibitsu Cauldron" features the possessing spirit of a jealous woman—first when she is alive and then after she has died. In "A Serpent's Lust," a jealous serpent in the form of a woman seeks revenge on her husband. A monk turns into an oni and then miraculously stays alive for a year while meditating, in "The Blue Hood." "On Poverty and Wealth" features a little man who introduces himself as the spirit of gold. "The Carp of My Dreams" differs from the other stories in that no anomalous being plays a major role; instead, the story deals with the anomaly of a man who crosses the boundaries between human and animal, and between the waking world and the world of dreams.

Tengu and oni, which have no exact Western equivalents, require some explanation. Tengu are goblins said to live deep in the mountains. In Japanese art, they often resemble birds but sometimes take human form, with wings and a beak or long nose. They were "regarded as harbingers of war" because of their "insatiable desire to be destructive and to wreak havoc upon people's lives."[51] It is fitting, then, that the malicious spirit of the former emperor Sutoku becomes a tengu to exact his revenge. The Minamoto leader Yoshitsune, who had defeated Sutoku's enemies, was said to have learned martial arts from a tengu. Tengu were apparently brought under control by the Tokugawa government, which issued commands to them and expected them to obey.[52] Oni are usually depicted as grotesque, humanlike beings with horns, fangs, and claws, and clad in a tiger-skin loincloth or, sometimes, a monk's robes, as in the Ōtsu prints that depict an *oni-nembutsu* (oni dressed as an itinerant monk).[53] Some oni serve as soldiers in the Buddhist hell, but oni can also be benevolent, as was Ryōgen (912–985), chief abbot of the Tendai sect, who is said to have become an oni after his death in order to protect the Enryakuji temple complex on Mount Hiei.[54] Finally, the word *oni* is often applied to a cruel or frightening person. The mad abbot in "The Blue Hood" becomes an oni in this last sense of the word.

The categories suggested by Campany in his study of Chinese anomaly accounts help clarify the nature of the anomalies in *Moonlight and Rain*.[55] As Campany says, "Most (but not all) anomalies . . . occur at or across boundaries"[56]—for example, between humans and animals or the living and the dead. Two of Akinari's stories involve "anomaly by transformation,"[57] in which a being is metamorphosed across a boundary that normally separates humans from animals and the apparent from the real: "The Carp of My Dreams," in which a man seems to become a fish,[58] and "A Serpent's Lust," in which a woman turns out to be a serpent.[59] A category not posited by Campany—the boundary between mineral and animal—also figures in "The Carp of My Dreams," when paintings turn into real fish. Most of the stories in *Moonlight and Rain* involve "anomaly by contact," specifically, "contact with the realm of the dead":[60] "Shiramine," "The Chrysanthemum Vow," "The Reed-Choked House," "The Owl of the Three Jewels," and "The Kibitsu Cauldron," which also features the vengeful, possessing spirit of a living person, a type not mentioned by Campany. "The Carp of My Dreams" belongs to the category of "contact through dreams."[61] In the last story, "On Poverty and Wealth," contact occurs between a human being and a spirit.[62] Finally, two stories involve "sexual contact with non-human (or non-living human) beings":[63] "The

Reed-Choked House," in which "marital relations established during life continue after death,"[64] and "A Serpent's
Lust." "The Blue Hood" generally follows the pattern that
Campany has described for Buddhist tales (for a detailed
explanation, see the introduction to "The Blue Hood").[65] In
most of Akinari's stories, then, the anomalies correspond
to categories that had been used for centuries by Chinese
writers. This is not only because Akinari adapted Chinese
stories, but also because Chinese lore had been trickling
into Japan, along with Chinese Buddhist and secular texts,
for more than a thousand years and naturally influenced
the methods of Japanese storytellers.

SETTINGS

The chronological and geographical settings of each story in
Moonlight and Rain are shown in the table. The names of
provinces are accompanied by the names, in parentheses, of
the corresponding modern prefectures.

	Title	Date	Location
1	"Shiramine"	1168	Sanuki (Kagawa)
2	"The Chrysanthemum Vow"	1486	Harima (Hyōgo)
3	"The Reed-Choked House"	1455–1461	Shimōsa, Ōmi (Chiba, Shiga)
4	"The Carp of My Dreams"	923–931	Ōmi (Shiga)
5	"The Owl of the Three Jewels"	ca. 1616	Mount Kōya, in Kii (Wakayama)
6	"The Kibitsu Cauldron"	ca. 1500	Kibi, Harima (Okayama, Hyōgo)
7	"A Serpent's Lust"	794–1185?	Kii, Yamato (Wakayama, Nara)
8	"The Blue Hood"	1471–1472	Shimotsuke (Tochigi)
9	"On Poverty and Wealth"	ca. 1595	Aizu (Fukushima)

Three things are striking about the settings. First, they are specific. Second, all the stories except "The Owl of the Three Jewels" take place before the establishment of the Tokugawa shogunate in 1603. Third, none of the stories is set in any of the three great cities of Akinari's time—Kyoto (the capital), Osaka (the center of commerce), and Edo (the seat of the shogunate)—where most of his readers lived. In other words, the stories are specifically located at a chronological, geographical, and, therefore, political distance from Akinari's world. Various reasons can be imagined for this distancing, and it affects the stories in various ways.

None of the stories is set "in a certain province," but always in a real place and, with the exception of "A Serpent's Lust," at a more or less precisely specified time, not "once upon a time" or its Japanese equivalent, *mukashi mukashi*. This specificity has the effect of grounding the strange beings and events in the real world, thus lending plausibility to the stories. Specificity also makes the geographical and chronological distancing more effective than vagueness would have done.

Improvements in highways and other means of transportation—not to mention prosperity and relative freedom from bandits and warlords—made domestic travel in Japan fairly safe and increasingly popular during the Edo period. By contrast, the dangers of travel in the fifteenth century are portrayed in "The Reed-Choked House." Akinari is known to have traveled widely in Japan, possibly as far as the Kantō region (now greater Tokyo).[66] Journeys and far-off destinations thus were subjects of intrinsic interest to the author and his intended audience. The opening words of the first story—"Allowed by the guards to pass through the Ōsaka Barrier, he found it hard to look away from the mountain's autumn leaves, but he traveled on to Narumi Shore"—put the reader on notice that the narrative is moving away from the capital and toward the provinces. More than a love of travel is involved, however. From the perspective of the capital—and of Osaka and Edo—the provinces were more or less exotic places and definitely less civilized than the great cities. This conventional attitude has a long history in Japan. In *The Tale of Genji*, even Uji, just a few miles outside the capital, is depicted (with some hyperbole) as a wild, danger-ous place. Nor is this attitude unique to Japan. As Campany has written, "From the point of view of a center of urban culture, the 'distance' between the center and its periphery is seldom a matter of mere geographical space, or of the calendrical time required for the journey out and back. The peripheral is, from a centrist perspective, the anomalous—the external other."[67] Thus when a story moves away from the capital, the reader is prepared to encounter strange and wonderful things; mysterious happenings are more believ-able when they occur far from home; and a provincial setting facilitates the Japanese reader's "suspension of disbelief," in Coleridge's phrase.

Nevertheless, anomalies, even when they occur in dis-tant provinces, represent disorder, and it would not do to suggest that the Tokugawa regime permitted disorder any-where in Japan—especially in such extreme forms as canni-balism, necrophilia, and sexual relations between humans and nonhumans.[68] This is why the chronological settings of the stories, before Tokugawa rule began, is at least as significant as the geographical settings. As a collection of pre-Tokugawa anomalies in the provinces, *Moonlight and Rain* indirectly draws attention to the orderliness of the Tokugawa era and reinforces the normality of the center, the big city. "The Owl of the Three Jewels," the only story that is set during Tokugawa times, is the exception that proves the rule: it opens with praise for the Tokugawa regime and portrays one of the predecessors of the Tokugawa as having been so bloodthirsty that he was reborn as an asura. The old days, according to these stories, were not nearly as good as the present.

STRUCTURE OF THE STORIES

Much of Campany's analysis of the structure of Chinese anomalous accounts is applicable to the *Moonlight and Rain* stories.[69] He identifies ten typical structural elements, the last three of which are not present in all the stories he studies. I use "The Owl of the Three Jewels" to illustrate these elements in *Moonlight and Rain*.

1. *Chronological and geographical settings.* The opening paragraph hints that "The Owl of the Three Jewels" takes place during the Edo period; this time frame is made explicit later: "more than eight hundred years" after the founding of Mount Kōya. The second paragraph identifies the place: "In a village called Ōka, in Ise."

2. *Specifier.* The story provides "some indication . . . of the specific situation or string of events . . . , so that the focus is narrowed to a particular occasion when an event happened. This focusing is usually accomplished in part by introducing a protagonist."[70] In "The Owl of the Three Jewels," a "man of the Hayashi clan transferred his affairs to his heir, shaved his head . . . , [and] changed his name to Muzen."

3. *Process.* "Some sort of familiar process or type of interaction is set underway—some human activity with a predictable sequence."[71] Muzen "looked forward to traveling here and there in his old age" and sets out on a journey to Mount Kōya with his son.

4. *Hints.* The story provides clues that "something anomalous is about to occur."[72] The most obvious in "The Owl of the Three Jewels" are Muzen's decision to spend the night in front of Kōbō Daishi's mausoleum and the riveting cry of the owl.

5. *Limen.* Campany's list of liminal markers includes several that figure in "The Owl of the Three Jewels": travel through mountains, sunset, and a gateway.[73] In addition, the extraordinary historical and spiritual associations of Mount

Kōya make it, ipso facto, a liminal place, and the mausoleum itself represents liminality.

6. *Pivot.* "Something distinctly odd now happens and the reader—usually joined at this point . . . by the protagonist—becomes unmistakably aware of the strangeness of the situation."[74] Muzen, "taking out his travel-inkstone, . . . wrote down the verse by lantern light, then strained his ears in hopes of hearing the voice of the bird again, when, to his surprise, he heard instead the stern voice of a forerunner, coming from the direction of the distant temples and gradually drawing closer."

7. *Climax.* "The full force of the anomaly hits home to both protagonist and reader."[75] The climax of "The Owl of the Three Jewels" comes when Jōha identifies Hidetsugu and the other ghosts: "It was so horrible that the hair on Muzen's head would have stood on end, had there been any hair, and he felt as though his innards and his spirit alike were flying away into space." The climax continues to the point where the ghosts reveal their true form as asuras and threaten Muzen and his son.

8. *Response.* "Some tales . . . continue by reporting the protagonist's response" to the climax.[76] In "The Owl of the Three Jewels," Muzen produces the verse required of him and then faints.

9. *Outcome.* "In tales in which there is some response by the protagonist, comment is usually made on how things worked out."[77] In "The Owl of the Three Jewels," Muzen and his son wake up, return to the capital, and seek medical treatment.

10. *Impact.* "Very occasionally—especially in Buddhist miracle tales and in stories concerning the origins of cults and temples—further comment is made on reactions by persons other than the protagonist, or on some later situation relevant to the tale. In every case these comments concern the lasting impact made by the narrated event on a person or group of people or on the landscape."[78] "The Owl of the Three Jewels," of course, concerns the origin

of Mount Kōya and the legends surrounding Kōbō Daishi. The story concludes: "One day as he was passing the Sanjō Bridge, Muzen thought of the Brutality Mound [containing the remains of Hidetsugu and his family] and felt his gaze being drawn toward the temple. 'It was horrible, even in broad daylight,' he recounted to people in the capital. The story has been recorded here just as he told it." These sentences describe the lasting impact of the events at Mount Kōya both on Muzen and on the landscape (in the form of the Brutality Mound). The impact on other people is suggested in the survival of the story as it has been passed down from Muzen.

The structure of "The Owl of the Three Jewels" thus resembles that of Chinese anomalous accounts. A similar analysis could be made of the other stories in *Moonlight and Rain*, all of which follow this pattern. It is characteristic of Akinari's tales that the last three elements—response, outcome, and impact—which are often absent in Chinese stories, not only are present but are developed at length (except in "The Kibitsu Cauldron," "A Serpent's Lust," and "The Blue Hood," where they are present but abbreviated). The third through seventh elements are repeated several times in "A Serpent's Lust," which thus might be regarded as several stories in one. The response section of "On Poverty and Wealth" is exceptionally long, consisting of Sanai's conversation with the spirit of gold.

Another way to describe the *Moonlight and Rain* stories is in terms of the structure of nō plays, as many commentators have noted.[79] Indeed, Akinari invited comparisons by using the title of a nō play—*Ugetsu*—in the title of the collection. Four elements of nō structure can be found in some or all of the stories.

1. *Michiyuki*. Originating in the nō theater and found in other performance and literary genres as well, a *michiyuki*

(going on the road) is a literary convention in which the route, sights, and impressions of a journey are evoked with a litany of familiar place-names, often modified by *makura-kotoba* (pillow-words) or other epithets. In addition to providing a display of beautiful rhetoric and enriching the audience's experience by prompting the memory and imagination to envision famous scenes and their associations, a michiyuki guides the reader into a world apart, where unexpected, wondrous beings and events are likely to be encountered. Three of the stories in *Moonlight and Rain* include conspicuous michiyuki: Saigyō's poetic journey at the beginning of "Shiramine," Muzen's journey with his son in "The Owl of the Three Jewels," and Kaian's journey in "The Blue Hood." A fourth story, "The Carp of My Dreams," includes a particularly beautiful passage—Kōgi's tour of Lake Biwa—that resembles a michiyuki, although it does not serve the same structural function.

2. *Shite and waki.* A typical nō play has two important characters: the *shite* (central figure) and the *waki* ([man at] the side). The shite is preceded on the stage by the waki, who is frequently a traveler or an itinerant monk. The waki arrives at a famous site, where he meets a local person—the shite—whom he questions about the history of the area. As the waki draws out the shite's story, it turns out that the shite is actually the ghost of a historical figure who is still clinging to this world because of obsessive anger, desire for revenge, or love. Often the shite asks the waki to pray for his or her release from obsession so that he or she might be reborn in Amida Buddha's Western Paradise. Characters in at least four of the stories in *Moonlight and Rain* resemble the waki and shite roles, in greater or lesser degrees. Saigyō, in "Shiramine," corresponds to the waki as his michiyuki takes him to Shiramine. There he encounters the ghost of Sutoku, who corresponds to the shite, and they engage in a *mondō* (dialogue), a common element in nō plays.[80] As in a nō play, Sutoku's true form is revealed near the end of the

story. In "The Chrysanthemum Vow," Samon resembles the waki insofar as he elicits a story from Sōemon, who corresponds to the shite. Samon ceases to behave like a waki at the end of the story, however. In "The Owl of the Three Jewels," Muzen corresponds to the waki (and his son to a *wakizure* [waki companion]) as he travels to Mount Kōya. Hidetsugu's ghost, of course, corresponds to the shite (and his followers to *shitezure*), and the fact that Hidetsugu turns out to be an asura encourages the reader to recall nō plays, such as *Yashima*, in which the shite is an asura. Finally, the itinerant monk Kaian functions as the waki in "The Blue Hood," and the mad abbot can be thought of as the shite. The *Moonlight and Rain* stories are not nō plays, of course, and it would be a mistake to press the waki–shite analogy too far, but the resemblance is unmistakable.

3. *Dreams.* In some nō plays of the *mugen* (dream mystery) type, it is conceivable that the waki dozes off at the end of the first part of the play and dreams of his subsequent encounter with a ghost. This possibility exists in "Shiramine" and "The Owl of the Three Jewels." In "Shiramine," Saigyō "began to doze" just before Sutoku makes his appearance, and the strange events in "The Owl of the Three Jewels" take place after Muzen and his son have laid out their bedding and as they are trying to go to sleep. The central event of "The Carp of My Dreams" occurs in a dream, but parallels with mugen nō are less obvious in this story than in the other two.

4. *Jo-ha-kyū.* The fourth structural element of nō plays that is shared by the *Moonlight and Rain* stories is the *jo-ha-kyū* (introduction-development-climax) rhythm—common not only in nō, but in all Japanese traditional performing arts—in which the performance begins slowly, the pace gradually quickens, and a swift, dramatic climax is reached at the end. The development, typically the longest section, also consists of three parts, resulting in five sections altogether. This structure is fairly clear in, for example, "The

Blue Hood." In the introduction (jo), Kaian reaches Tonda and meets his host. In the first part of the development (ha), the host explains Kaian's odd reception and the problem that has been troubling the village. Kaian responds in the second part of the development, goes to the mountain temple, and meets the abbot. In the third part of the development, Kaian confronts the abbot's madness. Finally, in the climax (kyū), Kaian returns to the temple a year later and meets the abbot again, resolving the crisis faced by both the village and the abbot. The same analysis could be applied fruitfully to "Shiramine," "The Owl of the Three Jewels," "The Kibitsu Cauldron," and "A Serpent's Lust."[81]

The themes or motifs of several of the stories recall specific nō plays as well. "The Owl of the Three Jewels" resembles a *shuramono* (asura play), such as *Yashima*, in which the angry ghost of a warrior returns to the scene of his defeat. "The Reed-Choked House" employs the traditional theme of a woman who waits loyally and patiently for her husband or lover—a motif that is common in Japanese court poetry and in nō plays such as *Matsukaze* (*Wind in the Pines*) and *Izutsu* (*The Well Curb*). "A Serpent's Lust," which explicitly alludes to the Dōjōji legend, naturally recalls the nō play *Dōjōji* and its serpent-woman.[82]

STRUCTURE OF THE COLLECTION

Contemporary publishers of short-story collections commonly put the best—or the most appealing, exciting, or evocative—story first, in order to hook readers and keep them reading. If the publisher of *Moonlight and Rain* had followed this practice, he might have chosen to begin with "The Reed-Choked House," "The Kibitsu Cauldron," or "The Blue Hood," rather than with the stately, poetic "Shiramine," which opens the collection as we have it. The organization of *Moonlight and Rain* is so unlike that with which Western readers are accustomed that Kengi Hamada, in his translation, apparently found it necessary to rearrange the stories to conform more closely to Western tastes, beginning his version with "The Reed-Choked House."[83] In fact, the structure of the collection—the grouping and ordering of the stories—is complex and certainly not random.

The nine stories are arranged in five books:

Book One
  "Shiramine"
  "The Chrysanthemum Vow"
Book Two
  "The Reed-Choked House"
  "The Carp of My Dreams"
Book Three
  "The Owl of the Three Jewels"
  "The Kibitsu Cauldron"
Book Four
  "A Serpent's Lust"
Book Five
  "The Blue Hood"
  "On Poverty and Wealth"

This organization recalls two parallels: first, Teishō's *A Garland of Heroes* and *Shigeshige yawa*, which likewise consist of nine stories in five books; and, second, the five-part jo-ha-kyū rhythm of nō. This structure applies not only to individual plays, but also to the arrangement of the five kinds of plays into a five-play nō program.[84]

To some extent, *Moonlight and Rain* can be compared with a program of nō plays.[85] The five types of plays and their sequence in a full program are shown in the table.

It is tempting to try to apply this program of five plays to the five books of *Moonlight and Rain*—to say that Book One corresponds to the first category of nō plays, for example—

Number	Name	Typical central character (shite)
1	*wakinō* or *kaminō*	A deity
2	*shuramono*	The ghost of a warrior
3	*katsuramono*	A beautiful young woman
4	*kyōjomono* or *genzaimono*	A mad person or a modern person
5	*kirinō* or *ki(chiku)mono*	A demon or another strange creature

but the analogy breaks down almost immediately, since "The Chrysanthemum Vow" has little in common with a wakinō or kaminō, nor are "The Reed-Choked House" and "The Carp of My Dreams" at all analogous to shuramono. The five books of *Moonlight and Rain* do, however, parallel the five-part rhythmic structure of the nō program, with a gradual heightening of pace and excitement. The stories in Book One unfold at an appropriately dignified pace, with elevated language and high-ranking characters: an eminent poet-monk and the ghost of a deified former emperor in "Shiramine" and a scholar and a samurai in "The Chrysanthemum Vow." The excitement picks up in Book Two and continues to grow, as the status of the characters declines, through Book Four. In Book Five, the pace and excitement reach a climax in "The Blue Hood," and the collection ends with an auspicious prophecy of good times under the Tokugawa government, in "On Poverty and Wealth." In addition, there are unmistakable parallels between the five types of nō plays and the central characters of some of the stories and the order in which they appear. The ghost of the former emperor Sutoku, in "Shiramine," can be thought of as a deity, insofar as all emperors were believed to be divine descendants of Amaterasu, the sun goddess, and this one was actually enshrined at Shiramine. The second story, "The Chrysanthemum Vow," involves the ghost of a samurai, and "The Reed Choked House" focuses on a beautiful woman. With "The Carp of My Dreams" the collection departs from any correspondence with the subject matter of a nō program, but "The Owl of the Three Jewels" resembles a shuramono and draws the collection back toward the nō pattern. "The Kibitsu Cauldron" can be seen as a combination of a katsuramono, kyōjomono, and kirinō, since Isora starts out as a beautiful young woman and ends up as a possessing spirit. Finally, each of the remaining stories focuses on an anomalous creature: a serpent-woman, a necrophiliac and cannibalistic monk, and the spirit of gold. The sequencing of the nine stories does, then, approximate a nō program in its gradually accelerating pace and in the nature of the central characters. While the presence of the jo-ha-kyū rhythm might be explained as the automatic choice of a Japanese artist of the time, the downward progression of characters suggests a deliberate imitation of the nō form.

There are other ways of looking at the organization of *Moonlight and Rain*.[86] The most persuasive is the linking structure described by the prominent Akinari scholar Takada Mamoru.[87]

Stories 1–2. The clash of wills between a ghost and a living man in "Shiramine" is followed by the meeting of minds between a ghost and a living man in "The Chrysanthemum Vow." (The first two stories are also linked by an interest in Confucianism and by the theme of loyalty—Saigyō's to Sutoku, and Sōemon's and Samon's to each other. The intimacy and loyalty that bond Saigyō to his former master, Sutoku, in "Shiramine" anticipate an even closer relationship between two men in "The Chrysanthemum Vow.")

Stories 2–3. The fraternal loyalty of a ghost in "The Chrysanthemum Vow" is echoed by the marital fidelity of a ghost in "The Reed-Choked House," in which the loyal ghost is the woman who waits, not the man who returns. (There is a link by contrast, as well, in that the man who vows to return by a certain date keeps his promise in "The Chrysanthemum Vow," but not in "The Reed-Choked House." The parallel between the two stories is even closer if we think of Samon and Sōemon as lovers: the steadfast love between two men in "The Chrysanthemum Vow" is followed by the undependability of a husband in "The Reed-Choked House." Upper-class men of exemplary character are replaced by a pusillanimous farmer and his devoted wife. Miyagi, the ideal wife, anticipates another idealized wife, with a twist, in "The Kibitsu Cauldron," and a mockery of the ideal wife plays a central role in "A Serpent's Lust.")

Stories 3–4. The image of water links "The Reed-Choked House" to "The Carp of My Dreams": the former ends with the legend of a girl who threw herself into the water, and the latter concerns an artist who dreams that he swims about like a fish. ("The Carp of My Dreams" is a lighthearted, peaceful story with a happy ending, a cheerful interlude after the solemnity of "Shiramine" and "The Chrysanthemum Vow" and the pathos of "The Reed-Choked House" and before the darkness of "The Owl of the Three Jewels." Like Saigyō, in "Shiramine," Kōgi was an eminent monk, and "The Carp of My Dreams" makes many references to Buddhist teachings. The water motif is picked up again in "A Serpent's Lust.")

Stories 4–5. Kōgi, in "The Carp of My Dreams," comes back from the strange world of a watery dream to tell his story; similarly, Muzen, in "The Owl of the Three Jewels," barely returns alive from the strange world of Mount Kōya and a brush with the asura realm to tell others about his experience. Daytime turns to night; fish is replaced by owl. (The stories are also linked by the prominent role that Buddhism plays in each. If Muzen dreams of his encounter with Hidetsugu, the connection becomes even closer. The implicit contrast in "The Owl of the Three Jewels" between the revered Kōbō Daishi and the murderous Hidetsugu—both of them famous historical figures—echoes the contrast between Saigyō and Sutoku in "Shiramine" and anticipates that between Kaian and the mad monk in "The Blue Hood.")

Stories 5–6. The story of a cruel man who fell to the asura realm, in "The Owl of the Three Jewels," is followed, in "The Kibitsu Cauldron," by that of a betrayed woman whose jealousy turns her into an angry possessing spirit, and this time the man does not survive. (The Shinto context of "The Kibitsu Cauldron," as well as the amoral spirit of Isora, form a sharp contrast with the Buddhism of "Shiramine," "The Carp of My Dreams," and "The Owl of the Three Jewels.")

Stories 6–7. The lascivious husband of "The Kibitsu Cauldron" is followed, in "A Serpent's Lust," by a lascivious and jealous serpent-woman who, like the jealous wife of "The Kibitsu Cauldron," tries to kill her husband. (The reference to serpent-women in the first paragraph of "The Kibitsu Cauldron" anticipates "A Serpent's Lust." Both Shōtarō, in "The Kibitsu Cauldron," and Toyoo, in "A Serpent's Lust," are led by a servant girl to meet a mysterious lady at a house that turns out to be something other than what it first appears to be. In both stories, one or more wise old men tries to help: in "The Kibutsu Cauldron," he is a yin–yang master, while in "A Serpent's Lust," the first is a Shinto priest; the second, an overrated Buddhist monk; and the third, a Buddhist sage. Pervasive water imagery in "A Serpent's Lust" echoes that in "The Reed-Choked House" and "The Carp of My Dreams.")

Stories 7–8. The destructive power of lust is an issue in "The Blue Hood," as in "A Serpent's Lust," but the focus shifts from a serpent-woman to a previously upright monk who becomes a fiend, and the weak husband is replaced by a Zen "priest of great virtue." (Buddhism returns as a central concern, as in "Shiramine," "The Carp of My Dreams," and "The Owl of the Three Jewels.")

Stories 8–9. "The Blue Hood" is linked to "On Poverty and Wealth" by the important role of Chinese verse—the lines with which Kaian leads the mad abbot to enlightenment, and the prophetic lines bestowed on Sanai by the spirit of gold.

Stories 9–1. The last story in *Moonlight and Rain*, "On Poverty and Wealth," is linked to the first story, "Shiramine," since both involve a philosophical dialogue between a human and a nonhuman, and the gold spirit's prediction of a happy future for the nation echoes, and contrasts with, Sutoku's grim predictions of war. (Another parallel between the first and last stories is that "Shiramine" alludes to the Hōgen, Heiji, and Gempei conflicts, while "On Poverty and Wealth" reviews the struggles of the Warring States and Azuchi–Momoyama periods before predicting peace and prosperity under the Tokugawa. Tributes to the Tokugawa are included in the "Preface" and "The Owl of the Three Jewels" as well.)

At least two other patterns in the structure of *Moonlight and Rain* are noteworthy. First, anomalous beings and events grow more dangerous as the collection progresses and then less threatening again. They present no danger to Saigyō, Samon, Katsushirō, and Kōgi, in the first four stories. In the fifth, however, Muzen is nearly killed, and Shōtarō dies in the sixth. The danger recedes slightly in the seventh story, in which Tomiko is killed but Toyoo escapes, and the eighth, in which Kaian is threatened but survives because of his great virtue. Danger is not an element in the ninth story. The other notable pattern is the contrast between a steadfast character and an undependable, erratic, or vicious one. The motif is established in "Shiramine," with Saigyō's unshakable loyalty and Sutoku's thirst for revenge, and is repeated in all the stories except "The Carp of My Dreams" and "On Poverty and Wealth." Further, the loyalty that Samon and Sōemon show for each other in "The Chrysanthemum Vow" contrasts with the weakness of the central male characters in "The Reed-Choked House," "The Kibitsu Cauldron," and "A Serpent's Lust," and the theme is driven home with the warning in "The Chrysanthemum Vow": "Bond not with a shallow man."

About the Translation

Tales of Moonlight and Rain has already attracted an impressive company of translators and adapters, and yet it is a truism that English translations of the work have been inadequate. Takada understated the problem: "Readers of *Ugetsu Monogatari* in translation may not be able fully to grasp the classic beauty of the . . . original's literary style, its elegant phraseology, and its precise mode of expression, replete with concatenations yet without redundancy."[88] To reflect adequately in translation the style and tone of the original text is a tall order. Akinari was a great master of Japanese, but few of us who translate from Japanese are great masters of English. His prose is terse, elliptical, sinewy, highly literary, allusive, scholarly, dignified, elegant, and sometimes obscure—never slack or insipid. His is a neoclassical, self-conscious, quirky style, with many usages borrowed from archaic Japanese texts and Chinese sources, resulting in a rich, dense text that is meant to be read slowly and savored. I have tried to let the text speak for itself as directly as possible, rather than embroidering it with interpretations and explanations. Some of the existing translations strike me as wordy and insufficiently dignified, because they have gone too far in accommodating the Western reader and so fail to convey the tone, pace, and elegance of the original. Leon M. Zolbrod wanted his translation "to read as if the original were written in common English."[89] In this, he echoed Dryden: "I have endeavoured to make Virgil speak such English as he would himself have spoken, if he had been born in England, and in this present age."[90] Commonsensical as it sounds, this is an impossible goal.[91] In any case, Akinari certainly did not write in common Japanese.

Translators of *Moonlight and Rain* who attempted to "[leave] the reader alone as much as possible and [move] the writer toward the reader"[92]—in other words, to "naturalize" Akinari's prose into modern English—have vitiated the text.

In my translation, I have tried to leave Akinari alone as much as possible without doing violence to my mother tongue. I have looked for ways to convey in English the distinctive qualities of Akinari's prose more successfully than some of my predecessors have done, even though I am aware of my limitations as an English stylist and of the ultimate impossibility of a close approximation. Akinari's original (as opposed to the modern, edited texts on which we base our translations) presents each tale as a steady narrative flow, uninterrupted by paragraphs or quotation marks and only occasionally guided by punctuation. One effect of this presentation (which was common at the time) is to blur the distinction between narrative and dialogue: early editions give the impression that both narrative and dialogue are told in the voice of the narrator. I considered dispensing with quotations marks and other modern techniques for setting off dialogue, but finally decided that this would make the translation too odd and remote for the tastes of most readers. For the same reason, I have also used English tenses, despite the advice of those who emphasize the inherent differences between Japanese and English narrative.[93] Probably these compromises will satisfy no one, but I hope that my translation will bring readers of English a little closer to the tone, texture, and excitement of Akinari's masterpiece.

Some readers may think that I have accepted Vladimir Nabokov's advice to provide "copious footnotes, footnotes reaching up like skyscrapers."[94] In the case of *Moonlight and Rain*, I believe that extensive notes are desirable to explain exotic references and to demonstrate the rich intertextuality of the stories. Even so, the notes are far from exhaustive. I have emphasized sources that readers are most likely to be familiar with, such as *The Tale of Genji*, and secondary material in English. I hope that the notes will be sufficient for the scholarly reader and not too tedious for the casual. Information that is immediately useful for understanding the text is provided in footnotes; longer notes, of interest primarily to students and scholars, appear at the end of each story. Truly comprehensive notes can be found in Uzuki Hiroshi's indispensable *Ugetsu monogatari hyōshaku*. Many of my notes paraphrase Uzuki's.

Rather than inflating the footnotes further, I have provided an introduction for each story, with information on its title, characters, places, time, background, and affinities. I have presented this information in a format commonly used in nō texts, partly because it is a convenient arrangement and partly because *Tales of Moonlight and Rain* reminds me of a collection of nō plays.

For English equivalents of court titles, I am indebted to William H. McCullough and Helen Craig McCullough's *A Tale of Flowering Fortunes*.[95]

Personal names and ages are given as in the original: family name precedes given name, and the calendar years in which a character has lived are counted, rather than the number of full years elapsed since the day of birth. The premodern Japanese calendar consisted of twelve lunar months, of which the first three coincided with spring, the next three with summer, and so on. The Seventh Month, therefore, corresponds not to July but to the first month of autumn.

The translation is based on the text, notes, and commentary in Uzuki's *Ugetsu monogatari hyōshaku*. I have also referred to *Ueda Akinari shū*, edited by Nakamura Yukihiko;[96] *Hanabusa sōshi, Nishiyama monogatari, Ugetsu monogatari, Harusame monogatari*, edited by Nakamura Yukihiko, Takada Mamoru, and Nakamura Hiroyasu; and the introductions, translations, and notes in Wilfred Whitehouse's "'Shiramine': A Translation with Comments" and "*Ugetsu Monogatari*: Tales of a Clouded Moon," Dale Saunders's "*Ugetsu Monogatari*, or Tales of Moonlight and Rain," Kengi Hamada's *Tales of Moonlight and Rain: Japanese Gothic Tales*, and Leon M. Zolbrod's *Ugetsu Monogatari: Tales of Moonlight and Rain*. The translation would not have been feasible without the tireless efforts of Japanese scholars who have made the text as accessible as it is.

The woodcuts that accompany each story are from the edition of 1776. All the translations, including those in the notes, are my own unless otherwise indicated.

NOTES

1. Roger Ebert, "Misguided Ambition, Forbidden Passion," *Chicago Sun-Times*, May 9, 2004.

2. See, for example, Nakano Mitsutoshi, "The Role of Traditional Aesthetics," trans. Maria Flutsch, in C. Andrew Gerstle, ed., *18th Century Japan: Culture and Society* (Sydney: Allen & Unwin, 1989), p. 124.

3. Nakano, "Role of Traditional Aesthetics," p. 125.

4. C. Andrew Gerstle, "Introduction," in Gerstle, ed., *18th Century Japan*, p. xii.

5. Gerstle, "Introduction," p. xii.

6. Conrad Totman, *Early Modern Japan* (Berkeley: University of California Press, 1993), p. 354.

7. Since a full biography of Akinari is available in English, I offer only an overview of his life here. For a thorough treatment of his life and works, see Blake Morgan Young, *Ueda Akinari* (Vancouver: University of British Columbia Press, 1982). Other useful English-language sources on Akinari include Donald Keene, *World Within Walls: Japanese Literature of the Pre-Modern Era, 1600–1867* (New York: Holt, 1976), pp. 371–395; the introductions to Wilfrid Whitehouse, trans., "'Shiramine': A Translation with Comments," *Monumenta Nipponica* 1, no. 1 (1938): 242–258, and "*Ugetsu Monogatari*: Tales of a Clouded Moon," *Monumenta Nipponica* 1, no. 2 (1938): 549–567, and 4, no. 1 (1941): 166–191; to Dale Saunders, trans., "*Ugetsu Monogatari*, or Tales of Moonlight and Rain," *Monumenta Nipponica* 21, nos. 1–2 (1966): 171–202; and to Leon M. Zolbrod, trans. and ed., *Ugetsu Monogatari: Tales of Moonlight and Rain: A Complete English Version of the Eighteenth-Century Japanese Collection of Tales of the Supernatural* (Vancouver: University of British Columbia Press, 1974); Takata [Takada] Mamoru, "*Ugetsu Monogatari*: A Critical Interpretation," in Kengi Hamada, trans., *Tales of Moonlight and Rain: Japanese Gothic Tales* (Tokyo: University of Tokyo Press, 1971; New York: Columbia University Press, 1972), pp. xxi–xxix; Haruo Shirane, ed., *Early Modern Japanese Literature: An Anthology, 1600–1900* (New York:

Columbia University Press, 2002), pp. 563–567; Noriko T. Reider, *Tales of the Supernatural in Early Modern Japan: Kaidan, Akinari, Ugetsu Monogatari*, Japanese Studies, vol. 16 (Lewiston, N.Y.: Mellen, 2002); James T. Araki, "A Critical Approach to the *Ugetsu Monogatari*," *Monumenta Nipponica* 22, nos. 1–2 (1967): 49–64; Susanna Fessler, "The Nature of the Kami: Ueda Akinari and *Tandai Shōshin Roku*," *Monumenta Nipponica* 51, no. 1 (1996): 1–15; and Dennis Washburn, "Ghostwriters and Literary Haunts: Subordinating Ethics to Art in *Ugetsu Monogatari*," *Monumenta Nipponica* 45, no. 1 (1990): 39–74.

8. Totman, *Early Modern Japan*, pp. 302, 353. On the Kaitokudō, see also Tetsuo Najita, *Visions of Virtue in Tokugawa Japan: The Kaitokudō, Merchant Academy of Osaka* (Chicago: University of Chicago Press, 1987).

9. Young, *Ueda Akinari*, p. 12.

10. On kokugaku, see, for example, Shirane, ed., *Early Modern Japanese Literature*, pp. 599–630; and Peter Nosco, *Remembering Paradise: Nativism and Nostalgia in Eighteenth-Century Japan*, Harvard Yenching Monograph Series, no. 31 (Cambridge, Mass.: Harvard University, Council on East Asian Studies, 1990).

11. On bunjin, see, for example, Lawrence E. Marceau, *Takebe Ayatari: A Bunjin Bohemian in Early Modern Japan* (Ann Arbor: Center for Japanese Studies, University of Michigan, 2004), pp. 1–21; Mark Morris, "Buson and Shiki: Part One," *Harvard Journal of Asiatic Studies* 44, no. 2 (1984): 381–425, and "Group Portrait with Artist: Yosa Buson and His Patrons," in Gerstle, ed., *18th Century Japan*, pp. 87–105; and Patricia J. Graham, *Tea of the Sages: The Art of Sencha* (Honolulu: University of Hawai'i Press, 1998).

12. Inoue Yasushi, *Ugetsu monogatari ron—gensen to shudai* (Tokyo: Kasama Shoin, 1999), p. 3.

13. For fuller discussions of Akinari's ukiyo zōshi, see Young, *Ueda Akinari*, pp. 16–33; and Keene, *World Within Walls*, pp. 372–375.

14. Young, *Ueda Akinari*, p. 79.

15. On the debate, see Young, *Ueda Akinari*, pp. 78–87.

16. On ga and zoku in the eighteenth century, see Nakano, "Role of Traditional Aesthetics."

17. Young, *Ueda Akinari*, p. 109.

18. Excerpts from *A Record of Daring and Prudence* are in Fessler, "Nature of the Kami," pp. 8–15.

19. Graham, *Tea of the Sages*, pp. 22, 87–90, 92.

20. Barry Jackman, trans., *Tales of the Spring Rain* (Tokyo: University of Tokyo Press, 1975; New York: Columbia University Press, 1979). See also Young, *Ueda Akinari*, pp. 128–139.

21. Quoted in Nakano, "Role of Traditional Aesthetics," p. 127.

22. Marceau, *Takebe Ayatari*, p. 103.

23. Nakano, "Role of Traditional Aesthetics," p. 129.

24. Nakano, "Role of Traditional Aesthetics," p. 128.

25. Totman, *Early Modern Japan*, p. 366.

26. On Akinari's desire to change zoku into ga, see also Morita Kirō, *Ueda Akinari bungei no kenkyū* (Osaka: Izumi Shoin, 2003), pp. 583–585. Akinari was not the first bunjin to make this transformation in fiction. In his preface to *Nishiyama monogatari* (*A Tale of the Western Hills*), Kinryū Keiyū (1712–1782) praised Takebe Ayatari (also a bunjin) for his ability to "achieve ga while adhering to zoku" (Nakamura Yukihiko, Takada Mamoru, and Nakamura Hiroyasu, eds., *Hanabusa sōshi, Nishiyama monogatari, Ugetsu monogatari, Harusame monogatari*, Nihon koten bungaku zenshū, vol. 48 [Tokyo: Shōgakukan, 1973], p. 251). Keiyū's preface and *Nishiyama monogatari* have been translated by Blake Morgan Young: Takebe Ayatari, "A Tale of the Western Hills: Takebe Ayatari's *Nishiyama Monogatari*," *Monumenta Nipponica* 37, no. 1 (1982): 77–121.

27. Young, *Ueda Akinari*, p. 88.

28. Totman, *Early Modern Japan*, p. 363.

29. Totman, *Early Modern Japan*, p. 363. See also Keene, *World Within Walls*, p. 388.

30. Morita, *Ueda Akinari bungei no kenkyū*, p. 59.

31. Nakamura Yukihiko, introduction to *Hanabusa sōshi*, in Nakamura, Takada, and Nakamura, eds., *Hanabusa sōshi, Nishiyama monogatari, Ugetsu monogatari, Harusame monogatari*, pp. 37–38; Shirane, ed., *Early Modern Japanese Literature*, pp. 563–564.

32. Details in this paragraph come from Young, *Ueda Akinari*, p. 32; and Morita, *Ueda Akinari bungei no kenkyū*, p. 57.

33. Morita lists nine persuasive reasons in *Ueda Akinari bungei no kenkyū*, p. 58. Takada Mamoru argues that the whole collection was completed in 1768, in "Kaisetsu" for *Ugetsu monogatari*, in Nakamura, Takada, and Nakamura, eds., *Hanabusa sōshi, Nishiyama monogatari, Ugetsu monogatari, Harusame monogatari*, pp. 46–48.

34. Morita, *Ueda Akinari bungei no kenkyū*, pp. 58–59.

35. The nō play *Ugetsu* has not been published in English translation.

36. Reider, *Tales of the Supernatural in Early Modern Japan*, p. 138. On the influence of Chinese fiction in the eighteenth century and Akinari's sources, see the extensive notes and commentaries throughout Uzuki Hiroshi, *Ugetsu monogatari hyōshaku*, Nihon koten hyōshaku zenchūshaku sōsho (Tokyo: Kadokawa, 1969), and, in English, Marceau, *Takebe Ayatari*, p. 12; Keene, *World Within Walls*, pp. 375–378; and Zolbrod, trans. and ed., *Ugetsu Monogatari*, pp. 61–72.

37. On intertextuality in *The Tale of Genji*, see Haruo Shirane, *The Bridge of Dreams: A Poetics of The Tale of Genji* (Stanford, Calif.: Stanford University Press, 1987), esp. pp. 17–23. On honkadori, see Robert H. Brower and Earl Miner, *Japanese Court Poetry* (Stanford, Calif.: Stanford University Press, 1961), pp. 14–15, 286–291.

38. Most modern readers depend on footnotes, but Akinari's intended audience would have recognized many of his borrowings without an editor's assistance.

39. Reider, *Tales of the Supernatural in Early Modern Japan*, p. 90.

40. Robert Ford Campany, *Strange Writing: Anomaly Accounts in Early Medieval China*, SUNY Series in Chinese Philosophy and Culture (Albany: State University of New York Press, 1996), pp. 270–271.

41. Uzuki, *Ugetsu monogatari hyōshaku*.

42. Keene, *World Within Walls*, p. 383.

43. Keene, *World Within Walls*, p. 379.

44. In the subtitle of Hamada, trans., *Tales of Moonlight and Rain*.

45. In the subtitle of Zolbrod, trans. and ed., *Ugetsu Monogatari*; and the title of Reider, *Tales of the Supernatural in Early Modern Japan*, p. 1.

46. Reider, *Tales of the Supernatural in Early Modern Japan*, p. 7.

47. According to Rania Huntington, "Use of the term 'supernatural' in the Chinese context is problematic, because foxes and ghosts were not seen as distinct from the natural world" (*Alien Kind: Foxes and Late Imperial Chinese Narrative* [Cambridge, Mass.: Harvard University Asia Center, 2003], p. 2, n. 3).

48. Young, *Ueda Akinari*, pp. 48–50; Fessler, "Nature of the Kami," passim; Reider, *Tales of the Supernatural in Early Modern Japan*, pp. 46–52.

49. Christine Brooke-Rose, *A Rhetoric of the Unreal: Studies in Narrative and Structure, Especially of the Fantastic* (Cambridge: Cambridge University Press, 1981), p. 63. See also Tzvetan Todorov, *The Fantastic: A Structural Approach to a Literary Genre*, trans. Richard Howard (Cleveland: Press of Case Western Reserve University, 1973).

50. Books on Chinese literature that are useful in a study of kaidan include S. Y. Kao, ed., *Classical Chinese Tales of the Supernatural and the Fantastic: Selections from the Third to the Tenth Century* (Bloomington: Indiana University Press, 1985); Judith T. Zeitlin, *Historian of the Strange: Pu Songling and the Chinese Classical Tale* (Stanford, Calif.: Stanford University Press, 1993); and Campany, *Strange Writing*. Zeitlin defines "the strange" as "a cultural construct created and constantly renewed through writing and reading; moreover, it is a psychological effect produced through literary or artistic means. In this sense, the concept of the strange differs from our notions of the supernatural, fantastic, or marvelous, all of which are to some extent predicated on the impossibility of a narrated event in the lived world outside the text. This opposition between the possible and the impossible has been the basis of most contemporary Western theories of the fantastic, most notably Tzvetan Todorov's influential study" (*Historian of the Strange*, p. 6).

51. Pat Fister, "*Tengu*, the Mountain Goblin," in Stephen Addiss, ed., *Japanese Ghosts and Demons: Art of the Supernatural* (New York: Braziller, in association with the Spencer Museum of Art, University of Kansas, 1985), p. 105.

52. For the text of one of these edicts, see Fister, "*Tengu*," p. 110.

53. *Ōtsu-e* (Ōtsu prints) were hand-colored woodblock prints sold as souvenirs to travelers in Ōtsu, on the edge of Lake Biwa, in Shiga Prefecture.

54. Juliann Wolfgram, "*Oni*: The Japanese Demon," in Addiss, ed., *Japanese Ghosts and Demons*, p. 94.

55. Campany, *Strange Writing*, pp. 237–271.

56. Campany, *Strange Writing*, p. 266.

57. Campany, *Strange Writing*, p. 250.

58. Campany's "human/animal" (*Strange Writing*, p. 251).

59. Campany's "apparent/real" (*Strange Writing*, pp. 253–254). Since "A Serpent's Lust" is adapted from a Chinese story, it is not surprising that it fits Campany's description perfectly: "an apparent woman or man . . . seduces the opposite-sex protagonist of the tale, then transforms into her or his 'true form'—some species of animal" (*Strange Writing*, p. 254).

60. Campany, *Strange Writing*, pp. 259, 260.

61. Campany, *Strange Writing*, p. 265.

62. Campany, *Strange Writing*, p. 261.

63. Campany, *Strange Writing*, pp. 263–264.

64. Campany, *Strange Writing*, p. 264.

65. Campany, *Strange Writing*, pp. 321–328.

66. On Akinari's travels, see Young, *Ueda Akinari*, pp. 10, 16, 70–74, 76.

67. Campany, *Strange Writing*, p. 9.

68. One of the social functions of fantastic literature, according to Todorov, is that it allows for the treatment of forbidden themes, among
which he lists necrophilia (*Fantastic*, p. 158). The same could be said
for the function of setting a story at a geographical and chronological
distance.

69. Campany, *Strange Writing*, pp. 224–230.

70. Campany, *Strange Writing*, p. 224.

71. Campany, *Strange Writing*, p. 225.

72. Campany, *Strange Writing*, p. 225.

73. Campany, *Strange Writing*, p. 225.

74. Campany, *Strange Writing*, pp. 225–226.

75. Campany, *Strange Writing*, p. 226.

76. Campany, *Strange Writing*, p. 229.

77. Campany, *Strange Writing*, p. 229.

78. Campany, *Strange Writing*, pp. 229–230.

79. Virtually all Japanese commentators have pointed out affinities
between individual stories and nō. In English-language studies, parallels between nō plays and individual stories are noted in Araki, "Critical Approach to the *Ugetsu Monogatari*," pp. 61, 62, 63; J. Thomas
Rimer, *Modern Japanese Fiction and Its Traditions: An Introduction*
(Princeton N.J.: Princeton University Press, 1978), pp. 134–136;
Washburn, "Ghostwriters and Literary Haunts," p. 44; and Shirane,
ed., *Early Modern Japanese Literature*, p. 567.

80. As Washburn points out, Saigyō is far more assertive than is a typical
waki in nō ("Ghostwriters and Literary Haunts," p. 44).

81. Rimer draws attention to the jo-ha-kyū pacing in "The Kibitsu Cauldron," in *Modern Japanese Fiction and Its Traditions*, p. 135.

82. The parallels of "The Reed-Choked House" and "A Serpent's Lust"
with nō are mentioned in Shirane, ed., *Early Modern Japanese Literature*, p. 567.

83. In *Tales of Moonlight and Rain*, Hamada also assigned titles of his own
invention to the stories, which he arranged in this order (with my
versions of the titles): "The Reed-Choked House," "A Serpent's Lust,"
"Shiramine," "The Owl of the Three Jewels," "The Kibitsu Cauldron,"

"The Chrysanthemum Vow," "The Carp of My Dreams," "The Blue Hood," and "On Poverty and Wealth."

84. The grouping of plays into five categories developed in the eighteenth century, according to Earl Miner, Hiroko Odagiri, and Robert E. Morrell, *The Princeton Companion to Classical Japanese Literature* (Princeton, N.J.: Princeton University Press, 1985), p. 308.

85. The comparison has been suggested by Zolbrod in the introduction to his translation of *Ugetsu Monogatari*, pp. 74–75.

86. Morita summarizes other Japanese scholars' approaches to the question of structure in *Ueda Akinari bungei no kenkyū*, pp. 550–554, after offering his own analysis on pp. 535–550.

87. The rest of this paragraph summarizes Takada's analysis (with my supplementary comments in parentheses) in "Kaisetsu" for *Ugetsu monogatari*, pp. 50–53.

88. Takata, "*Ugetsu Monogatari*," p. xxi. Along the same lines, Araki wrote, "Those in the West who have read the *Ugetsu monogatari* in translation may have felt that some of the tales are curiously composed, and may have questioned their excellence" ("Critical Approach to the *Ugetsu Monogatari*," p. 49); Zolbrod argued that "one can hardly claim that the tales have been available [in English translation] in a suitable form for the general public" (*Ugetsu Monogatari*, p. 82); and Keene noted that "it probably would not occur to anyone reading 'Shiramine' in translation that Akinari was a writer of the first quality, considered by the Japanese to be worthy of a lifetime's research" (*World Within Walls*, p. 381).

89. Zolbrod, trans. and ed., *Ugetsu Monogatari*, p. 83.

90. John Dryden, "On Translation," in Rainer Schulte and John Biguenet, eds., *Theories of Translation: An Anthology of Essays from Dryden to Derrida* (Chicago: University of Chicago Press, 1992), p. 26.

91. According to Friedrich Schleiermacher, "Indeed, the goal of translating in such a way as the author would have written originally in the language of the translation is not only unattainable but is also futile and empty in itself" ("On the Different Methods of Translating," trans. Waltraud Bartscht, in Schulte and Biguenet, eds., *Theories of Translation*, p. 50).

92. Schleiermacher, "On the Different Methods of Translating," p. 42.

93. See, for example, H. Richard Okada, *Figures of Resistance: Language, Poetry, and Narrating in The Tale of Genji and Other Mid-Heian Texts* (Durham, N.C.: Duke University Press, 1991).

94. Vladimir Nabokov, "Problems of Translation: *Onegin* in English," in Schulte and Biguenet, eds., *Theories of Translation*, p. 143.
95. William H. McCullough and Helen Craig McCullough, trans., *A Tale of Flowering Fortunes: Annals of Japanese Aristocratic Life in the Heian Period* (Stanford, Calif.: Stanford University Press, 1980), vol. 2, pp. 789–831.
96. Nakamura Yukihiko, ed., *Ueda Akinari shū*, Nihon koten bungaku taikei, vol. 56 (Tokyo: Iwanami, 1968).

TALES OF MOONLIGHT AND RAIN

PREFACE

The Preface is written in *kambun*, or Japanese-style Classical Chinese. This practice was common in premodern Japanese texts, especially during the early modern period, when interest in Chinese literature reached new heights. The style afforded an author the opportunity to show that he was both erudite and au courant. Akinari's publications before *Tales of Moonlight and Rain* were, however, written entirely in Japanese. Composing the Preface in kambun might have been a way to signal the greater seriousness of the work that follows.[1]

The Preface opens with references to two of the greatest classics of Chinese and Japanese fiction: *Shuihu zhuan* and *Genji monogatari*. The first, written in the fourteenth century in colloquial Chinese and attributed to Shi Nai'an and Luo Guanzhong (both fl. before 1400), has been translated by Pearl S. Buck (as *All Men Are Brothers*), J. H. Jackson (as *Water Margin*), Sidney Shapiro (as *Outlaws of the Marsh*), and John Dent-Young and Alex Dent-Young (as *The Marshes of Mount Liang*). *Genji monogatari*, written in the early eleventh century in colloquial Japanese by Murasaki Shikibu (976?–1015?), has been translated as *The Tale of Genji* by Arthur Waley, Edward G. Seidensticker, and Royall Tyler. The unhappy fates of Luo and Murasaki, as recounted by Akinari, are based on old legends. In the Confucian view, which held that literature should be didactic and edifying, the authors' "wrongful actions" consisted of leading readers astray by writing fiction.

Akinari therefore adopts a modest tone in the Preface, disparaging his "scribbled" stories as "idle," "flawed," "baseless," and unbelievable, especially in comparison with the masterpieces of his two illustrious predecessors. It is tempting, however, to conclude that Akinari's modesty is ironic; that he wanted his work to be considered in the same league as *Water Margin* and *The Tale of Genji*; that he hints at retribution in the present, in the form of his crippled fingers; and that his offspring may well turn out to be deformed.[2] Akinari's choice of one Chinese and one Japanese precedent is appropriate, since he drew heavily on both Chinese and Japanese sources in writing the stories in *Tales of Moonlight and Rain*. The Preface serves to signal this borrowing to his readers.

Akinari lauds the Tokugawa regime, which governed Japan during his lifetime, with a reference to "a time of peace and contentment." He compliments the regime again at the opening of "The Owl of the Three Jewels," the fifth story, and at the conclusion of "On Poverty and Wealth," the last story in the collection. Maybe government censors concentrated on beginnings and endings, as many readers do to this day. The mention of wars in three other stories—"Shiramine," "The Chrysanthemum Vow," and "The Reed-Choked House"—also served to remind Akinari's readers that they lived in a peaceful era. Akinari's praise for his rulers was probably sincere.

Akinari used the pen name Senshi Kijin in none of his other works. *Senshi* is written with characters that signify "clipping limbs" or "pruning," but also suggest "clipped fingers," an allusion to Akinari's two fingers deformed by smallpox when he was in his fifth year. *Kijin* can mean "an eccentric," but here probably signifies "a cripple." Thus the possible meanings of the pen name range from "an eccentric who prunes branches" to (more pertinently) "a cripple with clipped fingers." The pen name also alludes to Qu You's *Jiandeng xinhua* (*New Tales After Trimming the Lamp*, 1378), since the first character, read *sen* in Japanese, is also the first character in the title of the Chinese story collection.

aster Luo compiled Water Margin and sired three generations of deaf-mutes. Lady Murasaki wrote *The Tale of Genji* and fell for a time into a dreadful realm.[3] No doubt it was for their wrongful actions that they suffered so. Look at their writings: each depicts many ingenious scenes and stories; their silences and songs are true to life;[4] rising and falling, their language rolls smoothly along; and so their work resonates like fine music in the reader's heart. Even after a thousand years, the events of those times show clearly in the mirror of the present. I, too, have scribbled down some idle tales for a time of peace and contentment. A pheasant cries, dragons fight:[5] I know that these tales are flawed and baseless; no one who skims them will find them believable. How, then, can I expect retribution, whether in the form of harelips or flat noses?[6] In the late spring of Meiwa 5, on a night with a misty moon after the rains have cleared, I compose this at my window and give it to the bookseller. The title is "Tales of Moonlight and Rain." Written by Senshi Kijin.

NOTES

1.   Morita Kirō, *Ueda Akinari bungei no kenkyū* (Osaka: Izumi Shoin, 2003), p. 61.

2. This is the view of Uzuki Hiroshi, *Ugetsu monogatari hyōshaku*, Nihon koten hyōshaku zenchūshaku sōsho (Tokyo: Kadokawa, 1969), pp. 17–18; and Morita, *Ueda Akinari bungei no kenkyū*, pp. 60–62.

3. "for a time": reflects a legend that Murasaki Shikibu was rescued by memorial services sponsored by her admirers.

   "dreadful realm" (*akushu*): in Buddhism, people who had committed bad actions were thought to be reborn in one of the three most undesirable realms of the Six Realms: hell, the lowest (*jigoku*); the realm of hungry ghosts; and the realm of beasts.

4. "silences and songs": style, rhythm, and tone.

5. "A pheasant cries, dragons fight": examples of exceptionally strange stories, drawn from the Confucian classics *Shu Jing* (*Book of Documents*) and *I Jing* (*Book of Changes*), respectively.

6. That is, "I do not expect my descendants to suffer deformities in retribution, since I admit that my stories are weird and baseless and so will not deceive anyone, as Luo's and Murasaki Shikibu's writings have done."

BOOK ONE

SHIRAMINE

TITLE

The title, "Shiramine" (White Peak), refers to a mountain in the coastal village of Matsuyama, now part of the city of Sakade, Kagawa Prefecture (formerly, Sanuki Province), on the island of Shikoku. To a knowledgeable reader, it evokes the tragic story of Emperor Sutoku, who was banished to Shiramine, where he died, was buried, and finally was enshrined.

CHARACTERS

There are only two characters in "Shiramine," both men who are important historical figures.

The first is the revered poet-monk Saigyō (1118–1190), born Satō Norikiyo. In his youth, he served Emperors Toba and Sutoku as a palace guard, but he took Buddhist vows and became a monk in 1140, initially with the name En'i. He is remembered for his extensive travels in Japan and, especially, for his remarkable poetry. His work appears in his personal collection, *Sankashū* (*Poems of a Mountain Home*),[1] and in imperial anthologies, especially the great *Shinkokin-*

shū (*New Collection of Ancient and Modern Poems*, early thirteenth century). Many stories and legends have accrued to his name over the years.

The second character is the abdicated, exiled emperor Sutoku (1119–1164, r. 1123–1141). After his abdication, he was referred to as the new retired emperor (*shin'in*), to distinguish him from his father, Retired Emperor Toba (1103–1156, r. 1107–1123).

PLACES

On Shiramine, see "Title."

"Shiramine" begins with a michiyuki (going on the road), in which a journey is evoked with familiar place-names, most of which had acquired the status of utamakura (poetic sites)—place-names used frequently in poetry and listed in handbooks of poetic composition. The michiyuki begins with Ōsaka Barrier, situated on Mount Ōsaka, between Yamashiro and Ōmi Provinces (Kyoto and Shiga Prefectures). It was the first barrier to be encountered by a traveler heading east from Kyoto, the capital. Mention of the Ōsaka Barrier signals to the reader that the world of the story lies in the provinces, far from the familiar, civilized capital. The route progresses to the east and north of Kyoto, along the Tōkaidō (highway along the Pacific coast between Kyoto and Edo) and beyond, and then doubles back and heads to the west of the capital, to Shikoku. All the place-names are utamakura:

> Narumi Shore: coastline, now swallowed up by the southeastern part of the city of Nagoya.
> Mount Fuji: although now dormant, an active volcano through much of history.
> Ukishimagahara: marsh in Suruga Province (Shizuoka Prefecture).
> Kiyomi Barrier: in Suruga Province.

Ōiso and Koiso: towns in Sagami Province (Kanagawa Prefecture).

Musashino: plain on which greater Tokyo stands. I have followed Edward G. Seidensticker's example in translating *murasaki* (a gromwell [*Lithospermum erythrorhizon*]) as "lavender."[2]

Shiogama: in Rikuzen Province (Miyagi Prefecture), near Matsushima, which is said to be one of the three most beautiful spots in Japan.

Kisagata: inlet on the Sea of Japan, in Ugo Province (Akita Prefecture).

Sano: in Ueno Province (Gumma Prefecture). A *funabashi* (boat bridge) was constructed by tying boats together, side by side, across a river, and laying planks on top of them.

Kiso: in Shinano Province (Nagano Prefecture).

Naniwa: old name for Settsu Province, the area around what are now the cities of Osaka and Kobe.

Suma: in Settsu Province, in what is now the city of Kobe.

Akashi: west of Suma, in Harima Province (Hyōgo Prefecture). Suma and Akashi are famous as the settings and titles of chapters 12 and 13 of *The Tale of Genji*.

Mio Hill (Miozaka): in the northern part of the city of Sakade, now called Mizuozaka.

TIME

Autumn of 1168 (Ninnan 3).

BACKGROUND

The dramatic historical events in the background of "Shiramine" would have been familiar to Akinari's readers through the chronicle *Hōgen monogatari* (*Tale of the Disorder in Hōgen*, 1219–1220?) and many other sources, including plays and legends; but the events are complicated and perhaps hard to follow for contemporary readers, whether Japanese or Western. The disorder began in 1141, with the decision by Retired Emperor Toba to force Emperor Sutoku, his eldest son and successor, to abdicate in favor of another son, Sutoku's half brother Narihito (whom Akinari mistakenly calls Toshihito). According to *Tale of the Disorder in Hōgen*, "It was shocking to force the previous emperor to retire, although he had no special incapacity. . . . In truth, he left the Throne against his will."[3] Narihito became Emperor Konoe at the age of three, with Toba governing on his behalf. When Konoe died in 1155, a disagreement arose over the succession. New Retired Emperor Sutoku—and many others at court—assumed that Sutoku's son Shigehito would succeed Konoe as emperor, but instead Toba unexpectedly elevated his own fourth son, Masahito, to become Emperor Go-Shirakawa (1127–1192, r. 1155–1158). It was rumored that Bifukumon'in, Toba's consort and Konoe's mother, suspected that her son had died because of a curse from Sutoku and persuaded Toba to bypass Shigehito in favor of Masahito.

When Toba died in 1156, the first year of Hōgen, Sutoku thought that he saw his opportunity. Resentful that he and his line had been shut out of the imperial succession, he led a revolt, known as the Hōgen Insurrection, against Go-Shirakawa; but his uprising was quickly suppressed, and he was banished to Matsuyama, where he died in exile eight years later. In "Shiramine," Sutoku takes credit for two other conflicts as well. He looks back to the first of these, which occurred during his exile, and he predicts the second, which began twelve years after Saigyō's visit in 1168 to Sutoku's grave.

The first conflict is the Heiji Insurrection, a brief war that began and ended in the last month of lunar 1159, the first year of Heiji (January 1160 in the Gregorian calendar). Fujiwara Nobuyori (1133–1159), a favorite of Go-Shirakawa, had been promoted repeatedly, despite his mediocrity, and aspired to the high position of major captain of the imperial bodyguard (*konoe no taishō*); but he was thwarted by Fujiwara Shinzei, whose lay name was Michinori (1106–1159), a scholarly, unscrupulous official who served Emperors Toba, Sutoku, Konoe, and Nijō (r. 1158–1165) and who was especially close to Go-Shirakawa. Nobuyori responded by conspiring with Minamoto no Yoshitomo (1123–1160), who had supported Go-Shirakawa during the Hōgen Insurrection, in a plot to seize power. Although Nobuyori succeeded in killing his nemesis Shinzei, the coup failed, Nobuyori was executed, and Taira no Kiyomori (1133–1181) emerged as the most powerful figure in Japan. According to legend, the Heiji Insurrection was caused by Sutoku's vengeful spirit. In 1191 Go-Shirakawa ordered that a shrine be built next to Sutoku's grave in order to placate his spirit. A branch of the Shiramine Shrine stands in Kyoto.

The second conflict is the epochal Gempei (Minamoto–Taira) War of 1180 to 1185. Minamoto no Yoritomo (1147–1199), the third son of Yoshitomo, had been spared after the Heiji Insurrection and, in 1180, raised an army in eastern Japan to attack the rival Taira clan, headed by Kiyomori. At the same time, Yoritomo's cousin Minamoto (Kiso) no Yoshinaka (1154–1184) raised an army in northern Japan. In 1183 Yoshinaka succeeded in driving the Taira from the capital. They fled west toward their power base in the Inland Sea, but suffered a devastating defeat at Yashima, not far from Sutoku's grave, and on the nearby waters of Shido. Finally, in 1185, the Taira met with complete defeat at Dannoura, in the straits near Akamagaseki (modern Shimonoseki). Emperor Antoku (1178–1185, r. 1180–1185) was drowned during the battle. This pivotal conflict, which led to the establishment of military rule under a shogun, is the subject of *Heike monogatari* (*The Tale of the Heike*, mid-thirteenth century) and many other works in every genre.

AFFINITIES

The principal sources from which Akinari adapted material for "Shiramine" are the military chronicles *Tale of the Disorder in Hōgen*, *Heiji monogatari* (*Tale of the Heiji Insurrection*, 1221?), *The Tale of the Heike*, *Genpei jōsuiki* (or *seisuiki*; *Record of the Rise and Fall of the Minamoto and Taira*, thirteenth century), and *Taiheiki* (*Record of Great Peace*, fourteenth century); the *setsuwa* collection *Senjūshō* (*Selected Stories*, mid-thirteenth century), formerly attributed to Saigyō; Saigyō's *Poems of a Mountain Home*; the nō play *Matsuyama tengu* (*Goblin of Matsuyama*, late fourteenth–early fifteenth centuries); Tsuga Teishō's *Hanabusa sōshi* (*A Garland of Heroes*, 1749), which includes a story about a debate between Emperor Go-Daigo and one of his ministers; the *jōruri* play *Sutoku-in Sanuki denki* (*Biography of Retired Emperor Sutoku at Sanuki*, 1756); and *Honchō jinja kō* (*Studies of Japanese Shrines*), by Hayashi Razan (1583–1657). It is notable that all these sources are Japanese, except for the Chinese tale from which the story in *A Garland of Heroes* was derived.

In addition, the text quotes from or refers to Confucius; Mencius; *Wuzazu* (*Five Miscellanies*, 1618), by the late-Ming official Xie Zhaozhe (1567–1624), which was reprinted and widely read in Japan from the 1660s on; *Shi jing* (*The Book of Songs*, eleventh–sixth centuries B.C.E.); Laozi's *Daodejing* (*Classic of the Way and Its Power*, fourth or third century B.C.E.); and the *Diamond Sutra*. Other sources and related works listed by Uzuki Hiroshi include *Nihon shoki* (*Chronicles of Japan*, 720), *Shiramineji engi* (*History of Shiramine Temple*, 1406), and several Chinese works.[4]

OTHER OBSERVATIONS

Mishima Yukio considered "Shiramine" to be "a perfect masterpiece" and wrote that, with "The Carp of My Dreams," it

was his favorite story in the collection.[5] Tanizaki Jun'ichirō
singled out the opening of "Shiramine" as "a masterpiece
of classical style," "an exemplary piece of Japanese prose,
employing the special strengths of our language."[6] He did
so in part because Akinari provides no subject in the opening paragraphs, even though the knowledgeable reader will
guess that the subject is Saigyō. (Indeed, Saigyō is not clearly
identified until the end of the fourth paragraph, and then
only indirectly, by his lesser-known name of En'i.) As Tanizaki
points out, the original reads smoothly without subjects, but
English requires the use at least of pronouns.[7] "Shiramine"
can even be read as a first-person narrative, and has been
translated as such by Leon M. Zolbrod.[8] Thus it is impossible to capture in translation the "special strengths," and
particularly the ambiguity, of the language of "Shiramine."

*A*llowed by the guards to pass through the Ōsaka Barrier,
he found it hard to look away from the mountain's
autumn leaves, but he traveled on to Narumi Shore,
where plovers leave tracks in the sand; to the high peak of
Fuji, with its constant smoke; to Ukishimagahara, Kiyomi
Barrier, the rocky shores of Ōiso and Koiso, the lavender-
rich plains of Musashino, the tranquil morning landscape
at Shiogama, the fishermen's thatched huts at Kisagata, the
boat-bridge at Sano, the suspended bridges of Kiso—none
of these places failed to move him, but, wanting also to see
poetic sites in the western provinces, he went in the autumn
of Ninnan 3 past the reeds that shed their blooms at Naniwa,
felt the piercing winds on the shores of Suma and Akashi,
and finally arrived at Sanuki, where, in the woods at a place
called Mio Hill, he rested his staff for a time. Here he built a
hut, not for comfort after pillows of grass on the long road,
but as a way to practice contemplation and self-discipline.[9]

He learned that, near this village, at a place called Shiramine, was the grave of the New Retired Emperor, and wishing to pay his respects he climbed the mountain early in the
Tenth Month. Pines and cypress grew so thickly together that
a misty rain seemed to fall even on a fine day when white
clouds trailed across the sky. A steep hill called Chigogadake
towered behind the site, while clouds and mist rose from the
depths of the valley, blurring even objects close at hand. In
a small opening among the trees, soil had been piled high
with three stones laid on top, and the whole was overgrown
with wild roses and vines. This melancholy mound must be
the imperial grave, he thought, as a shadow fell on his heart
and he could barely distinguish dream from reality.

When he had seen him in person, the emperor had con-
ducted the business of the court from the Royal Seats in the
Shishinden and Seiryōden, while the one hundred officials
had listened in awe and obeyed his commands, exclaiming
at the wisdom of their lord.[10] Even after abdicating in favor of
Emperor Konoe, he had occupied a jeweled forest on Mount
Hakoya—and to think that now he lay dead beneath this
wild mountain thicket where no attendants could be seen,
only the tracks of passing deer! Emperor though he was,
the karma of former lives clung fearsomely to him, and he
could not evade his wrongdoing. From this came thoughts of
mutability, and no doubt tears began to flow.

Wishing to hold a memorial service through the night, he
sat on a flat stone before the grave and, while quietly chanting a sutra, composed this poem as an offering:

"The view of the waves at Matsuyama may not have changed,
but like the tidelands, traces of my lord have gradually
  disappeared."[11]

l. 19 "jeweled forest": an elegant term for a palace.
l. 19 "Mount Hakoya": a conventional term for the residence of a retired
  emperor, deriving from the name of a mountain where immortal sages
  dwelt. Both terms come from Chinese legends.

He continued tirelessly chanting the sutra. How damp with dew his sleeves must have grown! As the sun set, the night was menacing here, deep in the mountains. He was cold with his bed of stone and fallen leaves for nightclothes; his mind clear and his body chilled to the bone, he began to sense something bleak and awful. The moon rose, but the thick woods allowed no light to penetrate. In the darkness, his heart grew weary and he began to doze, when a voice called unmistakably, "En'i, En'i."

Opening his eyes and peering into the darkness, he saw the strange form of a person, tall and haggard, but could make out neither the face nor the color or pattern of the robes on the figure that stood facing him. Saigyō was, of course, a monk with a strong faith in the Buddhist Way, and so fearlessly he replied, "Who is there?" The other said, "I have appeared because I wish to reply to the verse you have recited:

The ship that drifted here on Matsuyama's waves
has quickly faded into nothingness.[12]

I am glad that you have come."

Realizing that this was the ghost of the New Retired Emperor, he pressed his forehead to the ground and said, with tears in his eyes, "But why do you wander like this, Your Majesty? It was because I envied your having shunned this degenerate world that I have tried to draw closer to the Buddha's Way through my observances tonight; but for you to appear here, while it is more than I deserve, is surely very

l. 1   "How damp with dew his sleeves": damp sleeves conventionally con-
note tears, as well as dew.

l. 22 "why do you wander like this": in other words, "Why does your spirit
cling to this world, without achieving enlightenment?"

l. 23 "shunned this degenerate world" (jokuse o enri shi): has been interpreted
in two ways: as a reference to Sutoku's having taken Buddhist vows after
his failed uprising, or as a reference to his having died and, presumably,
achieved buddhahood.

sad for you. You must set your mind on leaving this world behind, quickly forgetting its attachments, and rise, through your good karma, to the level of a perfect Buddha." Thus he remonstrated with all his heart.

The New Retired Emperor gave a great laugh: "You do not know. The recent turmoil in the land has been of my doing. While I was still alive I devoted myself to the Tengu Way and caused the insurrection of the Heiji era, and since my death I have placed a curse on the imperial family. Watch! Soon I will bring about a great war in the land."

Hearing these words, Saigyō checked his tears: "I am astonished to hear these ill-considered, woeful sentiments from you. You were always known for your wisdom, and you understand the nature of the Royal Way. Let me ask you a question. Did you decide upon the Hōgen Insurrection believing that it was in accord with the Heavenly Deity's oracle? Or did you plan it out of selfishness? Please explain this to me in detail."

The Retired Emperor's expression changed: "Listen. The status of emperor is the highest among men. When an emperor corrupts morality, then one must follow the Mandate of Heaven, respond to the people's wishes, and strike.[13] No one can say that I was motivated by selfishness when, long ago in the Eiji era, I humbly acceded to my imperial father's command and, though innocent of any crime, relinquished

l. 1 "sad for you": it is sad for Sutoku that he still clings to this world, unable to achieve buddhahood.

l. 7 Tengu Way (madō): madō (literally, "evil way") leads one away from or interferes with the Buddha's teachings. Commentators agree that ten-gudō (the tengu way) is meant here. On tengu, see the introduction.

l. 14 Royal Way (ōdō): a Confucian concept that emphasizes enlightened rule through the virtues of benevolence (J. jin, Ch. ren) and righteousness (J. gi, Ch. yi), as opposed to military rule (hadō).

l. 16 Heavenly Deity (Ame no kami): Amaterasu Ōmikami, the sun goddess, who is said to have prophesied that her progeny would rule Japan without interruption.

l. 24 Eiji: the years 1141/1142.

the throne to the three-year-old Toshihito. When Toshihito died in his youth, I and others assumed that naturally my son Shigehito would rule the country next, but we were thwarted by the jealousy of Bifukumon'in, and the throne was seized by the Fourth Prince, Masahito. This caused deep bitterness, did it not? Shigehito would be an able ruler. What talent does Masahito possess? Ignoring a person's virtues and consulting a consort about the future of the realm were my imperial father's crimes. Nevertheless, as long as he lived, I maintained my sincere devotion to him and gave no sign of discontent; but when he died, I asked myself how long matters could go on like this, and summoned my courage. A mere vassal's striking down his king led to eight hundred years of the Zhou,[14] because the vassal had followed Heaven and responded to the people's wishes; and so no one can call it unreasonable that men who have the status to govern should try to replace a reign in which hens announce the dawn. You took your vows and became infatuated with the Buddha in a selfish desire to escape earthly passions and achieve nirvana in the next life. Now are you trying to sway me by forcing morality into the law of cause and effect, and mixing the teachings of Yao and Shun with Buddhism?" He spoke harshly.

Showing no fear, Saigyō moved forward and spoke: "In what you have just said, you have applied the principles of

l. 1   Toshihito: the name should be Narihito.
l. 12 "courage": that is, courage to resort to force in order to rectify the wrong that Sutoku believed had been done to himself and his son.
l. 16 "men who have the status to govern": Sutoku is referring to himself and his son Shigehito.
l. 17 "hens announce the dawn": a proverb signifying that a wife has usurped her husband's authority, referring here to Bifukumon'in's influence over Toba.
l. 22 Sutoku rebukes Saigyō for having embraced Buddhism ("law of cause and effect") and for trying to force ancient Confucian morality, as represented by the legendary sage-kings Yao and Shun (ca. twenty-fourth century B.C.E.), into the mold of Buddhism.

morality but have not escaped from desire and contamination.[15] There is no need to speak of distant China. In our own country, long ago, Emperor Ōjin passed over an older son, Prince Ōsasagi, to make his youngest son, Prince Uji, the Heir Apparent. When the emperor died, each brother yielded to the other and neither would ascend to the throne. Prince Uji grew deeply concerned when this situation continued for three years, and, asking himself why he should go on living and causing trouble for the people, took his own life, whereupon his older brother had no choice but to become emperor.[16] He did so because he revered the position of emperor, observed filial and fraternal devotion, was utterly sincere, and had no personal desires.[17] Surely this is what is meant by 'the Way of Yao and Shun.' In our country, esteem for Confucianism, and its position as the sole basis of the Royal Way, began when Prince Uji summoned Wani of Paekche as his tutor,[18] and so we can say that the spirit of these princely brothers was precisely the spirit of the Chinese sages.

"Also, a book called *Mencius*, I am told, says that at the beginning of Zhou, King Wu brought peace to the people in a fit of rage. One should not say that a vassal killed his lord. Rather, he executed a man named Zhou who had trampled on benevolence and righteousness.[19] Although the Chinese classics, histories, and even poetry and prose collections have all been brought to Japan, this book called *Mencius* alone has not yet come. The reason is said to be that all the ships carrying this book have met with violent storms and sunk.[20] Why? Since the great goddess Amaterasu established our country and ruled, there has never been a break in the succession of emperors; but if the sly, specious teachings of *Mencius* were transmitted to Japan, then some future villain might overthrow the divine progeny and say that he had done no wrong: realizing this, the gods all hated the book and raised divine winds to capsize the ships. Thus many of the teachings of the sages of another country are not suited to our land. Further, is it not said in the *Songs* that brothers might quarrel at home but must defend against insults from outside?[21] You, however, not only forgot the love of your own flesh and blood when the Retired Emperor died, but unfurled banners and raised bows to fight over the succession before his body had grown cold in the funerary palace—surely there is no worse crime against filial devotion than this.[22] The world is a sacred vessel.[23] The truth is that one who greedily tries to seize it will fail: Prince Shigehito's accession may have been the wish of the people, but when you resorted to wayward methods and brought chaos to the world instead of spreading virtue and harmony, even those who loved you until yesterday suddenly became wrathful enemies today, you were unable to attain your goal, you received an unprecedented punishment, and you turned to dust in this remote province. I beg you to forget your old resentments and return to the Pure Land."

The Retired Emperor heaved a long sigh and said, "You have clearly stated the rights and wrongs of the matter and rebuked me for my crimes. What you say is not without reason. But what can I do? Banished to this island, confined in the Takatō house at Matsuyama,[24] I had no one to serve me but those who brought my three meals a day. Only the cries of the wild geese that cross the sky reached my pillow at night, and I longed for the capital, toward which they might be flying;[25] and it broke my heart to hear the plovers at dawn,[26] crying to each other at the tip of the sandbar. Crows' heads would turn white before the time came for me to return to the capital: I would surely wander this shore as a ghost. For the sake of the future world, I devoted myself to copying five

l. 17 Pure Land (Jōdo): a Buddhist paradise in the west, presided over by the Buddha Amitābha (J. Amida). Here Saigyō implores Sutoku's wandering ghost to put his grudges behind him, let go of his worldly attachments, achieve enlightenment, and enter the Pure Land.

Mahāyāna sutras,[27] but there was no place to keep them on this desolate strand, where no sound of conch or bell is ever heard. I sent the sutras with a poem to the prince at Ninwaji, asking that at least the traces of my brush be allowed to enter the capital.[28]

> A plover on the shore—his traces go to the capital
> but he himself only waits and cries at Matsuyama.[29]

But Lesser Counselor Shinzei, taking charge of the matter, told the emperor that the sutras might be intended as a curse, and so they were returned unopened, causing me great bitterness. Since ancient times in both Japan and China, there have been many examples of brothers who became enemies competing for the realm; but no matter who interfered in his decision, for the emperor to ignore the law that requires consideration for members of the family[30] and reject even the traces of my brush—the sutras I copied, aware of the depth of my guilt and repentant for my wrong-heartedness—is something I can never forgive. In the end, I decided to throw off my resentment by dedicating those sutras to the Tengu Way: biting my finger, I wrote a petition with the blood and sent it with the sutras to the bottom of the Shito Sea,[31] after which I shut myself away, meeting no one, and fervently petitioned that I might become King of the Tengu—and then came the Heiji Insurrection. First I induced in Nobuyori the arrogance to wish for high rank, and caused Yoshitomo to become his ally. Yoshitomo was a hateful enemy. Everyone in his family, beginning with his father, Tameyoshi, gave his life for my sake, while Yoshitomo alone drew his bow against me.[32] Victory was in sight, thanks to Tametomo's valor and

---

l. 2   "no sound of conch or bell": that is, there were no Buddhist temples, where conches and bells were used to mark the hour, among other functions.

the strategy of Tameyoshi and Tadamasa,[33] but attacked by
a fire borne on a southwesterly wind, we fled the Shirakawa
Palace,[34] after which I tore my feet on the crags of Mount
Nyoi[35] and endured the rain and dew, my body covered with
oak-cuttings from the mountain people, until finally I was
arrested and banished to this island—and all of these tor-
ments arose from Yoshitomo's perverse plot. In revenge, I
cursed him by giving him the heart of a tiger or a wolf and
had him conspire with Nobuyori, so that Nobuyori committed the crime of defying the earthly deity and was struck
down by Kiyomori, who has no talent for military affairs.[36]
Retribution for killing his own father, Tameyoshi, came to
Yoshitomo when he was deceived by one of his own retainers: this was heaven's punishment![37] As for Lesser Counselor
Shinzei: inciting his twisted heart, which had always led him
to show off his erudition and block the advancement of others, I made him the enemy of Nobuyori and Yoshitomo, so
that in the end he abandoned his home and hid in a hole
at Uji, where he was finally discovered and captured, and
his severed head was exposed on the riverbank at Rokujō.[38]
This brought to a close his crime of sycophancy in returning
my sutras. Caught up with my anger, I took Bifukumon'in's
life in the summer of the Ōhō era and placed a curse on
Tadamichi[39] in the spring of the Chōkan era, and in the
autumn of that year I left the world myself; but the flames
of my resentment still blazed undiminished, and I became
the Great King of Evil, the master of more than three hundred. When my followers see happiness in others, they turn

l. 8   "heart of a tiger or a wolf": that is, a cruel, grasping heart.
l. 10 "earthly deity": the emperor; here Cloistered Emperor Go-Shirakawa.
l. 23 Ōhō: the years 1161 to 1163. Bifukumon'in actually died in the winter of
       1160.
l. 24 Chōkan: the years 1163 to 1165.
l. 27 "three hundred": there were said to be more than three hundred tengu
       in Japan.

it to calamity; seeing the realm at peace, they incite turmoil. Kiyomori's karmic reward has been large in this life, so that all the members of his clan have achieved high position and rank, and he governs as he wishes; but since Shigemori assists him devotedly, their time has not yet come.[40] You watch—the Taira clan will surely not last long. In the end, I shall take my revenge on Masahito to the same extent that he was cruel to me." His voice had grown steadily more ominous. Saigyō said, "Tied so strongly to the evil karma of the Tengu World, Your Majesty is separated one trillion leagues

l. 6 Masahito: Ex-Emperor Go-Shirakawa.

"He sat facing him
silently."

from the Pure Land. I shall say nothing more." He sat facing
him silently.

Just then, the peaks and valleys shook; a wind seemed
to knock over the forest and lifted sand and pebbles twisting into the sky. In the next instant, a goblin-fire burst from
below the Retired Emperor's knees, and the mountains and
valleys grew as bright as at noontime. Staring at the royal
figure in this light, Saigyō saw a face as red as though blood
had been poured over it; a tangle of knee-length hair; angry,
glaring eyes; and feverish, painful breathing. The robe was
brown and hideously stained with soot; the nails on the
hands and feet had grown as long as an animal's claws: he

had exactly the aspect of the King of Evil himself, appalling and dreadful. Looking to the sky, the Retired Emperor cried, "Sagami, Sagami." In response, a goblin flew down in the form of a hawk-like bird, prostrated itself, and waited for its master to speak. The Retired Emperor said to the goblin-bird, "Why do you neither take Shigemori's life quickly nor torment Masahito and Kiyomori?" The goblin-bird replied, "The Ex-Emperor's luck has not yet run out, and Shigemori's devotion keeps him beyond our reach. After one zodiac cycle, Shigemori's life span will come to an end;[41] if you wait for him die then, the luck of his clan will perish as well." The Retired Emperor clapped his hands in delight: "I shall destroy all these enemies, here in the sea before me!"[42] The horror of his voice, echoing in the valleys and peaks, was beyond description.

Witnessing the baseness of the Tengu Way, Saigyō could not hold back his tears. Composing another poem, he urged the Retired Emperor again to embrace the Buddha's Way:

"Long ago you may have dwelt, my lord, in jeweled splendor, but what good is that to you now?[43]

Royalty and peasants—they are the same," he cried, pouring out his feelings.

The Retired Emperor appeared to be moved by these words: his expression softened, the goblin-fire flickered and went out, and his figure faded from sight; the goblin-bird, too, disappeared without a trace; the moon, nearly full, was hidden by the peak, and in the obscurity of the dark woods Saigyō felt as though he were wandering in a dream. Soon the dawn sky brightened and filled with the fresh chirping of morning birds, and so he chanted the *Diamond Sutra* as a final offering[44] and then descended the mountain and

1. 8   Ex-Emperor: Go-Shirakawa (Masahito).

returned to his hut, where he quietly reviewed the events of the night before. Realizing that there had been no discrepancies in the Retired Emperor's account of the Heiji Insurrection, the fates of various people, or the dates, he was deeply awed and spoke to no one about it.

Thirteen years later, in the autumn of the fourth year of Jishō, Taira no Shigemori fell ill and died, whereupon the Taira Lay-Priest Chancellor, angry at his lord, confined him in the Toba Detached Palace and then tormented him in the thatched palace at Fukuhara.[45] When Yoritomo, contending with the eastern winds, and Yoshinaka, sweeping away the northern snows, emerged, the whole Taira clan drifted on the western sea, finally reaching Shido and Yashima in Sanuki, where many brave warriors ended up in the stomachs of turtles and fish, and, pursued to Dannoura at Akamagaseki, their young lord entered the sea and all their commanders perished. It was a strange, terrifying story, differing in no detail from the Retired Emperor's prophesy. Later, a shrine was built for him, studded with jewels and brightly painted, where he is honored and revered. All who visit the province should put up offerings, purify themselves, and pay their respects to this deity.[46]

l. 6   "fourth year of Jishō": the year 1179.
l. 8   Taira Lay-Priest Chancellor: Kiyomori.
l. 8   "his lord": Ex-Emperor Go-Shirakawa.

NOTES

1. Saigyō, *Poems of a Mountain Home*, trans. Burton Watson (New York: Columbia University Press, 1991).
2. Murasaki Shikibu, *The Tale of Genji*, trans. Edward G. Seidensticker (New York: Knopf, 1976), p. 102, n. *.
3. William R. Wilson, trans., *Hōgen Monogatari: Tale of the Disorder in Hōgen*, Cornell East Asia Series, no. 99 (Ithaca, N.Y.: East Asia Program, Cornell University, 2001), p. 3.
4. Uzuki Hiroshi, *Ugetsu monogatari hyōshaku*, Nihon koten hyōshaku zenchūshaku sōsho (Tokyo: Kadokawa, 1969), pp. 707–708.
5. Mishima Yukio, "*Ugetsu monogatari* ni tsuite," in *Mishima Yukio zenshū* (Tokyo: Shinchōsha, 1975), vol. 25, pp. 272–273.
6. Tanizaki Jun'ichirō, *Bunshō tokuhon*, in *Tanizaki Jun'ichirō zenshū* (Tokyo: Chūō Kōronsha, 1974), vol. 21, pp. 137–138.
7. Tanizaki, *Bunshō tokuhon*, p. 175.
8. Leon M. Zolbrod, trans. and ed., *Ugetsu Monogatari: Tales of Moonlight and Rain: A Complete English Version of the Eighteenth-Century Japanese Collection of Tales of the Supernatural* (Vancouver: University of British Columbia Press, 1974), pp. 98–108.
9. "contemplation" (*kannen*): refers to contemplating and meditating on the truth of Buddhist teachings and the path to enlightenment.

    "self-discipline" (*shugyō*): refers to a monk's maintaining the rules for proper conduct, as taught by the Buddha.
10. The Shishinden (Hall of the Royal Seat) was the main ceremonial building of the emperor's residential compound, and the Seiryōden (Hall of Cool and Refreshing Breezes) was the emperor's private residence.

    "one hundred officials": a formulaic expression for the many military and civil officials serving the court.
11. This poem is identical, except for the last word, to one by Saigyō, which begins with a headnote: "I traveled to Sanuki and searched for the site of the Retired Emperor's residence at a harbor called Matsuyama, but there was no trace / no tideland":

    > The view of the waves at Matsuyama may not have changed,
    > but like the tidelands, my lord is gone without a trace.
    > (*Sankashū*, no. 1354)

    Both "tidelands" and "trace" translate the word *kata*, which Saigyō used as a pun.

12. *Sankashū*, no. 1353. Although this poem was written by Saigyō, there is a tradition that it was composed by the ghost of Emperor Sutoku when Saigyō visited his grave. Embedded in the poem is a second layer of meaning: "The exiled emperor who came, borne upon the waves of Matsuyama, died here before long."

13. It was the Confucian philosopher Mencius (372?–289? B.C.E.) who most clearly enunciated the concept that the people have the right to depose a ruler whose corruption has caused him to lose the Mandate of Heaven.

14. King Wu of Zhou, a vassal of the notorious King Zhou of Shang, defeated his overlord around 1122 B.C.E. and established the Zhou dynasty, which lasted for eight hundred to nine hundred years, depending on which dates are accepted.

15. "you . . . have not escaped from desire and contamination": in short, "You have not achieved enlightenment."

    "desire and contamination" (*yokujin*): in Buddhism, enlightenment is hindered by "five desires" and "six contaminants"—that is, five objects of desire (color, voice, smell, taste, and touch; alternatively, color, fame, food, fortune, and sleep) and the six "roots" of these desires (eyes, ears, nose, tongue, body, and consciousness). Together, they refer to the passions and desires that impede one's progress toward enlightenment.

16. Prince Ōsasagi, the fourth son of Emperor Ōjin (late fourth–early fifth centuries; legendary r. 270–310), became Emperor Nintoku (early fifth century; legendary r. 313–399).

17. "filial and fraternal devotion": along with sincerity, were traditional Confucian virtues: "Filial piety and fraternal submission!—are they not the root of all benevolent actions?" (Confucius, *Analects* 1:2, in James Legge, trans., *The Four Books: Confucian Analects, The Great Learning, The Doctrine of the Mean, and The Works of Mencius* [1879, 1923; reprint, New York: Paragon, 1966], p. 3).

18. Around 400, the scholar Wani immigrated from Paekche (a state in the southwest of the Korean Peninsula) to Japan, where he introduced Confucian texts and tutored Prince Uji.

19. King Wu "brought peace to the people of the Empire in one outburst of rage" (Mencius, *Mencius*, trans. D. C. Lau [Harmondsworth: Penguin, 1970], I.B.3, p. 63). The reference is to Wu's killing of the despotic King Zhou: "A man who mutilates benevolence is a mutilator, while one who cripples righteousness is a crippler. He who is both

a mutilator and a crippler is an 'outcast.' I have indeed heard of the punishment of the 'outcast Tchou [Zhou],' but I have not heard of any regicide" (Mencius, *Mencius* I.B.8, p. 68).

20. This is reported in book 4 of Xie Zhaozhe, *Five Miscellanies*: "The Japanese prize Confucian texts and believe in Buddhist teachings. They pay high prices for all the Chinese classics. Only *Mencius* is lacking, it is said. If anyone tries to carry this book to Japan, his ship will capsize and sink. This is a very strange thing."

21. *The Book of Songs*, one of the five Confucian classics, was compiled between the eleventh and sixth centuries B.C.E. The reference is to a passage in song no. 164: "Brothers may quarrel within the walls, / But outside they defend one another from insult" (Arthur Waley, ed. and trans., *The Book of Songs* [1937; reprint, New York: Grove Press, 1960], no. 194, p. 203).

22. Saigyō is referring to Sutoku's rebellion against his brother Go-Shirakawa after the death of their father, Toba.

    "funerary palace" (*mogari no miya*): a temporary palace building or shrine where the body of a deceased emperor or empress was kept while preparations were being made for the funeral.

23. Quoted from chapter 29 of Laozi, *Classic of the Way*: "Some want to control the world. I have seen that this is not possible. The world is a sacred vessel; one cannot control it." Saigyō (perhaps speaking for Akinari) embraces Chinese classics selectively, linking the original Confucian virtues of benevolence, righteousness, and filial and fraternal devotion, as well as the Taoist concept of *wu wei* (inaction), to the Japanese imperial tradition, and rejecting Mencius's theory of revolution.

24. The Takatō were a prominent family in Matsuyama.

25. In Chinese and Japanese legend, wild geese (*kari*) were often associated with messengers, partly because of their migratory habits. *Kari* is homophonous with a word meaning "temporary" or "transitory," and so carries Buddhist connotations as well.

26. Wild geese were associated with autumn; plovers, with winter. There is a progression from night (geese) to dawn (plovers) as well.

27. Through performing good karma (copying sutras), Sutoku sought to be reborn in better circumstances, preferably in Amida's Pure Land. Mahāyāna is the school of Buddhism prevalent in China, Korea, and Japan (in contrast to Theravāda, widespread in, for example, Thailand).

28. Ninwaji, now called Ninnaji, is a Buddhist monastery in Kyoto. Sutoku's younger brother Prince Motohito (Kakushō Hōshinnō) was the abbot of Ninnaji.

29. In this poem, which appears in *Hōgen monogatari*, Sutoku likens himself to a plover.

    "traces" (*ato*): signifies both "footprints" and "writing."

    matsu: both "pine tree" (in the place-name Matsuyama) and "to wait."

30. A provision in the Taihō Code, promulgated in 701, called for penalties to be reduced in the case of the emperor's close relatives.

31. The reference to Shito Sea (Shito no umi) is unclear. Shido no ura (Shido Bay), near the city of Takamatsu, and Shido no umi (Shido Sea), near the city of Sakade, have been suggested, but neither is written with the same characters as Akinari's "Shito no umi."

32. Minamoto no Tameyoshi (1096–1156) and six of his sons—except Yoshitomo—sided with Sutoku in the Hōgen Insurrection.

33. Minamoto no Tametomo (1139–1170), Tameyoshi's eighth son, was known for his courage and strength. Taira no Tadamasa (d. 1156) sided with Sutoku in the Hōgen Insurrection and was executed by his own nephew, Kiyomori.

34. Shirakawa Palace was Sutoku's headquarters during the Hōgen Insurrection. The fire was Yoshitomo's "perverse plot," mentioned at the end of the sentence.

35. Mount Nyoi (Nyoigamine), located on the eastern edge of Kyoto above the Ginkaku (Silver Pavilion), is now called Nyoigatake or Daimonjiyama.

36. *Tale of the Disorder in Hōgen* reports that Kiyomori, head of the Taira clan, was a "weak shot" (Wilson, trans., *Hōgen Monogatari*, p. 27).

37. In 1156 Yoshitomo had resisted the emperor's command to kill Tameyoshi, but finally ordered that it be done (Wilson, trans., *Hōgen Monogatari*, pp. 65–68). He was assassinated in 1160 by a retainer in whose house he had taken refuge.

38. Uji is a village south of Kyoto. Criminals were often executed, and their heads displayed, on the bank of the Kamo River near Rokujō (Sixth Avenue) in Kyoto.

39. Fujiwara Tadamichi (1097–1164), chancellor and regent, conspired with Bifukumon'in to deny the throne to Sutoku's son Shigehito and install Go-Shirakawa instead, and sided with the emperor (against Sutoku) during the Hōgen Insurrection.

40. Shigemori (1138–1179), Taira no Kiyomori's eldest son, was noted for his good character.

41. "zodiac cycle" (*eto hitomeguri*): normally refers to the sixty-year Chinese cycle, which combines five elements with twelve animals of the zodiac, but here a twelve-year cycle is meant.

42. "sea before me": refers to the Inland Sea (Setonaikai), where the Taira clan was defeated by the Minamoto in 1185.

43. Saigyō, *Sankashū*, no. 1355. The headnote reads, "Visiting a place called Shiramine, where the emperor's grave is located."

44. The *Diamond Sutra* (J. *Kongō [hannyaharamitta] kyō*, Skt. *Vajracchedikā-sūtra*) is fascicle 547 of the *Large Sutra on Perfect Wisdom* (J. *Daihannyaharamitta-kyō*, Skt. *Mahāprajñāpāramitā-sūtra*).

45. The Toba Detached Palace was a luxurious estate in what is now Fushimi Ward in Kyoto. For a few months in 1180, Kiyomori had the capital moved from Kyoto to Fukuhara, the present Hyōgo Ward in Kobe, whose palace was proverbially rough and primitive, compared with the elegant mansions of Kyoto.

46. "offerings" (*nusa*): hangings made of cloth or paper that are attached to the gates and eaves of a Shinto shrine.

"diety": a translation of *kami*. All Japanese emperors were considered kami, especially those who had been enshrined, as was Sutoku.

THE CHRYSANTHEMUM VOW

TITLE

The title, "Kikka no chigiri," refers to the Chrysanthemum Festival, observed on the ninth day of the Ninth Month, the last month of autumn in the old Japanese calendar. Although the festival originated in China, it has a long history in Japan, having first been observed there in 824.

The choice of the Chrysanthemum Festival as the day on which the central characters will reunite defines their relationship. In early modern Japan, the chrysanthemum blossom (*kikka*) was a common symbol of homosexual intercourse because it was thought to resemble an anus. Both *kiku no chigiri* (chrysanthemum vow) and *kiku asobi* (chrysanthemum play) are euphemisms for homosexual intercourse. The story's title, then, tells the alert reader that Samon and Sōemon are not just friends, but lovers.[1]

CHARACTERS

Like "Shiramine," "The Chrysanthemum Vow" has only two principal characters: the Confucian scholar Hasebe Samon and the samurai Akana Sōemon. Both men represent upper levels of society and are paragons of dependability and integrity. The cast also includes several supporting characters, most notably Samon's mother. Unlike the fictional protagonists Samon and Sōemon, as well as Samon's mother, En'ya Kamon-no-suke, Sasaki Ujitsuna, and Amako Tsunehisa lived in the fifteenth century.

PLACES

Most of "The Chrysanthemum Vow" takes place at the home of Samon in the town of Kako, the modern city of Kakogawa, Hyōgo Prefecture, about 65 miles west of Kyoto. Sōemon is from Matsue, a city in Shimane Prefecture (formerly, Izumo Province), across the mountains on the coast of the Sea of Japan, about 125 miles west-northwest of Kakogawa.

TIME

Spring, early summer, and autumn of 1486.

BACKGROUND

Far from stigmatizing the sexual bond between Samon and Sōemon, "The Chrysanthemum Vow" presents the two men as models of friendship, loyalty, dependability, courage, erudition, and self-sacrifice—the opposite of the shallow men against whom the story warns the reader. Samon and Sōemon are, in fact, idealized figures, as are the devoted samurai lovers in Ihara Saikaku's *Nanshoku ōkagami* (*The Great Mirror of Male Love*, 1687). Given the consistently dysfunctional heterosexual relationships featured in the subsequent tales, erotic friendship between men, as depicted in this story, becomes a sort of model for human relationships. This is not surprising in a society led by a samurai class that idealized male–male sexuality.

The attack on Toda (Tomita, in Akinari's unorthodox reading) Castle, mentioned in "The Chrysanthemum Vow," began on the last day of the Twelfth Month of 1485. The ruins of Toda Castle can still be seen in Shimane Prefecture.

AFFINITIES

Akinari adapted "The Chrysanthemum Vow," in part, from "Fan Juqing jishu sisheng jiao" (Fan Chü-ch'ing's Eternal Friendship), a Ming vernacular tale in the collection *Gujin xiaoshuo* (*Old and New Stories*, 1620–1621), edited by Feng Menglong.[2]

In keeping with the story's Chinese origins, Akinari also refers, directly or indirectly, to Mencius, Confucius, the *Li ji* (*The Book of Rites*, ca. 300 B.C.E.), and the *Shiji* (*Records of the Grand Historian*), by Sima Qian (145?–90? B.C.E.), as well as to *The Tale of Genji* and several waka.

*L*ush and green is the willow in spring; plant it not in your garden. In friendship, bond not with a shallow man. Though the willow comes early into leaf, will it withstand the first winds of autumn? The shallow man is quick to make friends and as quick to part. Year after year, the willow brightens in the spring, but a shallow man will not visit again.

In the province of Harima, in the post town of Kako, lived a Confucian scholar named Hasebe Samon. Content with an upright life of poverty, he abhorred the encumbrance of possessions, except for the books that he made his companions. With him was his elderly mother, as virtuous as the mother of Mencius.[3] She worked steadily, twisting and spinning thread to support Samon's desire for learning. He had a younger sister, too, who was provided for by the Sayo clan, of the same town. The Sayos had great wealth. Admiring the sagacity of the Hasebe mother and son, they took the sister as a bride, thus becoming family, and often would send goods to Samon and his mother; but insisting that they could not trouble others for their own sustenance, Samon and his mother never accepted the gifts.

One day Samon was visiting a man of the same town, talking with him of matters ancient and contemporary, when, just as the conversation was gaining momentum, he heard a sad moaning from the other side of the wall. He questioned his host, who replied, "The man seems to be from someplace west of here. He asked for a night's lodging, saying that he had fallen behind his traveling companions. He appeared to me to be a man of quality, a fine samurai, and so I allowed him to stay; but that night he was seized by a violent fever that made it difficult for him even to rise by himself, and so, taking pity on him, I have let him stay these three or four days; but I am not sure where he is from and think I might have made a terrible mistake. I do not know what to do." Samon said, "A sad story indeed. Your misgivings are understandable, of course, but a fever must be especially distressing to a man who takes ill on a journey, far from everyone he knows. I should like to have a look at him." His host restrained him: "I have heard that such diseases can spread and afflict others, and so I have forbidden everyone in my household to go in there. You must not put yourself in danger by going to him." With a smile, Samon replied, "Life and death are a matter of Destiny.[4] What disease will spread to another? It is the ignorant who say such things; I do not believe them." With this, he opened the door and went in. Looking at the man, he saw that his host had not been mistaken—this was no ordinary person, and the illness appeared to be grave: his face was yellow; his skin was dark and gaunt; and he lay in agony on an old quilt. Looking affably at Samon, he said, "Give me a cup of hot water, if you would." Samon went to his side. "Have no fear, sir, I shall help you," he said. Consulting his host, he selected some medicines and, by himself, determined the dosage and prepared a decoction, which he gave to the man to drink. He also had him eat some rice porridge. In short, he cared for the man with extraordinary kindness, as though he were nursing his own brother.

The samurai was moved to tears by Samon's warm compassion. "That you should be so kind to me, a complete stranger . . . Even if I die, I will show my gratitude," he said. Samon comforted him: "You must not use fainthearted words. Generally this disease has a certain term; once it has run its course, your life will be in no danger. I shall come every day to look after you," he vowed with all sincerity. Samon cared for the man devotedly, and the illness gradually abated. Feeling quite refreshed, the man thanked his host warmly and, esteeming Samon for his unobtrusive kindness, inquired into his vocation and then related his own circumstances: "I am from the village of Matsue, in the province of Izumo, and my name is Akana Sōemon. Since I have attained some slight understanding of military texts, the master of Tomita Castle, En'ya Kamon-no-suke, employed me as his tutor.[5] During that time, I was sent as a secret envoy to Sasaki Ujitsuna, in Ōmi.[6] While I was staying there, the former master of Tomita Castle, Amako Tsunehisa, enlisted the support of the Nakayama, launched a surprise New Year's Eve attack, and captured the castle. Lord Kamon-no-suke was among those killed. Since Izumo was, properly speaking, a Sasaki domain, and En'ya the administrator, I urged Ujitsuna to join the Mizawa and Mitoya clans to overthrow Tsunehisa; but Ujitsuna, despite his formidable appearance, was in fact a coward and a fool—far from carrying out my proposal, he ordered me to stay in his domain. Seeing no point in remaining there, I slipped away and started for home, only to be

stricken by this disease and forced against my will to impose on you, sir. Your kindness is more than I deserve. I shall devote the rest of my life to repaying you." Samon responded, "It is only human nature to help someone in distress;[7] I have done nothing to earn your very gracious thanks. Please stay on and recuperate." Taking strength from the sincerity of Samon's words, Akana stayed for some days, and his health returned almost to normal.

During this time, thinking what a good friend he had found, Samon spent his days and nights with Akana. As they talked together, Akana began to speak hesitantly of various Chinese thinkers, regarding whom his questions and under-

"Amako Tsunehisa . . . launched a surprise New Year's Eve attack, and captured the castle."

standing were exceptional, and on military theory he spoke with authority. Finding that their thoughts and feelings were in harmony on every subject, the two were filled with mutual admiration and joy, and finally they pledged their brotherhood. Being the elder by five years, Akana, in the role of older brother, accepted Samon's expressions of respect and said to him, "Many years have passed since I lost my father and mother. Your aged mother is now my mother, and I should like to pay my respects to her anew. I wonder if she will take pity on me and agree to my childish wish." Samon was overjoyed: "My mother has always lamented that I was alone. Your heartfelt words will give her a new lease on life when I convey them to her." With this, he took Akana to his house, where his mother greeted them joyfully: "My son lacks talent, his studies are out of step with the times, and so he has missed his chance to advance in the world. I pray that you do not abandon him, but guide him as his elder brother." Akana bowed deeply and said, "A man of character values what is right. Fame and fortune are not worthy of mention. Blessed with my honored mother's love, and receiving the respect of my wise younger brother—what more could I desire?" Rejoicing, he stayed for some time.

Although they had flowered, it seemed, only yesterday or today, the cherry blossoms at Onoe had scattered, and waves rising with a refreshing breeze proclaimed that early summer had arrived.[8] Akana said to Samon and his mother, "Since it was to see how things stand in Izumo that I escaped from Ōmi, I should like to go down there briefly and then come back to repay your kindness humbly as a servant living on bean gruel and water. Please allow me to take my leave for a time." Samon said, "If it must be so, my brother, when will you return?" Akana said, "The months and days will pass quickly. At the latest, I shall return before the end of this autumn." Samon said, "On what day of autumn shall I expect you? I beg you to appoint the time." Akana said, "Let us decide, then, that the Chrysanthemum Festival, the ninth day of the Ninth Month, shall be the day of my return." Samon said, "Please be certain not to mistake the day. I shall await you with a sprig of blossoming chrysanthemum and poor saké." Mutually they pledged their reunion and lamented their separation, and Akana returned to the west.

l. 18 "living on bean gruel and water": a hyperbolic expression of filial devotion that derives from a line attributed to Confucius in the *Book of Rites*: "To sip bean gruel and drink water, and to do so joyfully—this is what I call filial devotion."

l. 28 "poor saké": an expression of humility.

The ever-renewing months and days sped by, the berries colored on the lower branches of the oleaster, and the wild chrysanthemum in the hedge put out brilliant blossoms as the Ninth Month arrived. On the ninth day, Samon rose earlier than usual, swept the mats of his grass hut, placed two or three sprigs of yellow and white chrysanthemums in a small vase, and emptied his purse to provide saké and food. His aged mother said, "I have heard that Izumo, the Land of Eight Clouds, lies far to the north of the mountains, more than one hundred *ri* from here, and so we cannot be sure that he will arrive today. It would not be too late if you made your preparations when you see that he has come." Samon said, "Being a samurai of honor, Akana certainly will not break his vow. I am ashamed at what he would think if he should find me rushing to get ready only after I had seen him." Buying fine saké and cooking some fish, he prepared them in the kitchen.

On this day, the sky was clear and cloudless in every direction, and many groups of travelers appeared, talking as they went. "So-and-so enjoys good weather today as he enters the capital, an omen that our merchandise will fetch a good profit," said one as he passed. A samurai in his fifties said to his companion, a man in his twenties and wearing the same attire: "The weather is so good, the sea so calm. If we had hired a boat at Akashi and set out at dawn,[9] we would now be approaching the harbor at Ushimado Straits. You youngsters waste money with your timidity." The other soothed him, saying, "I should think that anyone would hesitate to cross here. Our lord had a terrible time, according to his attendants, crossing from Azukijima to Murozu on his way up to the capital. Do not be angry. I shall treat you to some *soba* noodles when we reach Uogahashi."[10] They moved on out of sight. A packhorse man said angrily, "Are you dead,

l. 5   "grass hut": signifies a humble dwelling and is not to be taken literally.
l. 9   "more than one hundred *ri*": signifies a great distance.

you nag? Open your eyes." Pushing the packsaddle back into place, he drove the horse on. Noon passed, too, but the one awaited had not come. As the sun sank in the west, the travelers' steps quickened in their search for lodging. Samon saw them, but his gaze was fixed on the distance, and he felt something like intoxication.

Samon's aged mother called to him: "Although the man's heart be not fickle like autumn, is it only today that the hue of the chrysanthemum is rich and warm?[11] If he is sincere about returning here, what reason have you to reproach him, though the gentle rains of early winter fall? Come inside, lie down, and wait again tomorrow." Unable to disobey, Samon reassured his mother and asked her to retire first, and then, just in case, he stepped out through the door and looked again. The Milky Way shone faintly; the solitary moon cast its light on him alone; a watchdog's bark reached him clearly from the distance; and the waves on the shore seemed to crash at his very feet.[12] As the moon set behind the hills and its light faded from the sky, he thought it time to go inside and was about to shut the door behind him when he glimpsed a figure in the shadows, moving toward him with the wind. Doubting his eyes, he looked again. It was Akana Sōemon.

Samon's heart leaped with joy. "I have been waiting for you since early this morning. How delighted I am that you have kept your pledge! Here, please come in," he said, but Akana merely nodded and did not speak. Samon led him to the south window and seated him there: "Since you were so late, my brother, our mother grew weary of waiting. 'He will come tomorrow,' she said, and went into her bedroom. I shall go to waken her." Akana stopped him with a shake of the head. Still he said nothing. Samon said, "You have traveled day and night; your heart must be weary and your legs tired. Please have a cup of saké and rest." He warmed the saké, arranged some dishes of food, and served them; but Akana covered his face with his sleeve, as though to avoid a foul smell. Samon said, "This is simple, homemade fare, inadequate to welcome you properly, but I prepared it with all my heart. Please do not refuse it." Akana still did not reply. Heaving a long sigh, he paused, then finally spoke: "My brother, what reason could I have to decline your heartfelt hospitality? I lack the words to deceive you, and so I shall tell the truth. You must not be startled. I am not a man of this world. A filthy ghost has taken this form briefly to appear before you."

Samon was astounded: "What makes you say this monstrous thing, my brother? I am certain that I have not been dreaming." Akana said, "Parting from you, I returned to my native place. Most of the people there had submitted to Tsunehisa's authority; no one remembered En'ya's kindness. I called on my cousin, Akana Tanji, at Tomita Castle. He explained the advantages and disadvantages and arranged for me to have an audience with Tsunehisa. Tentatively accepting my cousin's advice, I observed Tsunehisa's conduct closely and found that even though he is a man of great courage who trains his troops well, he is jealous and suspicious in his dealings with men of learning and, as a consequence, confides in no one and has no retainers willing to give their lives for him. I saw no point in lingering there, and so, explaining my chrysanthemum vow with you, asked for leave to go; but Tsunehisa looked displeased and ordered Tanji not to let me out of the castle. This state of affairs continued until today. Imagining how you would regard me if I broke my pledge, I pondered my options but found no way to escape. As the ancients said: A man cannot travel a thousand ri in one day; a spirit can easily do so. Recalling this, I fell on my sword and tonight rode the dark wind from afar to arrive in time for our chrysanthemum tryst. Please understand my feelings and take pity on me." As he finished speaking, his eyes seemed to fill with tears: "Now we part forever. Please serve our mother faithfully." With this, he rose from his seat and faded from sight.

In a panic, Samon tried to stop him, but, blinded by the dark wind, he could not tell where Akana had gone. Falling to his knees and then on his face, he began to wail loudly. His mother, startled from sleep, came to look and found Samon lying on the floor among the saké flasks and plates of fish that he had arranged by the seat of honor. Hurrying to help him rise, she asked, "What is wrong?" But he sobbed quietly, saying nothing. His mother spoke again: "If you resent your brother Akana now for breaking his pledge, you will have nothing to say if he comes tomorrow. Are you such a child that you can be so foolish?" Thus she admonished and encouraged him. Finally Samon replied, "My brother came tonight to fulfill our chrysanthemum pledge. When I welcomed him with saké and food, he refused them again and again and said, 'For this and that reason, I was about to break our pledge, and so I fell on my sword and came these one hundred ri as a ghost.' Then he vanished. As a result, I have roused you from your sleep. Please forgive me," he said and began to weep, the tears streaming down his face, whereupon his mother said, "I have heard that a man in prison dreams that he has been pardoned, and a thirsty man drinks water in his dreams. You must be like them. Calm yourself." But Samon shook his head: "Truly, it was nothing like an empty dream. My brother was here." Again he cried out in grief and threw himself down, weeping. His mother no longer doubted him, and together they passed the night raising their voices in lamentation.

The next day, Samon bowed in supplication to his mother and said, "Since childhood I have devoted myself to the writing brush and ink, but I have neither made a name for myself in public service nor been able to discharge my filial duty to my family; I have merely dwelt here uselessly between heaven and earth. My brother Akana gave his life for loyalty.

l. 32 "dwelt here uselessly": that is, he has not been a good Confucian, in either his public or his private life, except insofar as he loves learning.

Today I shall set out for Izumo, where I intend at least to bury his remains and fulfill his trust. Please take good care of yourself and give me leave to be away for a time." His mother said, "Go, my son, but come back soon and comfort me in my old age. Do not stay there so long that you make today the day of our final parting." Samon said, "Our lives are like foam on the water—we cannot know but what they might fade away, morning or evening, but I shall come back soon." Brushing away his tears, he left the house, went to beg the Sayos to look after his mother, and started down the road to Izumo. Even though he was hungry, he did not think of food; even though he was cold, he forgot about clothing; and when he dozed off, he lamented all night in his dreams. After ten days, he reached Tomita Castle.

He went directly to Akana Tanji's house and sent in his name, whereupon Tanji came to greet him and led him inside. Questioning Samon closely, he said, "Unless you heard of Sōemon's death from some winged creature, how could you know? It does not seem possible." Samon said, "A samurai does not concern himself with the vicissitudes of rank and fortune; he values only loyalty. Valuing his pledge, my brother Sōemon came one hundred ri as a ghost. I, in return, have traveled day and night to come down here. I should like to ask you, sir, about something I learned in my studies. Please answer clearly. In ancient times, when Gongshu Zuo of Wei lay ill in bed, the king of Wei himself came and, holding Zuo's hand, said, 'If the unavoidable should happen, whom shall I appoint to protect the country? Give me your guidance.' Zuo replied warmly, saying, 'Even though Shang Yang is young, he has rare ability. If your highness does not employ him, do not let him cross the border, even if you must kill him. If you allow him to go to another country, calamity will surely result.' Then Zuo secretly summoned Shang Yang and told him, 'I recommended you, but the king appeared not to accept my advice, and so I told him to kill you if he does not employ you. This is putting the lord first and the retainer after. You must go quickly to another country and escape harm,' he said.[13] How would you compare this case, sir, with that of you and Sōemon?" Tanji hung his head and said nothing. Samon moved closer: "My brother Sōemon was a loyal retainer for remembering En'ya's former kindness and not serving Amako. You, sir, having abandoned En'ya, your former master, and submitted to Amako, lack the righteousness of a samurai. My brother, cherishing his chrysanthemum pledge, gave up his life and traveled one hundred ri: this is the ultimate sincerity. You, sir, seeking favor with Amako, have tormented your own kin and caused his unnatural death: this is to lack the sincerity of a friend. Tsunehisa forced him to stay here; but if you had remembered your long-standing friendship, you would secretly have shown the utter sincerity of Zuo with Shang Yang. Instead you were driven by wealth and fame—this differs from the way of a samurai house and must be the way of the House of Amako as well. No wonder my brother had no wish to linger here. Now I, valuing loyalty, have come. Leave behind you a name stained by unrighteousness!" He had not finished speaking when he drew his sword and struck in one motion. Tanji fell with a single blow. Before the retainers could raise an alarm, Samon escaped without a trace. It is said that Amako Tsunehisa heard the story and, moved by the warmth of the brothers' loyalty, chose not to pursue Samon. Truly, one must not form bonds of friendship with a shallow man.

NOTES

1. The nature of Samon's and Sōemon's relationship has been debated by Japanese scholars. The most persuasive arguments in favor of a homosexual reading have been offered by Matsuda Osamu, "'Kikka no chigiri' no ron: *Ugetsu monogatari* no saihyōka (2)," *Bungei to shisō* 28 (1963); and Uzuki Hiroshi, *Ugetsu Monogatari hyōshaku*, Nihon koten hyōshaku zenchūshaku sōsho (Tokyo: Kadokawa, 1969), pp.

135–136. Neither of them mentions the title of the story in this context, although it is the title that clinches the matter. The most thorough treatment I have found in English is in Timon Screech, *Sex in the Floating World: Erotic Images in Japan, 1700–1820* (Honolulu: University of Hawai'i Press, 1999), pp. 151–154. See also Gary Leupp, *Male Colors: The Construction of Homosexuality in Tokugawa Japan* (Berkeley: University of California Press, 1996), p. 110; and Bernard Faure, *The Red Thread: Buddhist Approaches to Sexuality* (Princeton, N.J.: Princeton University Press, 1998), p. 259, n. 49, which quotes *Onna Imagawa oshiebumi* (*An Imagawa* [copybook and book of maxims] *Teaching Text for Women*, 1778?): "On the ninth day of the ninth moon occurs the union of the chrysanthemums, after a banquet during which many wines are served; one celebrates that day by practicing the way of the youths." "The way of the youths" translates *wakashudō* (sexual relations between a man and a boy).

2. John Lyman Bishop, trans., "Fan Chü-ch'ing's Eternal Friendship," in *The Colloquial Short Story in China: A Study of the San-Yen Collections* (Cambridge Mass.: Harvard University Press, 1956), pp. 88–102.

3. The virtue of the mother of Mencius was proverbial.

4. Samon is quoting Confucius, *Analects* 12:5.

5. "military texts": refers to the seven Chinese military classics, the best known of which is Sunzi, *Sunzi bing fa* (*The Art of War*, sixth century B.C.E.).

6. Ōmi Province corresponds to the modern Shiga Prefecture.

7. This sentiment derives from *Mencius* 2.A.6., in which Mencius argues that humans are altruistic by nature.

8. "Onoe": can mean simply "mountaintop" or refer to the Onoe district of Kakogawa. The text alludes to a poem composed in 1171 by Priest Gen'yū:

> The blossoms at Onoe [or, on the summit] will have scattered
>   in the spring breeze—
> waves lap at the row of cherries here on Takasago shore.
>   (*Fuboku wakashō*, vol. 25, no. 94)

Takasago is at the mouth of the Kako River.

9. An allusion to a poem by Mansei:

> To what shall I compare the world?
> Like a ship that rows out at dawn and vanishes, leaving no
>   wake. (*Man'yōshū*, no. 351)

10. Akashi is a port in Hyōgo Prefecture, on the Inland Sea, about twelve miles southeast of Kakogawa; Ushimado is a port in Okayama Prefecture, about thirty-seven miles southwest of Kakogawa, and just north of the island of Shōdoshima; Azukijima, now called Shōdoshima, is an island in the Inland Sea, in Kagawa Prefecture, about twenty miles by sea southwest of Murotsu; and Murozu, now called Murotsu, is a major port in the Inland Sea, in Hyōgo Prefecture, between Kakogawa and Ushimado.

11. An allusion to a poem by Sagami:

> When I saw the *hagi*'s lower leaves change color,
> I knew before all else the fickle heart of man in autumn.
> (*Shinkokinshū*, no. 1352)

Hagi (*Lespedeza japonica*) is Japanese bush clover.

12. An allusion to the "Suma" chapter of *The Tale of Genji*, in which the pounding of the surf at Suma seems to be at Genji's ear.

13. Akinari based this account on chapter 68, "Biography of Lord Shang," of Sima Qian's *Records of the Grand Historian*. Gongshu Zuo was prime minister of the kingdom of Wei (fourth century B.C.E.). Shang Yang, or Lord Shang (d. 338 B.C.E.), one of the fathers of the Legalist school of Chinese thought, left Wei and eventually reorganized the state of Qin, paving the way for the unification of the Chinese empire about a century later by the first Qin emperor (259–210 B.C.E.).

BOOK TWO

THE REED-CHOKED HOUSE

TITLE

The title, "Asaji ga yado," denotes a neglected house overgrown with *chigaya* reeds. The wording recalls a waka in the "Kiritsubo" (The Paulownia Court) chapter of *The Tale of Genji*:

> Even here above the clouds [at court] the autumn moon is blurred with tears.
> How then could it be clear, and how can you dwell, in a *house overgrown with reeds* [*asaji fu no yado*]?[1]

The phrase *asaji ga yado* appears in chapter 137 of Yoshida Kenkō's *Tsurezuregusa* (*Essays in Idleness*, early fourteenth century), which is more closely related to Akinari's story:

> Does the love between men and women refer only to the moments when they are in each other's arms? The man who grieves over a love affair broken off before it was fulfilled, who bewails empty vows, who spends long autumn nights alone, who lets his thoughts wander to distant skies, who yearns for the past in a dilapidated house [*asaji ga yado*]—such a man truly knows what love means.[2]

CHARACTERS

Like "Shiramine" and "The Chrysanthemum Vow," "The
Reed-Choked House" has only two important characters,
the fictional Katsushirō and Miyagi, supported by minor
figures. Unlike the previous stories, however, this tale
focuses on the lives of peasants, who were second on
the Tokugawa social scale, below the samurai class but
above artisans and merchants. Katsushirō and Miyagi are
remarkably literary peasants, given to quoting and alluding to court poetry. This has the effect of elevating them
to a status closer to that of the characters in the previous
two stories.

PLACES

"The Reed-Choked House" is centered on the village of
Mama, now part of the city of Ichikawa, just east of Tokyo,
in Chiba Prefecture (formerly, Shimōsa Province). Mama is
implicitly contrasted with the sophistication of Kyoto (the
capital) and Ōmi Province (Shiga Prefecture).

TIME

Spring of 1455 to summer of 1461.

BACKGROUND

The historical events mentioned in "The Reed-Choked
House" provide a factual background for the strange story,
but the details have no direct bearing on the lives of Katsushirō and Miyagi.[3]

AFFINITIES

"The Reed-Choked House" draws from a number of Chinese and Japanese sources, the most important being the story "In Which a Wife, After Her Death, Meets Her Former Husband" (27:24), in the late-Heian setsuwa collection *Konjaku monogatari shū* (*Tales of Times Now Past*, ca. 1120); Qu You's "Aiqing zhuan" (The Story of Aiqing), in *Jiandeng xinhua* (*New Tales After Trimming the Lamp*, 1378); Asai Ryōi's adaptation of "Aiqing zhuan": "Fujii Seiroku yūjo Miyagino o metoru koto" (In Which Fujii Seiroku Marries the Courtesan Miyagino), in *Otogibōko* (*Talisman Dolls*, 1666); and the "Yomogiu" (The Wormwood Patch) chapter of *The Tale of Genji*. The story also contains parallels to Zeami's nō play *Kinuta* (*The Fulling Block*) and allusions to a number of other Japanese classics, including *Ise monogatari* (*Tales of Ise*, ca. 947) and *Genji*. Many waka from imperial anthologies and other sources are alluded to or quoted.

OTHER OBSERVATIONS

"The Reed-Choked House," along with "A Serpent's Lust," was the basis for Mizoguchi Kenji's film *Ugetsu monogatari* (1953).

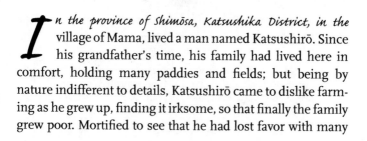

*I*n the province of Shimōsa, Katsushika District, in the village of Mama, lived a man named Katsushirō. Since his grandfather's time, his family had lived here in comfort, holding many paddies and fields; but being by nature indifferent to details, Katsushirō came to dislike farming as he grew up, finding it irksome, so that finally the family grew poor. Mortified to see that he had lost favor with many of his relatives, he considered various schemes to revive the family fortunes. In those days, a man named Sōji of Sasabe came down from the capital every year to stock up on dyed silk from Ashikaga.[4] Having distant relatives in the village, he often came to visit and had been on familiar terms with Katsushirō for some time. Katsushirō pleaded that he, too, wanted to become a merchant and go up to the capital. Sasabe agreed immediately. "Let me see, when will the next trip be?" he said. Delighted that he could now rely on Sasabe, Katsushirō sold off his remaining paddies, used the gold to buy a large supply of plain silk, and prepared for his journey to the capital.

Katsushirō's wife, Miyagi, was a woman of arresting beauty, intelligence, and steady disposition. Dismayed to hear that he had bought merchandise and was going to the capital, she used every argument she could think of to dissuade him; but she was helpless before his obstinacy, now worse than ever, and so, despite her misgivings about how she would fare in the future,[5] she applied herself with alacrity to his preparations. As they talked together that night about the painful separation to come, she said, "With no one to depend on, my woman's heart will know the extremities of sadness, wandering as though lost in the fields and mountains.[6] Please do not forget me, morning or night, and come back soon. If only I live long enough, I tell myself,[7] but in this life we cannot depend on the morrow, and so take pity on me in your stalwart heart." He replied, "How could I linger in a strange land, riding on a drifting log? I shall return this autumn, when the arrowroot leaf turns over in the wind.[8] Be confident and wait for me." Thus he reassured her; the night sky brightened with dawn; and

l. 27 "riding on a drifting log": signifies rootlessness and anxiety, as in the "Matsukaze" (The Wind in the Pines) chapter of *The Tale of Genji* (Murasaki Shikibu, *Genji monogatari*, ed. Yamagishi Tokuhei, Nihon koten bungaku taikei, vol. 14 [Tokyo: Iwanami, 1958], p. 199):

How many autumns have come and gone as I was dwelling here— why now should I return, riding on a drifting log?

leaving the East Country, where the roosters crow, he hurried toward the capital.[9]

In the summer of 1455, the shogun's deputy in Kamakura, Lord Ashikaga Shigeuji, had a falling out with the family of Uesugi, his own deputy, and so when troops burned his palace to the ground, he took refuge with an ally in Shimōsa. From that moment, the lands east of the barrier were thrown into chaos, and each man did just as he pleased.[10] The aged fled to the mountains and hid; the young were conscripted; women and children, hearing the rumors—"They will burn this place today! The enemy will attack tomorrow!"—fled weeping, now east, now west. Katsushirō's wife, Miyagi, too, wanted to escape, but relying on her husband's words—"Wait for me this fall"—she lived on, anxiously counting the days. Autumn came, but there was no word, not even in the wind. Sad and resentful that the heart of man proved to be as unreliable as this world itself, she composed in her despondency:

"No one will report my misery, I fear—
oh decorated cock of Meeting Hill, tell him autumn too has
passed."[11]

And yet she had no way to communicate with him, since many provinces separated them. Men's hearts grew more villainous in the turbulence of the world. Passersby, noting Miyagi's beauty, tried to seduce her with comforting words, but, firmly guarding her chastity, she would treat them distantly, close the door, and refuse to meet them. Her maidservant departed; her meager savings melted away; and that year, too, came to a close. The New Year brought no peace. What is more, in the autumn of the old year the shogun had bestowed the flag on Tō no Tsuneyori,[12] governor of Shimotsuke and lord of Gujō, Mino Province, who went down to the domain of Shimōsa, made plans with his kinsman Chiba no Sanetane, and attacked; but Shigeuji's forces defended their position resolutely, and so there was no end in sight. Bandits threw up strongholds here and there, set fires, and pillaged. No haven remained in the Eight Provinces; the losses were appalling.[13]

Katsushirō accompanied Sasabe to Kyoto and sold all his silk. Because it was an age when the capital delighted in luxury, he made a good profit.[14] As he prepared to return to the East Country, word spread that Uesugi troops had toppled the shogun's deputy and then had pursued and attacked him. Katsushirō's home village would be the battlefield of Zhoulu, bristling with shields and halberds. Even rumors close at hand are frequently untrue; his home was in a distant land beyond myriad layers of white clouds.[15] Anxiously, he left the capital at the start of the Eighth Month. Crossing the pass at Misaka in Kiso, he found that robbers had blocked the road, and to them he lost all his baggage.[16] Furthermore, he heard reports that new barrier stations had been established here and there to the east, where even travelers were not allowed to pass. In that case, there would be no way to send any message at all. His house had surely been leveled by the fires of battle. His wife would no longer be alive. His village would have become a den of ogres, he told himself, and so he turned back toward the capital; but as he entered the province of Ōmi, he suddenly felt unwell and came down with a fever. In a place called Musa lived a wealthy man named Kodama Yoshibei.[17] This being the birthplace of Sasabe's wife, Katsushirō pleaded for help; and Kodama did not turn him away, but summoned a physician and devoted himself to Katsushirō's care. Feeling well again at last, Katsushirō thanked Kodama deeply for his great kindness. He was still unsteady on his feet, however, and so he found himself still there when they greeted the New Year. Presently he made new friends in the town, where he was admired for his unaffected honesty, and formed close ties with Kodama and many others. Thereafter, he would call on Sasabe in the capi-

l. 9   Zhoulu: in the present Hebei Province, China, the scene of an ancient battle involving the legendary Yellow Emperor.

tal and then return to stay with Kodama in Ōmi, and seven years passed like a dream.

In 1461 the struggle between the Hatakeyama brothers in the province of Kawachi showed no sign of ending, and the turmoil approached the capital.[18] What is more, corpses piled up in the streets as an epidemic swept through the city in the spring. Thinking that a cosmic epoch must be coming to an end, the people lamented the impermanence of all things.[19] Katsushirō pondered his situation: "Reduced to this pointless existence, how long should I drag out my life, and for what, lingering in this distant land, depending on the generosity of people with whom I have no ties of blood? It is my own faithless heart that has let me pass long years and months in a field overgrown with the grass of forgetfulness, unmindful even of the fate of her I left at home.[20] Even if she is no longer of this world and has gone to the Land of the Dead, I would seek out her remains and construct a burial mound." Thus he related his thoughts to those around him and, during a break in the rains of the Fifth Month, said farewell. Traveling for more than ten days, he arrived at his village.

Although the sun had already sunk in the west and the rain clouds were so dark that they seemed about to burst, he doubted he could lose his way, having lived for so long in the village, and so he pushed through the fields of summer; but the jointed bridge of old had fallen into the rapids, so that there could be no sound of a horse's hoofs;[21] he could not find the old paths because the farmland had been abandoned to grow wild, and the houses that used to stand there were gone. Scattered here and there, a few remaining houses appeared to be inhabited, but they bore no resemblance to those in former days. "Which is the house I lived in?" he wondered, standing in confusion, when about forty yards away, he saw, by the light of stars peeking through the clouds, a towering pine that had been riven by lightning. "The tree that marks the eaves of my house!" he cried and joyfully moved forward. The house was unchanged and appeared to be occupied, for lamplight glimmered through a gap in the old door. "Does someone else live here now? Or is she still alive?" His heart pounding, he approached the entrance and cleared his throat. Someone inside heard immediately and asked, "Who is there?" He recognized his wife's voice, though greatly aged. Terrified that he might be dreaming, he said, "I have come back. How strange that you should still be living here alone, unchanged, in this reed-choked moor!"[22] Recognizing his voice, she quickly opened the door. Her skin was dark with grime, her eyes were sunken, and long strands of hair fell loose down her back. He could not believe that she was the same person. Seeing her husband, she burst into wordless tears.

Stunned, Katsushirō could say nothing for a time. Finally he spoke: "I would never have let the years and months slip by had I thought that you were still living here like this. One day years ago, when I was in the capital, I heard of fighting in Kamakura—the shogun's deputy had been defeated and taken refuge in Shimōsa. The Uesugi were in eager pursuit, people said. The next day, I took my leave from Sasabe and, at the beginning of the Eighth Month, left the capital. As I came along the Kiso road, I was surrounded by a large band of robbers, who took my clothing and all my money. I barely escaped with my life. Then the villagers said that travelers were being stopped at new barriers on the Tōkaidō and Tōsandō.[23] They also said that a general had gone down from the capital the day before, joined forces with the Uesugi, and set out for battle in Shimōsa. Our province had long since been razed by fire, and every inch trampled under horses' hoofs, they said, and so I could only think that you had been reduced to ashes and dust or had sunk into the sea. Returning to the capital, I lived on the generosity of others for these seven years. Seized in recent days with constant longing, I returned, hoping at least to find your remains, but I never dreamed that you would still be living in this world. I wonder if you might not be the Cloud of Shaman Hill or the Apparition in the Han Palace."[24] Thus he rambled on, tediously repeating himself.

Drying her tears, his wife said, "After I bid you farewell, the world took a dreadful turn, even before the arrival of the autumn I relied on,[25] and the villagers abandoned their houses and set out to sea or hid in the mountains. Most of the few who remained had hearts of tigers or wolves and sought, I suppose, to take advantage of me now that I was alone. They tempted me with clever words, but even if I had been crushed like a piece of jade, I would not imitate the perfection of the tile, and so I endured many bitter experiences. The brilliance of the Milky Way heralded the autumn, but you did not return.[26] I waited through the winter, I greeted the New Year, and still there was no word. Now I wanted to go to you in the capital, but I knew that a woman could not hope to pass the sealed barrier gates where even men were turned away; and so, with the pine at the eaves, I waited vainly in this house, foxes and owls my companions, until today.[27] I am happy now that my long resentment has been dispelled. No one else can know the resentment of one who dies of longing, waiting for another to come."[28] With this, she began to sob again. "The night is short," he said, comforting her, and they lay down together.

He slept soundly, weary from his long journey and cooled through the night as the paper in the window sipped the pine-breeze. When the sky brightened in the fifth watch of night, he felt chilly, though still in the world of dreams, and groped for the quilt that must have slipped off. A rustling sound wakened him. Feeling something cold dripping on his face, he opened his eyes, thinking that rain was seeping

l. 10 "crushed . . . tile": that is, "I would not prolong my life [the perfect tile] by being unfaithful, even though death [the crushed jade] might be the consequence."

l. 26 "fifth watch": the time between sunset and sunrise was divided into five equal watches of about two hours each. The fifth watch corresponded roughly to the period from 4:00 A.M. until daybreak.

in: the roof had been torn off by the wind, and he could see the waning moon lingering dimly in the sky. The house had lost its shutters. Reeds and plumed grasses grew tall through gaps in the decaying floorboards, and the morning dew dripped from them, saturating his sleeves. The walls were draped with ivy and arrowroot; the garden was buried in creepers—even though fall had not come yet, the house was a wild autumn moor.[29] And where, come to think of it, had his wife gone, who had been lying with him? She was nowhere in sight. Perhaps this was the doing of a fox? But the house, though dilapidated in the extreme, was certainly the one he used to live in: from the spacious inner rooms to the rice-storehouse beyond, it still retained the form that he had favored. Dumbfounded, he felt as though he had lost his footing; but then he considered carefully: since the house had become the dwelling place of foxes and raccoon-dogs—a wild moor—perhaps a spirit had appeared before him in the form of his wife. Or had her ghost, longing for him, come back and communed with him? It was just as he had feared. He could not even weep. "I alone am as I was before," he thought as he walked around.[30] In the space that was her bedroom, someone had taken up the floor, piled soil into a mound, and protected the mound from rain and dew. The ghost last night had come from here—the thought frightened him and also made him long for her. In a receptacle for water offerings stood a stick with a sharpened end, and to this was attached a weathered piece of Nasuno paper,[31] the writing faded and in places hard to make out, but certainly in his wife's hand. Without inscribing a dharma name or date, she had, in the form of a waka, movingly stated her feelings at the end:

l. 29 "dharma name" (*hōmyō* or *kaimyō*): a posthumous name, usually composed by a Buddhist priest and inscribed on a gravestone with the date of death.

"Nevertheless, I thought, and so deceived
I have lived on until today!"[32]

Realizing now for the first time that his wife was dead, he
cried out and collapsed. It added to his misery that he did
not even know what year, what month and day, she had met
her end. Someone must know, he thought, and so, drying his
tears, he stepped outside. The sun had climbed high in the
sky. He went first to the nearest house and met the master,
a man he had never seen before. On the contrary, the man
asked him what province he had come from. Katsushirō
addressed him respectfully: "I was the master of the house
next door, but to make my living I spent seven years in the
capital. When I came back last night, the house had fallen
into ruins and no one was living there. Apparently my wife
has left this world, for I found a burial mound, but there is
no date, which makes my grief all the more intense. If you
know, sir, please tell me." The man said, "A sad story indeed.
I came to live here only about one year ago and know nothing
of the time when she was living there. It would seem that she
lost her life long before that. All the people who used to live
in this village fled when the fighting began; most of those
who live here now moved in from somewhere else. There is
one old man who seems to have lived here for a long time.
Occasionally he goes to that house and performs a service to
comfort the spirit of the departed. This old man must know
the date." Katsushirō said, "And where does the old man
live?" The man told him, "He owns a field thickly planted
with hemp, about two hundred yards from here, toward the
beach, and there he lives in a small hut." Rejoicing, Katsushirō went to the house, where he found an old man of about
seventy, terribly bent at the waist, sitting in front of a hearth
on a round, wicker cushion and sipping tea. Recognizing
Katsushirō, the old man said, "Why have you come back so
late, my boy?" Katsushirō saw that he was the old man called
Uruma, who had lived in the village for a long time.

Katsushirō congratulated the old man on his longevity and
then related everything in detail, from going to the capital
and remaining there against his true desires, to the strange
events of the night before, and expressed his deep gratitude
to the old man for raising a burial mound and performing
services there. He could not stop his tears. The old man said,
"After you went far away, soldiers began to brandish shields
and halberds in the summer; the villagers ran off; the young
were conscripted; and, as a result, the mulberry fields turned
quickly into grasslands for foxes and rabbits.[33] Only your virtuous wife, honoring your pledge to return in the fall, would
not leave home. I, too, stayed inside and hid, because my legs

"Leaning on his staff,
he led the way."

had grown weak and I found it hard to walk two hundred yards. I have seen many things in my years, but I was deeply moved by the courage of that young woman, even when the land had become the home of tree spirits and other ghastly monsters.[34] Autumn passed, the New Year came, and on the tenth day of the Eighth Month of that year she departed. In my pity for her, I carried soil with my own hands, buried the coffin, and, using as a grave marker the brush marks she left at the end, performed a humble service with offerings of water; but I could not inscribe the date, not knowing how to write, and I had no way to seek a posthumous name, as the temple is far away. Five years have passed. Hearing your story now, I am sure that the ghost of your virtuous wife came and told you of her long-held resentment. Go there again and carefully perform a memorial service." Leaning on his staff, he led the way. Together they prostrated themselves before the mound, raised their voices in lamentation, and passed the night invoking the Buddha's name.

Because they could not sleep, the old man told a story: "Long, long ago, even before my grandfather's grandfather was born, there lived in this village a beautiful girl named Tegona of Mama.[35] Since her family was poor, she wore a hempen robe with a blue collar; her hair was uncombed, and she wore no shoes; but with a face like the full moon and a smile like a lovely blossom, she surpassed the fine ladies in the capital, wrapped in their silk brocades woven with threads of gold. Men in the village, of course, and even officials from the capital and men in the next province, all came courting and longed for her. This caused great pain for Tegona, who sank deep in thought and, the better to requite the love of many men, threw herself into the waves of the inlet here. People in ancient times sang of her in their poems and passed down her story as an example of the sadness of the world. When I was a child, my mother told the story charmingly, and I found it very moving; but how much sadder is the heart of this departed one than the young heart of Tegona of old!" He wept as he spoke, for the aged cannot control their tears. Katsushirō's grief needs no description. Hearing this tale, he expressed his feelings in the clumsy words of a rustic:

"Tegona of Mama, in the distant past—
this much they must have longed for her, Tegona of Mama."

It can be said that an inability to express even a fragment of one's thoughts is more moving than the feelings of one skilled with words.

This is a tale passed down by merchants who traveled often to that province and heard the story there.

NOTES

1. Murasaki Shikibu, *Genji monogatari*, ed. Yamagishi Tokuhei, Nihon koten bungaku taikei, vol. 14 (Tokyo: Iwanami, 1958), p. 41.

2. Yoshida Kenkō, *Essays in Idleness: The "Tsurezuregusa" of Kenkō*, trans. Donald Keene (New York: Columbia University Press, 1967), pp. 117–118.

3. George Sansom provides a good summary of the "absurd situation" in *A History of Japan*, vol. 2, *1334–1615* (Stanford, Calif.: Stanford University Press, 1961), p. 241.

4. Sasabe was a village northwest of Kyoto, later incorporated into the city of Fukuchiyama; Ashikaga, in Ibaraki Prefecture, north of Tokyo, was noted for its dyed silk.

5. An allusion to an anonymous, alternative version of *Man'yōshū*, no. 2985:

    Though I know not how I will fare in the [catalpa bow] future,
    my heart is with you.

6. An allusion to a poem by Sosei, who, having taken holy vows, wonders where to live away from society:

    Where shall I loathe this world?
    Whether in fields or in mountains my heart will surely wander. (*Kokinshū*, no. 947)

7. An allusion to a poem by Shirome: "Composed when parting from Minamoto no Sane at Yamazaki, as he set out for the hot springs of Tsukushi":

    If only life obeyed the wishes of our hearts
    what pain would we feel in our partings? (*Kokinshū*, no. 387)

8. This sentence contains a pun on *kaeru*, which means both "to return" and "to turn over." Arrowroot, being one of the "seven autumn grasses," signifies autumn.

9. "roosters crow" (*tori ga naku*): a pillow-word for Azuma, the East Country, an old name for the region now called Kantō, or greater Tokyo. The image is further enriched by the truism that roosters crow at dawn and the fact that the word "Azuma" is often written with characters signifying "my wife."

10. "lands east of the barrier": refers to the eight provinces to the east of the barrier station at Hakone: Sagami, Musashi, Awa, Kazusa, Shimōsa, Hitachi, Shimotsuke, and Kōzuke (corresponding to the mod-

ern Kantō prefectures of Kanagawa, Tokyo, Saitama, Chiba, Ibaraki, Tochigi, and Gumma).

11. "decorated cock of Meeting Hill": cocks decorated with mulberry-cloth ribbons were occasionally sent to the barrier stations around Kyoto, including the Ōsaka Barrier, as part of a purification ritual. On the Ōsaka Barrier, see the introduction to "Shiramine." Since "Ōsaka" (the barrier, not the city) means "Meeting Hill," poets frequently used the name in a double sense, as in this anonymous poem:

> Does the decorated cock of Meeting Hill, like me,
> long for someone, and that is why we cry in vain? (*Kokinshū*,
>   no. 536)

and in a poem by Kan'in: "Sent to the Middle Counselor Lord Minamoto no Noboru, when he was Vice-Governor of Ōmi":

> If only I were the decorated cock of Meeting Hill,
> crying, I could watch you come and go. (*Kokinshū*, no. 740)

12. "bestowed the flag on": in the autumn of 1455, the shogun Ashikaga Yoshimasa appointed Tsuneyori (1401–1494), a leading poet and commander, to subdue the disloyal Shigeuji and his supporters.

13. Shimotsuke corresponds to the modern Tochigi Prefecture; Mino Province, to Gifu Prefecture.

    "domain of Shimōsa": Akinari mistakenly wrote "Shimotsuke" instead of Shimōsa.

    "Eight Provinces": see note 10.

14. Yoshimasa's reign (1443–1490) was a golden age in culture, as the shogun led the way in promoting garden design, architecture, nō theater, and other arts. His Ginkaku (Silver Pavilion) in Kyoto, with its splendid garden, is the most famous relic of the period.

15. An allusion to a poem by Ki no Tsurayuki: "Composed for a person who was going to Michinokuni":

> Even far away where white clouds pile in myriad layers
> let not your heart grow distant from him who thinks of you.
>   (*Kokinshū*, no. 380)

16. Misaka in Kiso is an old name for Magome Pass, on the Nakasendō (highway through the mountains between Kyoto and Edo), at the border of Gifu and Nagano Prefectures.

17. Musa is now part of the city of Ōmi Hachiman, Shiga Prefecture, on the shore of Lake Biwa, about twenty miles northeast of Kyoto.

18. The Hatakeyama brothers Masanaga and Yoshinari fought for some years over which should hold the office of shogun's deputy (*kanrei*). Their dispute was one of several that led to the infamous Ōnin War (1467–1477), which devastated the capital. Kawachi corresponds to the eastern part of the modern Ōsaka Prefecture, just southwest of Kyoto.

19. "cosmic epoch" (*kō*): *kalpa*, a Sanskrit word for an almost unimaginably long period of time. Here the reference is to the second kalpa, during which there is life on earth. Epidemics and famines occurred throughout Japan in the 1450s. This sentence echoes Kamo no Chōmei's description of Kyoto in 1182, in *Hōjōki* (*An Account of a Ten-Foot-Square Hut*, 1212).

20. "grass of forgetfulness" (*wasuregusa*): a kind of daylily (*Hemerocallis aurantiaca*), mentioned in section 100 of *Tales of Ise*: "Long ago, as a man was passing by the Kōrōden, a high-ranking lady sent a message out to him, saying, Do you refer to the grass of forgetfulness as grass of remembrance? to which he replied with a poem:

> This may look to be a field overgrown with grass of forgetful-
> ness,
> but it is remembrance, and I shall continue to depend on you."

21. An allusion to an anonymous poem:

> I wish for a horse whose hoofs would make no sound.
> Across the jointed bridge of Mama in Katsushika would I
> always go to her. (*Man'yōshū*, no. 3387)

22. This paragraph contains several echoes of the "Yomogiu" (The Wormwood Patch) chapter of *The Tale of Genji*, in which the Hitachi Princess has waited for ten years for another visit from Genji (Murasaki Shikibu, *Genji monogatari*, NKBT, vol. 15, pp. 155–160). Her mansion has fallen into ruin, most of her servants have left, and she is almost without resources, when Genji happens to notice her dilapidated estate. He sends in his attendant, Koremitsu, to learn whether the princess still lives there. Koremitsu first lets his presence be known by clearing his throat, in response to which an aged voice asks, "Who is there? Who are you?" He recognizes the voice, that of an attendant. After identifying himself, he says, "If the princess has not changed, then my lord's desire to visit her, too, has not ceased." The aged voice replies, "If my lady had changed, would she still be living in this reed-choked moor [*asaji ga hara*]?" When Genji finally meets the princess again, he composes a waka for her:

> I found it hard to ignore the waves of wisteria blooms
> because the pine they drape on is the mark of your waiting
>   house.

23. Kiso road refers to the section of the Nakasendō between Nakatsu-gawa (Gifu Prefecture) and Shiojiri (Nagano Prefecture). The Tōkaidō ran along the Pacific coast between Kyoto and Edo; the Tōsandō, through the mountains between Kyoto and the northern tip of Honshū.

24. "Cloud of Shaman Hill": refers to a story in the *Wenxuan* (*Anthology of Writing*, sixth century), edited by Xiao Tong, in which King Xiang of Chu dreams that he has slept with a woman at Shaman Hill (Wushan, in Sichuan) who turns out to have been a cloud (Sun Yü, "The Kao T'ang Fu," in *The Temple and Other Poems*, trans. Arthur Waley [New York: Knopf, 1923], pp. 65–72).

    "Apparition in the Han Palace": derives from a story in the *Han shu* (*History of the Former Han Dynasty*), by Ban Gu (32–62), in which the Han emperor Wu, grieving the death of a beloved lady, commands a sorcerer to summon her spirit.

    Both tales bespeak a confusion of illusion and reality.

25. "autumn I relied on" (*tanomu no aki*): a pun on *tanomu no hi* (the day relied upon / the day of the fruits of the field), a harvest and gift-exchanging festival on the first day of the Eighth Month. Compare a poem by the Sesshō Daijōdaijin: "On the returning geese":

> Do not forget, oh geese who rise from the sheltering marsh
>   by the fields,
> the wind on the rice leaves in the evening of autumn.
>   (*Shinkokinshū*, no. 61)

26. The Milky Way, which brightens as the air becomes less humid in the autumn, is associated with the Tanabata festival, the seventh night of the Seventh Month, the only night when, in Sino-Japanese legend, the Oxherd (the star Altair) may cross the River of Heaven (the Milky Way) to meet his love, the Weaver Maid (the star Vega).

27. Miyagi employs the usual pun on *matsu*, which means both "pine tree" and "to wait." The pine also echoes the tree that leads Katsu-shirō to his house, and Genji to the mansion of the Hitachi Princess, where he finds foxes and owls.

28. An allusion to a poem by Taira no Kanemori:

If unknown to him I die of longing while I wait for him to come,
for what shall I say I have exchanged my life? (*Goshūishū*, no.
656)

29. An allusion to a poem by Priest Henjō:

The house is ruined, the people are grown old—
garden and brushwood-fence have both become a wild
autumn moor. (*Kokinshū*, no. 248)

30. An allusion to a poem by Ariwara no Narihira:

The moon is not that moon nor the spring the spring of old,
and I alone am as I was before. (*Tales of Ise*, sec. 4; *Kokinshū*,
no. 747)

31. Nasuno, in Shimotsuke Province (Tochigi Prefecture), produced a
thick, sturdy paper of high quality.

32. Miyagi's waka is borrowed from the collection of the courtier and
poet Fujiwara no Atsutada (905?–943): *Gon Chūnagon Atsutada kyō shū*,
in Hanawa Hokiichi, comp., *Gunsho ruijū* (*Classified Collection of Various
Books*) (1819), vol. 9, no. 235.

33. The proverb *Sōden henjite sōkai to naru* (mulberry fields [sōden]
change into blue seas [sōkai]) refers to the world's mutability.

34. "home of tree spirits and other ghastly monsters": another echo of
the mansion of the Hitachi Princess in "The Wormwood Patch" chapter of *The Tale of Genji*.

35. The legend of Tekona (or Tegona, the pronunciation that Akinari preferred) of Mama is told in the *Man'yōshū*, nos. 431–433, 1807–1808.
The old man's narrative is based on a long poem by Takahashi Mushi-
maro, "Of the Maiden of Mama of Katsushika" (*Man'yōshū*, no. 1807).
See *The Manyōshū: The Nippon Gakujutsu Shinkōkai Translation of
One Thousand Poems* (New York: Columbia University Press, 1965),
pp. 223–224.

THE CARP OF MY DREAMS

TITLE

The title, "Muō no rigyō," comes from the first paragraph of the story, in which Kōgi gives this name to one of his paintings.

CHARACTERS

"The Carp of My Dreams" has only one important character, the Buddhist monk Kōgi, who narrates the story within the story. According to the setsuwa collection *Kokon chomonjū* (*Stories Heard from Writers Old and New*, 1254), edited by Tachibana Narisue, there was a painter-monk named Kōgi at Miidera, but nothing else is known of him.

PLACES

Miidera, also known as Onjōji, an important Buddhist temple established in the seventh century on a hill overlooking Lake Biwa, in what is now the city of Ōtsu, just east of Kyoto, is the setting of "The Carp of My Dreams." During his underwater journey around Lake Biwa, Kōgi passes a number of famous sights, including several of the famous Eight Views of Lake Biwa (Ōmi hakkei):

Mount Nagara: behind Miidera, west of the southern end of Lake Biwa.

Great Bay of Shiga: southwestern part of Lake Biwa, offshore from the former Shiga capital. This section echoes a poem by the monk Jakuren:

> Strollers tread the ice along the shore,
> crossing without getting wet at the Great Bay of Shiga.
> (*Shokukokinshū*, no. 641)

Mount Hira: west of Lake Biwa. "Evening Snow at Hira" is one of the Eight Views of Lake Biwa.

Katada: village on the western shore of Lake Biwa, now part of the city of Ōtsu. "Wild Geese Descending at Katada" is one of the Eight Views.

Mount Kagami (mirror-mountain): southeast of Lake Biwa.

Okino Isle: slightly southwest of the center of Lake Biwa.

Chikubu Isle: near the northern end of Lake Biwa, famous for its Benzaiten shrine, enclosed by a red-lacquered fence.

Asazuma Boat: ferry connecting the Nakasendō (highway through the mountains between Kyoto and Edo), on the northeastern shore of Lake Biwa, with Ōtsu, on the southwestern shore. Onboard prostitutes provided companionship for travelers.

Mount Ibuki: east of the northern end of Lake Biwa, paired with the Asazuma Boat in a poem by Saigyō:

> It makes me anxious: will the Asazuma Boat not face
> the brunt of the gale blowing down from Mount Ibuki?
> (*Sankashū*, no. 1005)

Yabase: village on the southeastern shore of Lake Biwa, connected by ferry to Ōtsu. "Sailboats at Yabase" is one of the
Eight Views.

Seta: river at the southernmost tip of Lake Biwa, spanned
by a bridge. "Sunset at Seta Bridge" is one of the Eight
Views. Carp-Kōgi is frightened by the guard's footfalls on
the planks of the bridge.

TIME

Summer (peach season), one year during the Enchō era
(923–931).

BACKGROUND

In contrast to the late twelfth and mid-fifteenth centuries,
during which the first three stories take place, the Enchō era,
a little more than a century into the Heian period (794–1185)
and the time frame of "The Carp of My Dreams," was a
period of relative stability and calm in Japan.

There was a priest named Enchin, or Chishō Daishi (814–
891), who restored Miidera and was famous for his Buddhist
paintings.

AFFINITIES

Akinari adapted "The Carp of My Dreams" from two Chinese stories in Ming collections: "Xue lu-shi yu fu zheng
xian" (Junior Magistrate Xue's Piscine Metamorphosis),
in Feng Menglong's *Xingshi hengyan* (*Constant Words to
Awaken the World*, 1628), and "Yu fu ji" (Account of a Piscine
Metamorphosis), in Lu Ji's *Gujin shuohai* (*Sea of Tales Old
and New*, sixteenth century).[1] Uzuki Hiroshi has identified

three stories—"Concerning Priest Myōtatsu of Ryūgeji in Dewa Province" (13:13), "In Which a Man from the Province of Settsu Who Killed an Ox Returns from the Underworld Through the Power of Releasing Living Beings" (20:25), and "In Which a Man from the Province of Sanuki Goes to the Underworld and Comes Back" (20:17)—in the late-Heian set-suwa collection *Konjaku monogatari shū* (*Tales of Times Now Past*, ca. 1120) as being closely related to "The Carp of My Dreams," in that they deal with people who come back from death because of merit accumulated by releasing captured creatures.[2] Ultimately, the roots of the story can be traced back to two passages in the Chinese Taoist classic *Chuang Tzu* (fourth–third centuries B.C.E.):

> Once Chuang Chou dreamt he was a butterfly, a butterfly flitting and fluttering around, happy with himself and doing as he pleased. He didn't know he was Chuang Chou. Suddenly he woke up and there he was, solid and unmistakable Chuang Chou. But he didn't know if he was Chuang Chou who had dreamt he was a butterfly, or a butterfly dreaming he was Chuang Chou.[3]

> Chuang Tzu and Hui Tzu were strolling along the dam of the Hao River when Chuang Tzu said, "See how the minnows come out and dart around where they please! That's what fish really enjoy!"
>
> Hui Tzu said, "You're not a fish—how do you know what fish enjoy?"
>
> Chuang Tzu said, "You're not I, so how do you know I don't know what fish enjoy!"[4]

OTHER OBSERVATIONS

Kōgi's clockwise circuit of Lake Biwa—a kind of michiyuki—is a rhetorical tour de force and a masterpiece of imaginative, scenic description. Mishima Yukio called it "the ultimate in the poetry that Akinari attempted."[5]

*L*ong ago, in the Enchō era, there was a monk at Miidera named Kōgi, who was recognized as a master painter. He did not limit himself to painting buddhas, landscapes, or birds and flowers. On days when he was free from temple chores, he would go out on the lake in a small boat and give money to fishermen in exchange for fish that they had caught with their nets and hooks, and then he would release the fish into the bay,[6] watch them swim about, and paint them; and as he did this over the years, he became extremely precise and skilled. Once, as he concentrated on a painting, he grew sleepy and dreamed that he had gone into the water and was swimming about with all kinds of fish, large and small. As soon as he woke up, he painted exactly what he had seen and fastened the painting to his wall. He called it *The Carp of My Dreams.* Marveling at how wonderful his paintings were, people jostled for a place in line to acquire them, but Kōgi, though he happily gave his flowers, birds, and landscapes to anyone who wanted them, stubbornly held on to his paintings of carp. Playfully he would say, "This monk will never give away the fish he has reared to ordinary laymen who kill living things and eat fresh meat."[7] Word of his paintings and of this joke spread throughout the realm.

One year he fell ill and, after seven days, suddenly closed his eyes, stopped breathing, and lost consciousness. His disciples and friends came together to grieve, but, finding that his chest was still a little warm, they gathered around him to keep watch, thinking that he might recover; and after three days, his arms and legs seemed to move a little, and he suddenly heaved a long sigh, opened his eyes, and sat up as though awakening from sleep. "I have forgotten human affairs for a long time," he said to the people around him. "How many days have passed?" His disciples said, "Master, you stopped breathing three days ago. People from throughout the temple, and others you have always been close to, came to discuss your funeral, but noticing that your chest was still warm, we watched you without putting you in a coffin, and now that you have come back to life, we are all rejoicing that, fortunately, we did not bury you." Kōgi nodded: "Someone go to the house of our *dānapati* the Taira officer and report that I have mysteriously come back to life. The officer is now pouring saké and preparing thinly sliced fish, but ask him to interrupt his banquet for a moment and come to the temple. Say that I will tell him a most unusual tale, and look closely at what everyone there is doing. Repeat exactly what I have told you, nothing else." The messenger was dubious, but he went to the mansion, gave the message to an intermediary, and then stealthily looked inside. The officer, his younger brother Jūrō, his retainer Kamori, and others were seated in a circle, drinking saké. The messenger was startled, because the scene was exactly as his master had said it would be. When they heard the message, the people in the officer's house were greatly surprised. Putting down his chopsticks, the officer went to the temple, attended by Jūrō and Kamori.

Raising his head from the pillow, Kōgi thanked his visitor for coming, and the officer congratulated Kōgi on his recovery. Then Kōgi said, "Listen to what I have to say. Have you ever bought fish from that fisherman named Bunshi?" Startled, the officer replied, "Yes, I have indeed. How did you know?" Kōgi said, "The fisherman entered your gate with a basket containing a fish more than three feet long. You were in the south wing, playing go with your younger brother. Kamori was sitting beside you, eating a large peach and watching the game. Delighted by the big fish that the man had brought,

l. 9   *dānapati* (J. *dan'otsu*): the Sanskrit word for a lay believer who supports the monastic community with donations.

you gave him a tray of peaches and shared your saké with him. The cook proudly took out the fish and cut it into thin slices. Am I right so far?" Hearing this, the officer and his men, suspicious and confused, pressed him to explain how he knew these things in such detail. Kōgi told them.

"The suffering caused by my illness became unbearable. Unaware that I had stopped breathing, I leaned on my staff and went out through the gate, hoping to relieve the feverishness a little, whereupon my illness began to ease and I felt like a caged bird returning to the land of clouds. Making my way through mountains and villages, I arrived again at the edge of the lake. When I saw the pale-jade water, I felt reality slip away and thought that I would have a swim, and so, shedding my robe, I threw myself in, plunged to the depths, and swam here and there, frolicking as I pleased, even though I am not one who grew accustomed to the water as a child. I realize now that it was all a foolish dream. But a man cannot float in the water with the ease of a fish. I began to wish that I could disport myself like a fish. Nearby was a large fish, who said, 'The master's wish is easily granted. Please wait here.' He disappeared into the depths, but soon a man wearing a crown and robes ascended toward me, sitting astride the same large fish and leading many other fish behind him. He said to me, 'I bear a message from the Lake God: "You, old monk, have acquired much merit by releasing creatures that were captured by men. Now you have entered the water and wish to swim about like a fish. For a time, we will give you the garb of a golden carp and let you enjoy the pleasures of the water world. But you must be careful not to be tempted by the fragrance of bait, get caught on a line, and lose your life."' Having said this much, he disappeared. Astonished, I looked at myself, and found that I had acquired glowing, golden scales and turned into a carp.

"Not thinking this particularly strange, I swished my tail, moved my fins, and rambled about as I pleased.[8] First I rode the waves that were raised by the wind blowing down from

Mount Nagara, and then, wandering along the edge of the Great Bay of Shiga, I was startled by people strolling back and forth, so close to the water that their skirts got wet, and so I tried to dive in the depths where high Mount Hira casts its reflection, but I found it hard to hide myself when the fishing flares of Katada at night drew me as though I were dreaming. The moon resting on the waters of the berry-black night shone clear on the peak of Mount Kagami and drove the shadows from the eighty corners of the eighty ports to cast a lovely scene.[9] Okino Isle, Chikubu Isle—the vermillion fence reflected in the waves startled me. Soon I was awakened from my dreams among the reeds as the Asazuma Boat rowed out in the wind from Mount Ibuki; I dodged the practiced oar of the Yabase ferryman and many times was driven away by the bridge-guard of Seta. When the sun grew warm, I rose to the surface; when the wind was strong, I swam in the depths.

"Suddenly feeling hungry, I searched here and there for something to eat. I swam around frantically, unable to find anything, until I came upon the line that Bunshi was dangling in the water. His bait was wonderfully fragrant. Then I remembered the Lake God's warning. I am a disciple of the Buddha. How should I stoop to eating fish bait, just because I have been unable to find food for a while? I swam away. With time, the hunger grew steadily worse, and I reconsidered, thinking: I can hardly bear it any longer. Even if I swallowed the bait, would I be so reckless as to get caught? I have known Bunshi for a long time; why should I hold back? I took the bait. Bunshi promptly hauled in the line and caught me. 'Hey! What are you doing?' I cried, but, pretending not to hear me, he passed a cord through my chin, tied up his boat in the reeds, placed me in a basket, and went in through your gate. You were in the south room, playing go with your younger brother. Kamori sat nearby, eating fruit. Seeing the large fish that Bunshi had brought, everyone was delighted and congratulated him. At that point, I spoke to all of you. 'Have you forgotten Kōgi? Release me, please! Let me go

back to the temple,' I cried, again and again, but you pretended not to hear and just clapped your hands in delight. The cook pressed both of my eyes hard with the fingers of his left hand, took up a well-sharpened knife in his right hand, placed me on the chopping block, and was about to cut, when I screamed in agony. 'Is there any precedent for hurting a disciple of the Buddha this way? Help me, help me!' I cried, but no one listened. When I felt that I was about to be cut, I awakened from my dream."

Everyone was deeply moved and amazed. "Thinking about the master's story," said the officer, "I remember seeing the fish's mouth move each time, but there was no voice

"When I felt that I was about to be cut, I awakened from my dream."

at all. It is marvelous to have seen such a thing with my own eyes." Sending a messenger running to his house, he had the remaining slices of fish thrown into the lake.

After this, Kōgi recovered completely and lived for many years before he died of old age. As his end approached, he took the many carp that he had painted and released them into the lake, where the fish left the paper and silk to swim about in the water. For this reason, none of Kōgi's paintings survived. A disciple named Narimitsu inherited Kōgi's divine skill and became famous in his time. It is recorded in an old tale that he painted a chicken on a sliding door at the Kan'in Palace, and when a live chicken saw the painting, he kicked it.[10]

NOTES

1. The Tang story on which the former is based has been translated by Lin Yutang as "The Man Who Became a Fish," in *Famous Chinese Short Stories* (New York: Day, 1948), pp. 273–278. On Chinese vernacular fiction, see, for example, Feng Meng-Lung, ed., *Stories from a Ming Collection: Translations of Chinese Short Stories Published in the Seventeenth Century*, trans. Cyril Birch (New York: Grove, 1958); and Patrick Hanan, *The Chinese Vernacular Story* (Cambridge, Mass.: Harvard University Press, 1981).

2. Uzuki Hiroshi, *Ugetsu monogatari hyōshaku*, Nihon koten hyōshaku zenchūshaku sōsho (Tokyo: Kadokawa, 1969), pp. 298–299.

3. Burton Watson, trans., *Chuang Tzu: Basic Writings* (New York: Columbia University Press, 1964), p. 45.

4. Watson, trans., *Chuang Tzu*, p. 110.

5. Mishima Yukio, "*Ugetsu monogatari* ni tsuite," in *Mishima Yukio zenshū* (Tokyo: Shinchōsha, 1975), vol. 25, p. 273.

6. In Buddhist teachings, releasing captured creatures is meritorious.

7. Taking life is the first of the five proscribed actions in Buddhism. The others are stealing, licentiousness, lying, and consuming alcohol. These bad karma (actions) impede one's gradual progress toward enlightenment and buddhahood.

8. The michiyuki follows, studded with utamakura, as carp-Kōgi swims clockwise around Lake Biwa and evokes famous sights from the point of view of a fish.

9. "berry-black night" (*nubatama no yoru*): *nubatama*, the seed of the blackberry lily (*Belamcanda chinensis*), also called leopard lily, is a pillow-word conventionally used to modify the terms "night," "black," "darkness," "evening," "hair," and, by extension, "dream" and "moon."

    "eighty corners of the eighty ports" (*yaso no minato no yasokuma*): *yaso* (eighty) here means "many"; *yaso no minato* could be a place-name (Yaso Port), but I take it here to mean "many ports."

10. "old tale": story 11:16 in Narisue, *Stories Heard from Writers Old and New*. Narimitsu probably lived in the middle of the tenth century. The Kan'in Palace, originally the mansion of Fujiwara Fuyutsugu (775–826), in Kyoto, served as an imperial palace in the twelfth and thirteenth centuries.

BOOK THREE

THE OWL OF THE THREE JEWELS

TITLE

The title, "Buppōsō," refers to two different birds: *buppōsō*, a broad-billed roller (*Eurystomus orientalis*), and *konohazuku*, the Japanese scops owl (*Otsu scops japonicus*). The call of the owl is thought to sound like *buppan* (Buddhist dharma) or *buppōsō*—Buddha, dharma, *saṅgha* (the Buddha, his teachings, and the community of monks, nuns, and laity), which constitute the "Three Jewels" of Buddhism. Accordingly, this owl is sometimes called buppōsō or *sambōchō* (three-jewel bird).

CHARACTERS

The number of characters in "The Owl of the Three Jewels" expands beyond the one or two in the previous stories to include the fictional merchants Muzen and his son, the ghost of the famous poet Satomura Jōha, the ghosts of Toyotomi Hidetsugu and his retainers, and Kōbō Daishi, whose spirit hovers over the story, constantly in the minds of the characters and readers.

Kōbō Daishi, or Kūkai (774–835), the founder of the Shingon (True Word) sect of Buddhism, is perhaps the greatest figure in the history of Japanese religion. In the story, he is referred to as the "Great Teacher." The honorific title Kōbō Daishi (Great Teacher Who Spread the Dharma) was conferred on him posthumously by Emperor Daigo in 921.

Toyotomi Hidetsugu (1568–1595) was the nephew and adopted son of the national unifier Toyotomi Hideyoshi (1537–1598). Although Hidetsugu succeeded Hideyoshi as regent (*kampaku*) in 1592, he fell out of favor after the birth of Hideyoshi's natural son, Hideyori, in 1593; two years later, he was ordered to commit suicide at Mount Kōya with sixteen of his retainers. Hidetsugu had a deep interest in nō, poetry, and other classics, but also was so bloodthirsty that he earned the nickname Sasshō Kampaku (Killer Regent), a pun on *sesshō kampaku*, in which the word *sesshō* is the title of a regent who serves a child emperor. The Portuguese Jesuit missionary Luis Frois (1532–1597) reported that Hidetsugu "had one weakness, namely a passionate delight in killing."[1]

Satomura Jōha (1524–1602) was the leading poet of his time and the last major renga master. The title by which he identifies himself, Bridge of the Dharma (Hokkyō), was applied to holy men, especially those who were also writers, painters, or physicians who served as a "bridge" for ordinary people who sought to understand the dharma. Jōha is known to have been invited to compose renga with Hidetsugu.

PLACES

"The Owl of the Three Jewels" begins in Ōka, now the town of Taki, located to the west of the Ise Shrines in Mie Prefecture. Muzen and his son travel to Kyoto and then to Mount Kōya (Kōyasan), where most of the story takes place.

Like "Shiramine" and "The Blue Hood," "The Owl of the Three Jewels" includes a michiyuki:

Nijō: district just to the south of the imperial palace in Kyoto. Having a second house at this location is a sign of Muzen's wealth.

Yoshino: mountainous area of Nara Prefecture, south of Kyoto, celebrated since ancient times for its magnificent cherry blossoms. Part of "A Serpent's Lust" also takes place in Yoshino.

Mount Kōya: mountain with a vast complex of monasteries, the headquarters of the Shingon sect of Buddhism, about sixty-two miles southwest of Kyoto, in Wakayama Prefecture (formerly, Kii Province).

Tennokawa: village through which pilgrims coming from the east passed on the road to Mount Kōya.

Mani: "holy mountain of Mani" (*mani no miyama*) sometimes refers to the whole of Mount Kōya, but here may refer specifically to the mountain called Mani, east of the Mount Kōya temple complex. *Mani* is originally a Sanskrit word meaning "pure" or "jewel."

TIME

Early summer in a year after 1616, early in the Tokugawa period: "more than eight hundred years" after the founding of Kōyasan.

BACKGROUND

In 804, as a student monk, Kūkai sailed to China, where he met with great success in his studies of esoteric Buddhism. Legend has it that, just before his return to Japan in 806, he threw a three-pronged *vajra* (J. *sanko*) toward Japan. It landed in a pine tree—the Vajra Pine (Sanko no matsu), which stands in the center of the main compound on Mount Kōya. (The vajra [Sanskrit for "diamond"], originally an Indian weapon resembling a two-headed mallet with three blades on each end, evolved in tantric and esoteric Buddhism into a ceremonial implement.) Kūkai established the monastic complex at Mount Kōya in 816. Most of the story takes place at the Lantern Hall (Tōrōdō) in front of Kōbō Daishi's mausoleum at Mount Kōya, where his followers believe he lies in a state of animated suspension. Pilgrims to the Mausoleum recite the chant *Namu Daishi Henjō Kongō*: "I put my faith in the great teacher who brings light to all the people, Universal Adamantine Illuminator."[2]

The Lantern Hall and Mausoleum are at some remove from the central compound at Kōya, which is called the Platform (Danjō). About 5 acres in area, the Platform contains the Great Pagoda, the Golden Hall, other important buildings, and the Vajra Pine. A 1¼-mile path lined with thousands of gravestones, including those of some of the most famous figures of Japanese history, leads east from the Platform through giant cedars to the Mausoleum. The path, the Lantern Hall, the Mausoleum, and other buildings together are referred to as the Inner Sanctuary (Oku-no-in). The flames in the Lantern Hall are said to have burned continuously since 1016. A narrow stream called the Tamagawa (Jewel River) flows in front of the Lantern Hall, where it is spanned by a short bridge.

Poetry in both Chinese and Japanese plays an important role in "The Owl of the Three Jewels." Muzen is an amateur poet in the "haikai style," which refers to a style of renga in which links of seventeen (5–7–5) and fourteen (7–7) syllables alternate. Muzen's verse, given in the story, could stand alone as a haiku or serve as the *hokku* (first link) of a linked-verse sequence. It was presumably composed by Akinari, who began writing and publishing haikai in his youth. The other poet in the tale is Jōha. The prominence of poetry in the story, especially Jōha's explication of Kōbō Daishi's waka, reflects Akinari's kokugaku interests.

AFFINITIES

Several sources of inspiration for "The Owl of the Three Jewels" have been identified: two stories in Qu You's *Jiandeng xinhua* (*New Tales After Trimming the Lamp*, 1378); Asai Ryōi's adaptation of one of them, "Yūrei shoshō o hyōsu" (Ghosts Evaluate Various Generals), in *Otogibōko* (*Talisman Dolls*, 1666); "Fushimi Momoyama bōrei no gyōretsu no koto" (A Procession of Ghosts at Fushimi Momoyama), in *Kaidan tonoibukuro* (*Ghost Stories: A Sack of Courtly Bedclothes*, 1768), edited by Ōe Bunpa; *Taiheiki* (*Record of Great Peace*, fourteenth century); Oze Hoan's *Taikōki* (*Chronicle of the Taikō* [*Hideyoshi*], 1617); and Hayashi Razan's *Honchō jinja kō* (*Studies of Japanese Shrines*).

OTHER OBSERVATIONS

For an analysis of "The Owl of the Three Jewels," see "Structure of the Stories," in the introduction.

The story echoes the indirect praise for the Tokugawa regime that appears in the Preface: "the ancient Tranquil Land" alludes, with an elegant old epithet for Japan (*urayasu no kuni*), to the tranquillity of the period and, with "ancient" (*hisashiku*), refers both to the unbroken line of emperors and to the long rule of the Tokugawa family, which had continued peacefully for more than 150 years by the time the story was written. The indirect praise continues, as the first paragraph refers to the popularity and relative safety of domestic travel, which before the Tokugawa regime had been fraught with danger, as depicted in "The Reed-Choked House." In a broader sense, the entire story pays tribute to the Tokugawa, who brought peace and stability to the country after the turbulent Toyotomi era, of which the story is such a vivid reminder. The praise is echoed again in the last story, "On Poverty and Wealth."

*I*n the ancient *Tranquil Land, people toil and enjoy their*
tasks and in their leisure hours relax under blossoms
in the spring, visit brocade forests in the fall, and, thinking they must know Tsukushi of the unknown fires, rest their
heads on rudders, and then turn eager thoughts to the peaks
of Fuji and Tsukuba.[3]

In a village called Ōka, in Ise, a man of the Hayashi clan
transferred his affairs to his heir, shaved his head (though he
had suffered no particular misfortune), changed his name
to Muzen, and, being robust and free of any disease, looked
forward to traveling here and there in his old age. Lamenting
that his youngest son, Sakunoji, was boorish and inflexible
by nature, he took the boy to stay for more than a month at his
second house, in the Nijō district, thinking that he would show
him how people of the capital behaved; then, late in the Third
Month, they viewed the blossoms in the depths of Yoshino,
where they rested for seven days at a temple he knew; and,
being nearby, he thought that they would go also to Mount
Kōya, which they had never seen, and so they pushed their
way through the lush green leaves of early summer, crossed
the mountains from a place called Tennokawa, and arrived at
the holy mountain of Mani. Exhausted from the steep path,
they were surprised to see the sun beginning to set.

After worshipping at the Platform and all the various
halls and mausoleums, they asked for lodging, but no one
responded. When they questioned a passerby about the rules

l. 4   Tsukushi: an old name for the island of Kyushu.
l. 4   "unknown fires" (*shiranuhi*): a pillow-word that conventionally modifies
       Tsukushi.
l. 5   "heads on rudders" (*kajimakura*): refers to a journey by ship.
l. 8   "shaved his head": signifies the taking of Buddhist vows.
l. 10 Muzen: a Buddhist name meaning, literally, "dreamlike."

of the place, they were told, "People with no connection to a temple or to a monks' residence go down to the foot of the mountain to spend the night. No one puts up travelers for the night on this mountain." What would they do? Although he was healthy, Muzen was an old man who had just toiled up a steep path, and now, hearing this, he felt completely spent. Sakunoji said, "It is growing dark, our legs are sore—how can we go back down that long road? A young person does not mind lying down on the grass, but I worry that you would take sick." Muzen said, "The poignancy of travel lies in just this sort of thing. Even if we went down the mountain tonight, dejected, exhausted, and injuring our legs, we would not be back at home. There is no telling what awaits us on the road tomorrow, either. This mountain is the holiest place in Japan. There are no words to describe the boundless virtue of the Great Teacher. Having come this far, we must pass the night in prayer at a temple, asking for an easy rebirth in the next life, and now is the perfect opportunity—we shall spend the night praying at the Mausoleum." Passing through the shadows on the path beneath the cedars, they ascended to the veranda of the Lantern Hall, which stands before the Mausoleum; spread out their rain gear to make a place to sit; and chanted calmly while the night gradually deepened, making them feel lonesome and desolate.

The temple grounds were an auspicious, holy place, a clearing one-third of a mile on each side without a shabby grove in sight, where even the smallest pebble had been swept away;[4] but here, far removed from the temples, no sound of incantations, bells, or ringing-staffs could be heard. Luxuriant trees pushed through the clouds; the sound of water flow-

l. 29 "incantations" (J. *darani*, Skt. *dhāraṇi*): Sanskrit phrases—the "true words" of Shingon—believed to have mystical power.

l. 29 "ringing-staffs" (*shaku[jō]*): wooden staffs with brass heads, decorated with metal loops that ring when moved. Originally used by itinerant holy men in India to frighten off snakes, they evolved into ceremonial staffs carried by priests.

ing beside the path was light and clear, deepening the melancholy. Unable to sleep, Muzen spoke: "The Great Teacher's godlike moral influence brings enlightenment even to the soil, rocks, grass, and trees, and coming down to us today after more than eight hundred years it is ever more splendid and noble. Among his many achievements all around the country is this mountain, the greatest of all Buddhist temples. When the Teacher was living, he crossed to distant China, where something happened that moved him deeply. Saying 'Wherever this lands will be the holy spot from which I shall spread my Way,' he threw a vajra into the far-off sky, and this mountain is where it came to rest. I have heard that it lodged in the Vajra Pine at the front of the Platform. They say there is no grass, tree, spring, or rock on this mountain that is not sacred. That we are able unexpectedly to take lodgings here this night is the result of a happy bond, transcending a single life.[5] Although you are young, you must never neglect your faith." He spoke softly, his voice clear and wistful.

In the woods behind the Mausoleum, it seemed, a bird cried *buppan, buppan,* and the echo sounded close at hand. Muzen felt suddenly wide awake: "Extraordinary. The bird that just sang must be the one called buppōsō. I heard a long time ago that it nests on this mountain, but I have never met anyone who had actually heard its voice. The fact that we have been able to hear this while we lodge here tonight may be an omen that our misdeeds will vanish and we will take good karma into the next life. They say that this bird chooses immaculate places to live. It is well known that it nests on Mount Kashō in the province of Kanzuke, Mount Futara in the province of Shimozuke, the peak of Daigo in Yamashiro, Mount Shinaga in Kawachi,[6] and especially on this mountain, as a *gāthā* poem by the Great Teacher says:

---

l. 32 "*gāthā* poem" (*shige*): praise (Skt. *gāthā*) for the Buddha's virtue and an explanation of his teachings, in the form of a Chinese poem.

In the quiet forest, sitting alone in my hut at dawn
I hear the call of the Three Jewels in one bird.
The bird has a voice, I have a mind—
voice, mind, clouds, water, all perfectly enlightened.[7]

Another old poem says:

As the peak of Matsuno-o quietly greets the dawn
I look up and hear the bird cry *buppōsō*.[8]

It has been handed down that, long ago, the gods of Matsuno-o commanded this bird always to serve the priest Enrō of Saifukuji, because he was without equal as a believer in the *Lotus Sutra*, and so we know that the bird lives in that sacred precinct as well.[9] Tonight, strangely enough, we have already heard the voice of the bird. How can I fail to be moved in these circumstances?"[10] After cocking his head in thought for a time, he recited a seventeen-syllable verse in the haikai style, of which he had long been fond:

"The cry of the bird is mysterious, too—lush foliage on the
   secret mountain."[11]

Taking out his travel-inkstone, he wrote down the verse by lantern light, then strained his ears in hopes of hearing the voice of the bird again, when, to his surprise, he heard instead the stern voice of a forerunner, coming from the direction of the distant temples and gradually drawing closer. "Who could be coming to worship so late at night?" he said, in puzzlement and fear. Exchanging glances, father and son held their breath as they peered toward the voice. Soon a young samurai outrider approached them, stomping roughly on the planks of the bridge.

Startled, they hid on the right side of the hall, but the samurai quickly discovered them. "Who are you?" he said. "His Excellency is coming. Get down quickly." In a panic,

they climbed down from the veranda and prostrated themselves on the ground. Soon they could hear the sound of
many shoes, particularly the resounding echo of clogs, as
a nobleman dressed in court robes and cap ascended to the
hall, followed by four or five samurai, who sat to his right
and left. The nobleman said to his attendants, "Why is so-
and-so not here?" "He should be here soon," one of them
replied. Again footsteps could be heard, and another group,

---

l. 3 "clogs" (*asagutsu*): made of black-lacquered paulownia and lined with
silk, worn by court nobles.
l. 4 "court robes and cap" (*eboshi nōshi*): the everyday wear of nobles.

"Soon a young samurai outrider approached them, stomping roughly on the planks of the bridge."

including a dignified samurai and a lay-priest with a shaved head, bowed and ascended to the hall. Addressing the samurai who had just arrived, the nobleman said, "Hitachi, why are you late?" The samurai replied, "Shirae and Kumagae were hard at work, saying that they would offer saké to Your Excellency, and so I wanted to prepare some fresh fish to go with it. This is why I have arrived late to serve Your Excellency."[12] When the fish had been arranged and presented, the nobleman said, "Mansaku, you pour."[13] A beautiful young samurai respectfully approached on his knees and raised the saké flask. As the cup was passed from person to person, the party appeared to grow lively. The nobleman spoke again: "I have not heard Jōha's stories for a long time. Summon him." The order seemed to be passed from man to man, until a large monk with a flat face and prominent features, wearing a priest's robes, appeared from behind the prostrate Muzen and sat at the end of the row. The nobleman questioned him on various ancient matters, about which he replied in detail. Greatly impressed, the nobleman said, "Give him a reward."

One of the samurai asked the monk a question: "I have heard that this mountain was established by a priest of high virtue, that there is no soil, rock, grass, or tree here that is not sacred. Yet there is poison in the waters of the Jewel River.[14] A man who drinks this water will die. For this reason, I have heard, the Great Teacher composed a poem:

Forgetting, the traveler will surely scoop and drink—
the waters of the Jewel River deep in Takano.[15]

Why is it that, despite his high virtue, he did not dry up this poisonous stream? What is your analysis of this strange matter?" Smiling, the monk said, "The poem was selected for inclusion in the *Fūgashū*.[16] In the headnote, the author explained, 'There being many poisonous insects upstream in the river called "Jewel River," on the path to the Inner Sanctuary of Takano, I cautioned against drinking from the stream and later wrote this poem.' And so it is just as you have recalled. Further, your question is reasonable because the Great Teacher, having mysterious, god-like powers, made the invisible gods open up roads where there had been none before; he cut through rocks more easily than digging in the soil, imprisoned great serpents, and subdued goblin-birds—when we consider that he accomplished these great deeds, which are revered by all under heaven, we cannot accept the headnote as the truth. There are, of course, streams called Jewel River in various provinces,[17] and all the poems composed about them praise the purity of their waters, leading us to conclude that this Jewel River, too, is not a poisonous stream; that the spirit of the poem is 'Even if someone coming here to worship has forgotten the existence of such a famous river on this mountain, he will be delighted by the purity of the stream and scoop some water up to drink'; and that somebody concocted the headnote later, having heard a groundless report about poison. If we pursue our doubts further, we will see that the poem is not in the style of the early days of the present capital.[18] Generally, in the old language of this country, 'jeweled chaplet,' 'jeweled curtain,' 'jeweled robe,' and the like were words of praise for a beautiful form or purity, so that pure water, too, was praised as 'jewel water,' 'jewel well,' and 'jewel river.'[19] Why would anyone have attached 'jewel' to the name of a poisonous stream? People who embrace Buddhism blindly and fail to grasp the spirit of poetry often make this kind of mistake. It is very perceptive of you to question the meaning of this poem, especially as you are not a poet yourself," he concluded, praising the man warmly. The nobleman and all the others lauded the reasonableness of this explanation.

From behind the hall came the cry *buppan, buppan,* sounding quite near. Raising his cup, the nobleman said, "That bird rarely calls. Tonight's party is better than ever. Jōha, how about it?" The monk bowed and said, "A link from me would surely sound fusty to your ears, my Lord. A traveler passing the night here has been reciting haikai in the current style. It would seem fresh to you, my Lord; please summon him and listen." "Call him," said the nobleman. A young samurai turned to Muzen and said, "You have been summoned. Approach." Unsure whether he was dreaming or awake, Muzen crept forward, trembling with fear. The monk turned to him. "That verse you just composed—present it to my Lord," he said. Muzen replied fearfully, "I do not remember what it

l. 24 "how about it": the nobleman is asking Jōha for a verse.

was. Please forgive me." The monk pressed him: "You said 'the secret mountain,' did you not? His Excellency is waiting. Quickly." More terrified than ever, Muzen said, "Who is the person you call His Excellency, holding a banquet by night, deep in this mountain? It is very mysterious." The monk answered, "The man I refer to as His Excellency is the regent, Lord Hidetsugu. The others are Kimura Hitachi-no-suke, Sasabe Awaji, Shirae Bingo, Kumagae Daizen, Awano Moku, Hibino Shimotsuke, Yamaguchi Shōun, Marumo Fushin, the lay-monk Ryūsai, Yamamoto Tonomo, Yamada Sanjūrō, Fuwa Mansaku, and, addressing you, Jōha, Bridge of the Dharma.[20] It is due to a strange and fortunate bond that you are able to behold His Excellency. Now hurry and give him your verse." It was so horrible that the hair on Muzen's head would have stood on end, had there been any hair, and he felt as though his innards and his spirit alike were flying away into space. Trembling, he drew a clean sheet of paper from his pilgrim-bag, wrote on it with a faltering brush, and presented it. Tonomo took the paper and recited in a loud voice:

> "The cry of the bird is mysterious, too—lush foliage on the secret mountain."

"Clever," said the nobleman. "Someone provide a linking stanza."[21] Yamada Sanjūrō moved forward and said, "I shall try." Cocking his head in thought for a moment, he produced:

> "Burning poppy seeds till dawn of a short night on the dais.[22]

How is this?" He showed it to Jōha. "Well done," the monk said, and presented it to his lord, who said, "Not bad." Well pleased, he took a drink and passed the cup around.

Suddenly turning pale, the man called Awaji said, "The

asura time is here already. The asuras say that they have come to escort you. Please rise." Instantly, the faces of the entire party turned as red as though blood had been poured over them. In high spirits they cried, "Again tonight we shall take Ishida, Masuda, and the rest by surprise."[23] Hidetsugu turned to Kimura. "I have shown myself to these two nobodies," he said. "Take them with us to the asura realm." The senior retainers intervened and spoke with one voice: "Their life spans have not yet run out. Do not repeat your evil deeds," but their words, and the figures of all the party, seemed to fade into the distant sky.

Muzen and his son fainted and lay motionless for a time, and then, as the eastern sky brightened, they were revived by the chill of the dew; but still terrified in the partial darkness, they fervently chanted the name of the Great Teacher,[24] until, finally seeing the sun emerge, they rushed down the mountain, returned to the capital, and sought treatment with medicines and acupuncture. One day as he was passing the Sanjō Bridge, Muzen thought of the Brutality Mound and felt his gaze being drawn toward the temple.[25] "It was horrible, even in broad daylight," he recounted to people in the capital. The story has been recorded here just as he told it.

l. 1   "asura" (J. *ashura* or *shura*): in Buddhism, former human beings reborn as demons in the asura realm, which among the Six Realms is the one reserved for those who have been arrogant and jealous or have indulged in dissipation and fighting. The cruel and dissolute Hidetsugu has been reborn in the asura realm, where he and the other inhabitants are condemned to constant fighting.

NOTES

1. Quoted in George Sansom, *A History of Japan*, vol. 2, *1334–1615* (Stanford, Calif.: Stanford University Press, 1961), p. 366.

2. Translated by Oliver Statler, *Japanese Pilgrimage* (New York: Morrow, 1983), p. 28.

3. Fuji and Tsukuba are, by convention, the two principal peaks of eastern Japan. With the stability and prosperity of Japan and improved transportation under the Tokugawa regime, domestic travel became increasingly popular.

4. "clearing one-third of a mile on each side": the main compound at Kōya is, in fact, about one-third of a mile west to east, and about 120 yards north to south.

5. Muzen is saying that their good fortune is the result of a bond from a former life.

6. Mount Kashō is in the city of Numata, Gumma Prefecture; Mount Futara, now called Mount Nikkō, is in Tochigi Prefecture (it is said that Kūkai changed the name from Futara to Nikkō during a visit in 820); Mount Daigo is in Fushimi Ward, southeastern Kyoto; and Kawachi is the modern Osaka Prefecture. Shinaga apparently was the name of a mountain in Taishi, Minami-kawachi County.

7. This verse, which is in Chinese, appears in volume 10 of Kōbō Daishi, *Shōryōshū* (*Collected Inspirations*, 835), with the title "A Poem on Hearing [a] Buppōsō at Night at Ryūkōin on Mount Kōya." Paraphrased, the poem reads: "In the quiet forest, meditating alone in my hut at dawn, I hear the call of a three-jewel bird singing *buppōsō*, 'Buddha, dharma, saṅgha,' the Three Jewels. In its voice the bird embodies the Three Jewels, and I, hearing it, have a mind that responds. In this holy place, the animate voice and mind, the inanimate clouds and water all have attained perfect enlightenment." Ryūkōin, one of the Kōya sub-temples, stands just northeast of the main compound.

8. This poem, a waka, is by Fujiwara Mitsutoshi (1210–1276) and appears in *Fubokushō* (*The Japanese Collection*, ca. 1310). Mount Matsuno-o (Matsuo) is in Ukyō Ward, west of the Matsuno-o Shrine, Kyoto.

9. The deities enshrined at the Matsuno-o Shrine are Ōyamakui-no-kami and Ichikishimahime-no-mikoto. Enrō (1130–1208), an eminent priest of the Tendai sect, became abbot of Saifukuji, a temple that stood south of the Matsuno-o Shrine, in 1176. The *Lotus Sutra* (J. *Myōhōrengekyō*) is the basic scripture of the Tendai sect and perhaps the most important text in East Asian Buddhism.

10. Muzen echoes Kūkai, who, in his poem, said that his mind responded to the bird's call. Having heard the bird, Muzen is inspired to compose a poem.

11. "secret mountain": refers to Mount Kōya, the center of the Shingon sect of esoteric Buddhism.

12. At this point, a reader familiar with Japanese history will realize that the nobleman must be Toyotomi Hidetsugu. Kimura Hitachi-no-suke Shigekore (d. 1595) was a retainer and confidant of Hidetsugu; Shirae Bingo-no-kami (d. 1595) and Kumagae Daizen-no-suke Naoyuki (d. 1595) also were retainers of Hidetsugu. Hitachi-no-suke, Bingo-no-kami, and Daizen-no-suke are honorary court titles. Unlike many of Hidetsugu's other retainers, who died with him at Kōya, Kimura, Shirae, and Kumagae took their lives elsewhere; in this story, they have rejoined their master at Mount Kōya, but have arrived late.

13. Fuwa Mansaku (1579–1595), Hidetsugu's page, was noted for his beauty. He took his own life at Kōya, before his master.

14. Conventional wisdom held at the time that the waters of the Tamagawa (Jewel River) were poisonous.

15. This poem, a waka, is attributed to Kōbō Daishi and appears in the *Fūgashū* (*Collection of Elegance*, 1346), no. 1778. The headnote that precedes it reads (as Jōha says): "There being many poisonous insects upstream in the river called 'Jewel River,' on the path to the Inner Sanctuary of Takano, I cautioned against drinking from the stream and later wrote this poem." "Takano" is an alternative reading of the characters for Kōya. My translation of the poem follows Jōha's interpretation, which reflects Akinari's own reading (*Tandai shōshinroku* [*A Record of Daring and Prudence*, 1808], sec. 46) and differs from earlier readings in rejecting the headnote and interpreting the poem without reference to it. For readers who accept the headnote as authentic, the ambiguity of the first part of the poem has led to two distinct readings: "Forgetting [that the river is poisonous], did the [dead] traveler scoop and drink?" and "Even forgetting [that the river is poisonous], should the traveler scoop and drink? [No, he should not.]"

16. The *Fūgashū* is number seventeen of the twenty-one imperially commissioned anthologies of poetry.

17. The six most famous Jewel Rivers (Tamagawa)—all of them utamakura—are in the prefectures of Kyoto, Shiga, Osaka, Wakayama (at Kōya), Tokyo, and Miyagi.

18. Kyoto became the capital in 794, when Kōbō Daishi, the putative author of the poem, was five years old, or about a generation before

the great *Kokinshū* poets Henjō (816–890?), Narihira (825–880), and Komachi (fl. ca. 833–857). The natural assumption is that Kōbō Daishi would have composed poetry in the style of his own time.

19. "jeweled chaplet . . . jewel river": *tamakazura* (the title of the "Jeweled Chaplet" chapter of *The Tale of Genji*), *tamadare*, *tamaginu*, *tamamizu*, *tamanoi*, and *tamagawa*.

20. Sasabe Awaji-no-kami served as Hidetsugu's second when the disgraced regent committed suicide; Awano Moku-no-suke, Hibino Shimotsuke-no-kami, Yamaguchi Shōun, Marumo Fushin, Ryūsai, Yamamoto Tonomo-no-suke, and Yamada Sanjūrō were retainers of Hidetsugu who committed suicide just before or after their master. Yamamoto and Yamada were young pages. Awaji-no-kami, Moku-no-suke, Shimotsuke-no-kami, and Tonomo-no-suke are honorary court titles.

21. "linking stanza" (*tsukeku*): in renga (linked-verse), a tsukeku is a stanza that links with the preceding stanza. Renga poets had to observe strict rules.

22. This stanza, presumably composed by Akinari, evokes the image of a *goma* ritual, common in Shingon Buddhism, in which a priest chants spells and incantations while burning poppy seeds and slips of wood on a dais, to symbolize the flames of wisdom extinguishing bad karma. Reference to the goma ritual echoes "secret mountain" (Mount Kōya) in the first stanza, in that both allude to esoteric Buddhism. In other ways, too, the linking stanza conforms to the rules of renga:

"dais": the *gomadan* in the Goma Hall (Gomadō), one of the buildings in the Inner Sanctuary at Kōya.

"till dawn": recalls the cry of the buppōsō at dawn in the first stanza.

"short night": like "lush foliage," in the first stanza, alludes to summer.

23. Ishida Mitsunari (1560–1600) and Masuda Nagamori (1545–1615), close retainers of Toyotomi Hideyoshi, were said to have conspired to turn Hideyoshi against Hidetsugu in the first place and were among those who signed the order for Hidetsugu's suicide.

24. That is, they chanted *Namu Daishi Henjō Kongō*.

25. On the grounds of the Buddhist temple Zuisenji, southeast of the bridge spanning the Takase River at Sanjō, in Kyoto, stands the Hidetsugu Brutality Mound (Hidetsugu Akugyakuzuka), in which are buried Hidetsugu's head and the remains of his wife, concubines, and children—some thirty people in all—who were executed on Hideyoshi's orders.

THE KIBITSU CAULDRON

TITLE

The title, "Kibitsu no kama," refers to the rice-cauldron oracle at the Kibitsu Shrine, in Okayama Prefecture.

CHARACTERS

All the characters in "The Kibitsu Cauldron" are fictional. The protagonists are Shōtarō, a farmer; his wife, Isora, the daughter of a Shinto priest; his lover, Sode, a prostitute; and Hikoroku, Sode's cousin.

PLACES

"The Kibitsu Cauldron" begins in the Kibi region, in the village of Niise, now called Niwase, Okayama Prefecture. Kibi consisted of the provinces of Bizen, Bitchū, Mimasaka, and Bingo, corresponding to Okayama Prefecture and part of Hiroshima Prefecture. The nearby Kibitsu Shrine, a major Shinto shrine in western Japan, is located in the town of Magane, Okayama Prefecture. It enshrines Ōkibitsuhiko-no-mikoto, son of Emperor Kōrei (legendary dates, 290–215 B.C.E.).

The rest of the story takes place in the village of Arai, now part of the city of Takasago, Hyōgo Prefecture, about fifty miles east of Niise/Niwase on the road to the capital.

TIME

Autumn, around 1500, or three generations from 1441 (the year of the Kakitsu Incident).

BACKGROUND

The Cauldron Purification ritual (Mikamabarai) is held in a small building on the grounds of the Kibitsu Shrine. Inside, a large iron rice cauldron rests on a clay hearth. When the water boils, fueled by burning pine needles, the cauldron makes a rumbling sound, the volume of which is taken to indicate good or bad fortune.

In "The Kibutsu Cauldron," Isora is depicted as the ideal wife of the time, as prescribed in such books as *Onna daigaku* (*The Great Learning for Women*, 1716), attributed to Kaibara Ekiken (1630–1714): she rises early, retires late, faithfully serves her husband and parents-in-law, and secretly empathizes with her husband's concubine. The most dramatic example in Japanese literature of a wife's concern for her husband's lover is in Chikamatsu Monzaemon's play *Shinjū Ten no Amijima* (*Love Suicides at Amijima*, 1720), in which the wife overcomes her jealousy and secretly corresponds with the mistress. The tradition of the good wife who supports an unfaithful husband goes back at least as far as section 23 of *Ise monogatari* (*Tales of Ise*, ca. 947). The husband of the lady in *Ise* is so moved by her loyalty that he stops visiting the

other woman.[1] Shōtarō pretends to be moved by his wife's
devotion, but soon proves to be unworthy of her.

AFFINITIES

There is a long history of tales similar to "The Kibitsu Cauldron" in China and Japan. Commentators have identified a
number of sources on which Akinari drew in writing this
story, including, especially, Qu You's "Mudan deng ji" (Peony
Lantern), in *Jiandeng xinhua* (*New Tales After Trimming the
Lamp*, 1378), and its Japanese adaptation, Asai Ryōi's "Botan
no tōrō" (The Peony Lantern), in *Otogibōko* (*Talisman Dolls*,
1666);[2] "Onna no ichinen kite otto no mi o hikisoite torite
kaeru koto" (A Woman's Vindictive Spirit Comes, Draws
near Her Husband, and Takes Him Away with Her), in *Zen-
aku mukui hanashi* (*Stories of Karmic Retribution, Good and
Evil*, ca. 1700?), which combines tales 27:20 and 24:20 of the
late-Heian setsuwa collection *Konjaku monogatari shū* (*Tales
of Times Now Past*, ca. 1120); and Hayashi Razan's *Honchō
jinja kō* (*Studies of Japanese Shrines*). Some of the details in
the opening paragraph are derived from book 8 of Xie Zhaozhe's *Wuzazu* (*Five Miscellanies*, 1618).

A *jealous wife is intractable, but with age one knows her*
merits." Alas! Whose words are these? Even if the
harm she does is mild, she interferes with making
a living and ruins everything, and the neighbors' censure is
hard to escape; and when the harm is severe, she loses her
family, brings down the realm, and everywhere becomes a
laughingstock. There is no telling how many people since
ancient times have suffered this poison. The kind who, after
death, vents her wrath by turning into a serpent or a vio-

lent thunderbolt will never rest, though her flesh be pickled in salt. But such cases are rare. The husband who behaves uprightly and instructs his wife carefully can surely escape this affliction; and yet with some trivial thing, he will incite her perverse nature and bring grief upon himself. It is said that "what controls a bird is the human will; what controls a wife is her husband's manliness." Truly, this is so.

In the province of Kibi, county of Kaya, village of Niise lived a man named Izawa Shōdayū. His grandfather served the Akamatsu clan in Harima, but left their mansion at the time of the Kakitsu Incident and came here, where the three generations down to Shōdayū prospered, plowing in the spring and harvesting in the fall.[3] Shōdayū's only son, Shōtarō, disliked farming and disobeyed his father's precepts, indulging in saké and sensual pleasure. Lamenting this, his parents held secret conversations: "If we could only find a pretty girl from a good family for him to marry, he would behave himself." They searched tirelessly throughout the province, until, happily, a matchmaker said, "The daughter of Kasada Miki, the head priest at Kibitsu, has an elegant, refined nature and is devoted to her parents; moreover, she composes poetry and plays the koto masterfully. Since the family is a good one, descended from Kibi no Kamowake, this would be a splendid match for your family. I would hope that a marriage could be arranged. What do you think?" Shōdayū was delighted: "You have brought wonderful news. This could be the means to a thousand years of good fortune for my family; but the Kasadas are a noble house in this province, while we are nameless peasants. We cannot compare in social standing; I fear that they would not accept a proposal from us." The old matchmaker smiled: "You are

---

l. 1 "pickled in salt": one form of punishment in ancient China was to mince and pickle a criminal's flesh.

l. 23 Kibi no Kamowake: Kibi Kamowake-no-mikoto, the younger half brother of Ōkibitsuhiko-no-mikoto, the deity enshrined at Kibitsu.

far too modest. I will be congratulating you soon, without a doubt." He went to speak with Kasada, who was delighted as well; and when Kasada talked with his wife, she said, in high spirits, "Our daughter is already seventeen, and my heart has had no rest, night or day, wishing that we might find a good man for her to marry. Choose a date quickly, and exchange the betrothal gifts." Since she was so enthusiastic, they soon agreed to the engagement and reported to Izawa. The families exchanged generous gifts, chose a propitious day, and prepared for the wedding ceremony.

Further, in order to pray to the god for happiness, Kasada assembled shrine maidens and priests to make an offering of hot water. It has long been the custom for worshippers at the Kibitsu Shrine to make abundant offerings, present hot water to the god, and seek a divination of good or bad fortune. When the maidens complete their ritual prayers and the water comes to a boil, the cauldron will, if the prospects are good, produce a sound like the lowing of cattle. If the prospects are bad, the cauldron will make no sound. This is called the Kibitsu Cauldron Purification. In the matter concerning the Kasada family, however, there was no sound, not even the feeble chirping of insects in the autumn grass. Could it be that the god would not accept their prayers? This awakened misgivings in Kasada, who consulted his wife about the oracle. She had no doubts whatever: "It is because the priests' bodies were impure that the cauldron made no sound. Do they not say that, once betrothal gifts have been exchanged, the red cord is tied and the engagement must not be broken, even if the families are enemies or come from different lands? And especially in the case of the Izawas—I hear that they are a strict family, descended from men who knew one end of a bow from the other; surely they would

---

l. 28 "red cord . . . broken": this sentiment derives from a Chinese tale about an old man who possessed a red cord that he would use to bind the legs of a man and a woman. Once bound, they would inevitably marry.

not accept a refusal from us now. And our daughter is counting the days, having somehow learned that her fiancé is very
good looking. There is no telling what she might do if she
heard this inauspicious talk. If it came to that, our regrets
would be futile." Her use of every argument to remonstrate
with her husband no doubt resulted from her disposition
as a woman. Kasada did not pursue his doubts any further,
because he favored the match, and he went along with his
wife. Having completed their preparations, the two families
assembled and congratulated the bride and groom, singing of
the crane's one thousand years, the tortoise's ten thousand.

After Isora, Kasada's daughter, went to live with the Izawas, she served them with all her heart, rising early, retiring
late, always ready to help her parents-in-law, and accommodating to her husband's nature, so that the older Izawas were
overjoyed at her admirable devotion and fidelity. Shōtarō,
too, was moved by her sincerity, and their life as husband
and wife was happy. And yet, there was no getting around
his willful, dissolute nature. At some point, he grew close
to a woman of pleasure named Sode, at Tomonotsu;[4] finally,
he redeemed her contract and installed her in a house at a
nearby village, where he would spend days at a time without returning home. Resentful of this, Isora remonstrated
with him, sometimes using her in-laws' anger as an excuse,
sometimes lamenting her husband's fickleness; but he paid
no attention and stayed away for more than a month. Shōdayū, unable to stand idly by in the face of Isora's devotion,

---

l. 4   "If it came to that": the implication seems to be "if she lost her mind" or,
even, "if she took her own life."

l. 11 "the crane's one thousand years, the tortoise's ten thousand": proverbially, cranes live for one thousand years; tortoises, for ten thousand.
The families use these conventional phrases to wish for a long, happy
marriage.

l. 20 "woman of pleasure" (*asobimono* or *ukareme*): an indentured prostitute,
whose contract could be redeemed by a patron who wanted to take her
as a wife or mistress.

reprimanded Shōtarō and confined him in a room. This saddened Isora, who behaved more steadfastly than ever, waiting on her husband faithfully morning and night and sending things secretly to Sode.

One day, when his father was away from home, Shōtarō
appealed to Isora, saying, "When I see how truly faithful you
are, I feel nothing but remorse for my misdeeds. I shall send
that woman back to her home village and assuage Father's
anger. She is from the Inami Plain, in Harima. It made me
sad to see her in that wretched position, without parents, and
I took pity on her. If I abandon her, she will surely go back to
entertaining men at some port again. I have heard that people
are more compassionate in the capital, and so I want to take
her there and help her find service with a man of substance,
even if it means that she continues in the same wretched status. She must be in terrible straits now, with me shut up like
this. Who will see to her expenses on the road and her clothing? Could you manage these things and help her?" Isora
responded joyfully to his courteously phrased entreaties. "Put
your mind at rest," she said. Secretly exchanging her own
clothing and accessories for cash and using some pretense
to plead for money from her mother, she gave everything to
Shōtarō. Once he had the money, he slipped out of the house
and fled with Sode toward the capital. Isora, having been so
cruelly deceived, now was overwhelmed by resentment and
distress and took to her bed, seriously ill. The Izawas and
Kasadas hated him and pitied her, and fervently hoped that
medical treatment would effect her recovery; but even porridge was more than she could swallow, and she weakened
day by day, until finally there was no hope.

In Harima Province, district of Inami, village of Arai,
there was a man called Hikoroku. Because he was her
cousin, Sode and Shōtarō called on him first and stopped to
rest their feet for a while. Hikoroku said to Shōtarō, "Even
in the capital, not everyone is trustworthy. Stay here. We
will share our rice and find a way to make a living together."

Relieved to hear these welcome words, Shōtarō decided
that he and Sode would live here. Hikoroku, delighted to
have new companions, rented the run-down house adjoin-
ing his for them to occupy. Sode, however, seemed to come
down with a cold; she began to be vaguely unwell and then
appeared to have lost her mind, as though possessed by
some malign spirit. In his distress that this disaster had
befallen them, and only a few days after their arrival, Shōtarō forgot even to eat as he looked after her. Sode only
wailed, apparently feeling an unbearable pressure on her
chest,[5] and then, whenever the fever subsided, she would
seem the same as always. Could it be an angry spirit? Had
something happened to her whom he had abandoned in
his village? Shōtarō's heart ached. Hikoroku encouraged
him: "How could that be? I have seen many cases of people
suffering from an ague. When the fever goes down a little,
you will forget all about it, as though it had been a dream."
His easy manner was reassuring. Their care, however, had
not the slightest effect, and on the seventh day Sode passed
away. Looking up at the sky and stamping his feet on the
ground, Shōtarō wailed with grief like one insane, saying
that he wanted to accompany her in death. Hikoroku tried
to comfort him. "Nothing more can be done," he said, and
finally they turned her into smoke on a remote field. Gathering the bones, they constructed a grave, erected memorial
tablets, and, summoning a priest, prayed earnestly for her
enlightenment in the next life.

Now Shōtarō, lying prostrate, longed for the Land of the
Dead, but he could not employ the Way of Calling Back the
Spirit;[6] looking up, he thought of his home, but it seemed
even more distant than the Underworld: there was no ferry
before him, and he had lost the road that would take him
back; all day he lay in bed, and each evening he visited the
grave, where the grass had already grown thick and the
voices of the insects were vaguely forlorn. As he was telling
himself that the loneliness of autumn was for him alone,[7]

he saw the same grief elsewhere under the clouds in the sky,[8] for there was a new grave near this one and a sorrowful woman making an offering of flowers and water. "How sad for a young woman like you to be wandering on this desolate field," he said. She turned to look at him and said, "I come every evening, but you are always here before me. You must have parted from someone very dear to you. It makes me sad to think how you must feel." Tears were streaming down her cheeks. Shōtarō said, "Yes, ten days ago I lost my beloved wife, and I feel helpless and alone. Coming here is my only consolation. I suppose it is the same for you." The woman said, "This is my master's grave; we buried him here some days ago. I bring incense and flowers in place of my widowed mistress, who is so heartbroken that she has taken seriously ill." Shōtarō said, "It is only natural that she should fall ill. Who was the deceased, and where do you live?" The woman said, "My master was from a prominent family in this province, but he lost his holdings because of slander and came to live miserably on the edge of this field. My mistress is known as a great beauty, even in neighboring provinces; it was because of her that my master lost his house and land."[9] His heart stirred by this account, Shōtarō said, "Then, is your mistress's lonely dwelling close by? Perhaps I should visit her, so that we can comfort each other by expressing the sadness we share. Please take me with you." "The house is a little way off the road by which you came. She has no one to turn to; please visit her often. She must be waiting anxiously."[10] With this, she stood and led the way.

Walking about 250 yards, they came to a little path. Another 100 yards brought them to a small, thatched house in a gloomy wood. Light from the moon, past its first quarter, streamed brightly through a dreary bamboo gate, illuminating a meager, neglected garden.[11] The feeble light of a candle shone desolately through a paper window. "Please wait here," she said, and went inside. Standing next to a moss-covered

well, he peered into the house. Through the narrow space where a sliding door had been left open, he saw the glow of elegant, black-lacquered shelves as the flame wavered in a draft, exciting his curiosity. The woman came out: "When I told my mistress of your visit, she said, 'Please come in; I will speak with you from behind a screen,' and she has crept to the edge.[12] Please come inside." She led him in through the garden. The door to a twelve-foot-wide reception room was open just enough for a person to enter; inside stood a low folding screen, from which protruded the edge of some old bedding; apparently, the lady of the house lay there. Facing the screen, Shōtarō said, "I have heard that you not only

"Let me show how I
repay your cruelty."

suffered a bereavement, but also have fallen ill—I, too, have
lost my precious wife, and so, thinking that we might call
on each other in our mutual grief, I have presumed to visit
you." The lady pushed aside the folding screen a little. "So
we meet again, after all this time," she said. "Let me show
how I repay your cruelty." Astonished, he looked closely. It
was Isora, whom he had left behind in his home village. Her
face was ghastly pale, the bleary, tired eyes appalling, and a
pale, wasted hand pointed horribly this way. Crying out, he
collapsed and lost consciousness.

He came to after a time. Opening his eyes just a little,
he saw that what had appeared to be a house was in fact

a Samādhi Hall in the desolate field, and only a statue of the Buddha stood inside, darkened with age. Following the barks of a dog coming from the faraway village, he ran back home and told Hikoroku what had happened. "You were probably tricked by a fox," said Hikoroku. "A deceiving spirit will possess you when you feel low. A grief-stricken weakling like you needs to pray to the gods and buddhas and calm your heart. There is a venerable yin–yang master in the village of Toda. Have him purify you and ask him for some talismans." Leading Shōtarō to the yin–yang master, he explained the situation in detail, from the beginning, and requested a divination. The master considered his divination and said, "Misfortune is already pressing close upon you. This is no easy matter. The spirit first took a woman's life, and yet its resentment is not dissipated. Your life, too, could end tonight or tomorrow morning. Because seven days have passed since the spirit left this world, you must shut yourself inside for forty-two more days and exercise the greatest restraint on your behavior during that period. If you obey my warning, you just might escape death; if you go astray, for even a moment, you will not escape." After giving him this firm warning, the master took up a brush, wrote characters in the seal-style on Shōtarō's back and limbs, and gave him a number of paper talismans written in cinnabar. "Affix these charms to every door and pray to the gods and buddhas," he instructed. "Make no mistake,

l. 1 Samādhi Hall (Sanmaidō): *samādhi* is a Sanskrit word meaning "concentration"—the calm state in which all desires and distractions are absent and the mind is prepared for enlightenment. A Samādhi Hall is a place where one tries to achieve samādhi or, as here, a cemetery chapel where visitors pray for the enlightenment of the dead.

l. 8 "yin–yang master": in the Edo period, yin–yang masters practiced divination using the *I jing* (*The Book of Changes*) and physiognomy, performed Shinto purifications, and recited Buddhist incantations for the protection of their clients.

l. 18 "forty-two more days": in Buddhism, the spirit of the dead was believed to wander in this realm for forty-nine days.

lest you lose your life." Feeling both fearful and jubilant,
Shōtarō returned to his house, where he affixed the cinnabar charms to the doors and windows and shut himself in,
exercising the greatest restraint.

That night, during the third watch, he heard a horrid voice.
"Oh! I loathe him! Sacred charms have been put up here," it
muttered. That was all. Terrified, Shōtarō bewailed the length
of the night. At dawn, reviving, he immediately pounded
on the wall that separated his house from Hikoroku's and
recounted the events of the night before. Finally grasping the
uncanny accuracy of the yin–yang master's words, Hikoroku,
too, stayed up the following night and waited for the third
watch. The wind in the pines sounded fierce enough to topple
things over, and then the rain began to fall. As this extraordinary night progressed, the two men called to each other,
back and forth through the wall, until the fourth watch came.
Then a crimson light pierced the window-paper of Shōtarō's
house. "Oh! I loathe him! They have been affixed here, too!"
The voice was even more horrible so late at night; the hair on
Shōtarō's head and body stood on end, and he fainted away.
At daybreak, he talked about the night before; at nightfall,
he longed for daybreak: the days and weeks seemed to pass
more slowly than a thousand years. Every night, the spirit
circled the house or screamed from the ridgepole, its angry
voice more horrible each night than the night before.

This continued until the forty-second night. It would all
be over in one more night, and Shōtarō exercised special
restraint. At last, the sky of the fifth watch brightened. Feeling as though he had awakened from a long dream, Shōtarō
immediately called to Hikoroku, who came to the wall and
asked, "How are you?" "My strict confinement is over now,"
Shōtarō said. "I have not seen your face for a long time. I

---

l. 5   "third watch": the time between sunset and sunrise was divided into five
        equal watches of about two hours each. The third watch corresponded
        roughly to the period from midnight to 2:00 A.M.

long to see you and to comfort my heart by talking with you about the pain and fear of these past days. Get up. I shall step outside." Hikoroku, being a rash and thoughtless man, replied, "What could happen now? Come over here." He had not yet opened the door halfway when a scream pierced his ears from the eaves next door, and he fell back on his rump. Thinking that something must have happened to Shōtarō, he picked up an ax and went out into the main street, where he found that the night, which they thought had ended, was still dark; the moon cast a dim light from high in the sky, the wind was cold, and Shōtarō's door stood open, but he was nowhere to be seen. Maybe he had fled back inside? Hikoroku ran in to see, but it was not the sort of residence that offered any place to hide. Was he lying in the street? Hikoroku searched, but found nothing. What could have happened to him? he thought, both puzzled and afraid. Holding up a torch, he looked all around, until, next to the open door, he saw fresh blood dribbling from the wall onto the ground. And yet neither corpse nor bones were to be seen. In the moonlight, he glimpsed something at the edge of the eaves. When he held up the torch to look, he found a man's topknot hanging there, and nothing else. The pity and horror were more than can be expressed with brush and paper. When dawn came, he searched the nearby fields and hills, but he could find no trace of Shōtarō.

He reported this to the Izawa family, who tearfully informed Kasada. Thus it was said, as people passed the story down, that the accuracy of the yin–yang master's divination, and the ultimate rightness of the cauldron's unfavorable oracle, were truly precious and sacred.

NOTES

1. Helen Craig McCullough, trans., *Tales of Ise: Lyrical Episodes from Tenth-Century Japan* (Stanford, Calif.: Stanford University Press, 1968), pp. 87–89.

2. Asai Ryōi, *The Peony Lantern: "Botan no tōrō" from* Otogi bōko *(1666)*, trans. Maryellen Toman Mori, An Episodic Festschrift for Howard Hibbett, vol. 3 (Hollywood, Calif.: Highmoonoon, 2000).

3. The Akamatsu clan governed Harima Province, now part of Hyōgo Prefecture, from the mid-fourteenth century until 1441, the first year of Kakitsu, when Akamatsu Mitsutsuke assassinated the shogun and was, in turn, forced to commit suicide, in what is known as the Kakitsu Incident. The family later regained power in Harima and governed there until 1521.

4. The port of Tomonotsu, now part of the city of Fukuyama, Hiroshima Prefecture, is about twenty miles west of Niise/Niwase.

5. "Sode only wailed . . . chest": this wording is almost identical to that in the "Aoi" (Heartvine) chapter of *The Tale of Genji*, in which Genji's wife is possessed by the spirit of the Rokujō lady (Murasaki Shikibu, *The Tale of Genji*, trans. Edward G. Seidensticker [New York: Knopf, 1976], p. 165). Sode's plight also recalls an incident in the "Yūgao" (Evening Faces) chapter of *Genji*, in which one of Genji's lovers dies, apparently in the grasp of a possessing spirit (pp. 71–72).

6. The Way of Calling Back the Spirit was a ritual practiced in ancient China: when a person died, someone would ascend to the roof and hold the deceased's clothing toward the north while calling his or her name three times.

7. An allusion to a poem by Ōe no Chisato:

Looking at the moon I am saddened by a thousand things— though the autumn is not for me alone. (*Kokinshū*, no. 193)

8. "clouds in the sky" (*amakumo no*): a pillow-word, here modifying "elsewhere" (*yoso*).

9. The reasons are unclear, but presumably have to do with the slander mentioned in the previous sentence.

10. Most commentators interpret this sentence (*machiwabitamawan mono o*) as something the woman says to herself: "She will be waiting for me, [I had better go]." Uzuki Hiroshi agrees, but suggests that the words are a double entendre, directed at Shōtarō as well: "She will be waiting for *you*" (*Ugetsu monogatari hyōshaku*, Nihon koten hyōshaku zenchūshaku sōsho [Tokyo: Kadokawa, 1969], p. 431).

11. This description echoes that of the residence of the lady of the "evening faces," in the "Evening Faces" chapter of *The Tale of Genji* (Murasaki Shikibu, *Tale of Genji*, pp. 68–69).

12. It was customary for upper-class women to receive men from behind a screen. It is unclear whether the lady has crept to the edge of her bedding, the edge of the room, or the edge of the veranda—or all three. Uzuki opts for "the edge of the room, in other words, near the veranda" (*Ugetsu monogatari hyōshaku*, p. 436). In what follows, it is also unclear where the screen is and where Shōtarō is when he addresses the lady behind the screen. The woodblock illustration accompanying this scene in the edition of 1776 appears to have Shōtarō and the maid kneeling in the garden and the lady kneeling or sitting on her bedding, just inside the open door, as she pushes the folding screen aside.

BOOK FOUR

A SERPENT'S LUST

TITLE

The title, "Jasei no in," refers to a monstrous serpent's lust for a handsome youth, Toyoo.

CHARACTERS

As in "The Kibitsu Cauldron," all the characters in "A Serpent's Lust" are fictional. The principal figures are Toyoo, the studious son of a fisherman, and Manago, the serpent-woman who seduces him.

PLACES

"A Serpent's Lust" begins at Cape Miwa, now part of the city of Shingū, Wakayama Prefecture (formerly, Kii Province), on the southeastern shore of the Kii Peninsula. The story then moves to several other sites.

Tsubaichi (Tsuba Market), now part of Miwa-chō, in the city of Sakurai, Nara Prefecture (formerly, Yamato Province), was a market town at the foot of Mount Miwa on the approach to Hasedera, the celebrated Buddhist temple at Hatsuse (now Hase, in Sakurai).

Yoshino is a region in Nara Prefecture, south of Sakurai, celebrated since ancient times for its beautiful mountain scenery and vast groves of blossoming cherry trees. Mount Mifune and the Natsumi River (an alternative name for part of the Yoshino River) are among the famous sights. Yoshino is also mentioned in "The Owl of the Three Jewels."

The Buddhist temple Dōjōji stands about one mile from Komatsubara, now part of the city of Gobō, on the southwestern coast of the Kii Peninsula, through which pilgrims passed on their way to and from the temple.

TIME

Late autumn of one year, spring of the following year, and later in the same year, apparently. Although the date of "A Serpent's Lust" is unclear, there are hints that it takes place during the Heian period (794–1185).

BACKGROUND

Shingū is home to the Kumano Gongen Hayatama Shrine, which is about three miles north of Cape Miwa and one of the "Three Mountains of Kumano": the Shinto shrines of Hongū, Shingū, and Kumano Nachi, which together constituted a popular destination for pilgrims in the Heian period. The retired emperor Go-Shirakawa—a younger brother of Sutoku, one of the protagonists in "Shiramine"—is said to have made the pilgrimage, a round trip requiring nearly a month, as often as thirty-four times.

The Buddhist temple at Hatsuse, now called Hasedera, is dedicated to the bodhisattva Avalokiteśvara (J. Kanzeon or Kannon) and was another popular destination for aristocratic pilgrims. It appears frequently in Heian literature. In a well-known example in *The Tale of Genji*, Tamakazura and her party undertake a pilgrimage to Hatsuse, having been told that it is "known even in China as the Japanese temple among them all that gets things done." They stay at Tsubaichi, where by chance they are reunited with Ukon.[1]

Another association makes Tsubaichi especially appropriate to "A Serpent's Lust." The deity of Mount Miwa "was notorious in early literature for his liking for beautiful women" and "was regarded as a snake—or at least as frequently assuming the form of a snake. Today, Mount Miwa is the center of a flourishing religious cult; the mountain, itself considered sacred, is infested with snakes, who consume the offerings left by the pious, and stories of supernatural marriage are grouped together by Japanese scholars as 'Mount Miwa type' tales."[2]

The Buddhist temple Dōjōji is famous for its association with the legend of the young monk Anchin, from Kurama, and Kiyohime, the daughter of the steward of Masago in the village of Shiba. According to the legend, Kiyohime fell in love with the handsome Anchin when he spent the night at her father's house during a pilgrimage to Kumano. When he failed to return to her, as he had promised, her jealous anger transformed her into a serpent and she pursued him to Dōjōji, where he had taken refuge inside the temple bell. She coiled herself around the bell and roasted him to death with the heat of her passion.

AFFINITIES

Akinari based "A Serpent's Lust" principally on "Bai Niangzi yong zhen leifengda" (Eternal Prisoner Under the

Thunder Peak Pagoda), a Ming vernacular tale in the collection *Jingshi tongyan* (*Warning Words to Penetrate the Age*, 1625), edited by Feng Menglong, and several other Chinese stories.[3] It also shows many signs of Akinari's intimate knowledge of the *Man'yōshū*, *The Tale of Genji*, and other Japanese classics.

Much of the description of the temple in Yoshino, for example, derives from two passages in the "Wakamurasaki" (Lavender) chapter of *The Tale of Genji*:

The sun rose high in the sky. Stepping outside, he looked out from the high vantage point and could clearly see monks' residences here and there below.[4]

The sky at dawn was very thick with haze, and mountain birds were chirping everywhere. The blossoms of trees and grasses whose names he did not know scattered in a profusion of color.[5]

The story of Kiyohime and Anchin is familiar in many versions, including the nō play *Dōjōji* and kabuki plays.

OTHER OBSERVATIONS

Despite their superficial resemblances, the angry, vengeful spirit of Isora, in "The Kibitsu Cauldron," and the serpent-woman Manago, in "A Serpent's Lust," are essentially different. The former is the spirit of a good woman who has been wronged by her husband. While Isora is still alive, her spirit appears to act without her knowledge, like the spirit of the Rokujō lady in *The Tale of Genji*. After Isora dies, her spirit, now free of human morality, takes revenge on Shōtarō for his betrayal. The latter, though, is not a woman, but a monstrous serpent that has temporarily assumed human form. Manago is motivated by simple lust for a young man.

The serpent-woman in this story is repeatedly associated with images of water. Manago first appears during a rainstorm that has blown in from the southeast—*tatsumi*, the direction of the dragon (east-southeast) and the serpent (south-southeast)—and she first meets Toyoo in the rain, on a seashore. Rain falls at night when she and Toyoo are reunited near the Hatsuse River. She is seated next to the falls at Miyataki, on the Natsumi River, when a Shinto priest recognizes her as a serpent. As she dives into the river, water boils up into the sky and a heavy rain begins to fall. Later, a Buddhist monk mixes orpiment with water in order to combat the serpent, and when the serpent repels him, Tomiko's family unsuccessfully tries to revive him with water.

"A Serpent's Lust" has survived in the twentieth-century popular imagination. It was adapted to the silent screen in 1921 in *Jasei no in*, directed by Thomas Kurihara, with a screenplay by Tanizaki Jun'ichirō. A partial translation of the screenplay appears in Joanne R. Bernardi's *Writing in Light*.[6] More famously, "A Serpent's Lust," along with "The Reed-Choked House," was the basis for Mizoguchi Kenji's film *Ugetsu monogatari* (1953). This was followed, in 1958, by *Hakujaden* (*Legend of the White Snake*), released in the West in 1961 as *Panda and the Magic Serpent*. It was the first full-length, color, animated film made in Japan and was based on "Eternal Prisoner Under the Thunder Peak Pagoda," the Chinese story that inspired "A Serpent's Lust."

*O*nce—*what era was it?*—*there was a man named* Ōya no Takesuke, of Cape Miwa in the province of Kii.[7] Enjoying the luck of the sea, he employed many fishermen, caught fish of every kind and size, and lived with his family in wealth. He had two sons and a daughter. Tarō, the eldest, had an unaffected, honest nature and managed the family business well. The second child, the daughter, had been welcomed as a bride by a man of Yamato and gone to live with him.[8] Then there was the third child, Toyoo. A gentle boy, he favored the courtly, refined ways of the capital and had no heart for making a living. Distressed by this, his father deliberated: if he left part of the family fortune to Toyoo, it would soon find its way into the hands of others. Or he could make Toyoo the heir of another family; but the bad news, which surely would come sooner or later, would be too painful. No, he would simply rear Toyoo as the boy wished, eventually to become a scholar or a monk, and let him be Tarō's dependent for the rest of his life. Having reached this conclusion, he did not go out of his way to discipline his younger son.

Toyoo traveled back and forth to study with Abe no Yumimaro, a priest at Shingū. One day late in the Ninth Month, the sea was remarkably calm, with no trace of wind or wave, when suddenly clouds appeared from the southeast and a gentle rain began to fall. Borrowing an umbrella at his mentor's house, Toyoo started toward home, but just as the Asuka Shrine came into distant view, the rain fell harder, and so he stopped at a fisherman's hut that happened to be nearby. The old man of the house scrambled out to meet him: "Well, well, the master's younger son. I am honored that you have come to such a shabby place. Here, please sit on this." He brushed the filth off a round wicker cushion and presented it. "I shall stay for only a moment," Toyoo said. "Anything will do. Please do not go to any trouble." He settled down to rest. A lovely voice came from outside, saying, "Please be kind enough to let me rest under your eaves." Curious, Toyoo turned to look and saw a woman of about twenty, resplendently beautiful in face, figure, and coiffure, wearing a kimono printed in fine colors with the distant-mountain pattern, and accompa-

l. 8   "heir of another family": he could marry Toyoo into another family, whose adopted son and heir he would become.

nied by a lovely servant girl of fourteen or fifteen to whom she had entrusted a package of some kind. Drenched to the skin, she appeared to be at her wits' end, but her face flushed with embarrassment when she saw Toyoo. His heart leaped at her elegance, and he thought, "If such a noble beauty lived around here, I would surely have heard of her before this. No doubt she is from the capital, here for a look at the sea on her return from a pilgrimage to the Three Mountains. But how careless of her not to have a male attendant." Moving back a little, he said, "Do come in. The rain will soon end." The woman said, "Just for a moment, then; please excuse me." The hut was small, and when she sat directly before him, he saw that her beauty at close range was scarcely that of a person of this world. His heart soaring, he said to her, "You appear to be of noble family. Have you been on a pilgrimage to the Three Mountains? Or perhaps you have gone to the hot springs at Yunomine? What could there be for you to see on this desolate strand? Someone wrote of this place in ancient times:

How distressing this sudden fall of rain—
and there is no shelter at Sano Crossing of Cape Miwa.[9]

Truly, the verse expresses the mood of today. This is a shabby house, but my father looks out for the man here. Please relax and wait for the rain to clear. And where are you lodging on your travels? It would be impertinent for me to escort you there, but please take this umbrella when you go." The woman said, "Your words cheer me, and I am most grateful. My clothing will surely dry in the warmth of your kindness. I do not come from the capital but have been living near here for many years. Thinking that today would be fair, I made a pilgrimage to Nachi,[10] but frightened by the sudden rain, I came bursting into this house, not knowing that you had already taken shelter here. I have not far to go; I shall start now, during this lull in the rain." "Do take the umbrella, please," Toyoo urged. "I will come for it sometime later. The rain shows no sign of letting up. Where is your home? I shall send someone for the umbrella." She replied, "Ask at Shingū for the house of Agata no Manago. Soon the sun will set. I shall be on my way, then, shielded by your kindness." She took the umbrella and left. He watched her go and then borrowed a straw hat and raincoat from his host and returned home; but her dew-like figure lingered in his mind, and when at dawn he finally dozed off, he dreamed of going to Manago's house, where he found an imposing gate and a mansion, with shutters and blinds lowered and the lady residing gracefully inside. Manago came out to welcome him. "Unable to forget your kindness, I have longed for you to visit," she said. "Please come inside." Leading him in, she entertained him elaborately with saké and small dishes of food. Enraptured, he finally shared her pillow, but then day broke and his dream faded. "How I wish it had been true," he thought. In his excitement, he forgot breakfast and left the house in high spirits.

Arriving at Shingū, Toyoo asked for the house of Agata no Manago, but no one had heard of it. He continued his inquiries wearily into the afternoon, when the servant girl approached him from the east. Overjoyed to see her, he said, "Where is your house? I have come for the umbrella." The girl smiled and said, "You were good to come; please follow me." She led the way and in no time said, "Here it is." He saw a high gate and a large house. Everything, even the shutters and the lowered blinds, was exactly as he had seen in his dream. Marvelous, he thought as he went through the gate. Running ahead, the servant girl said, "The gentleman has come for his umbrella, and I have led him here." Manago came out, saying, "Where is he? Show him this way." Toyoo said, "There is a Master Abe in Shingū, with whom I have been studying for some years. I am on my way to see him and thought that I would stop here for the umbrella. It was rude of me to call unexpectedly. Now that I know where you live, I shall come again." Manago detained him. "Maroya, do not allow him to leave," she said. The servant girl stood in his way, saying, "You forced us to take the umbrella, did you not? In return, we shall force you to stay." Pushing him from behind, she guided him to a south-facing room. Woven mats had been placed on the wooden floor; the curtain stands, the decorated cabinet, and the illustrated draperies—all were fine antiques.[11] This was not the home of any ordinary person. Manago entered and said, "For certain reasons, this has become a house without a master, and so we cannot entertain you properly. Let me just offer you a cup of poor saké." Maroya spread delicacies from the mountains and the seas on immaculate stands and trays, presented a flask and an unglazed cup, and poured for him. Toyoo thought that he was dreaming again and must awaken. That everything was real made it all the more wonderful for him.

When both guest and host were feeling the effects of drink, Manago raised her cup to Toyoo. Her face was like the surface of a pond that warmly greets the spring breeze and reflects the limbs of the cherry, laden with luscious pink blossoms; and her voice was as bewitching as the song of the warbler, fluttering from treetop to treetop, as she said, "If I keep my shameful thoughts to myself and fall ill as a result, which god will carry the undeserved blame?[12] Do not imagine that I speak flippantly. I was born in the capital but lost my parents early and was reared by my nurse. Already three years have passed since I married a man named Agata, an assistant to the governor of this province, and came down here with him. This spring, before completing his term, my husband died of some trifling disease, leaving me with no one to rely on. When I learned that my nurse, back in the capital, had become a nun and set out on ascetic wanderings, that place, too, became for me an unknown land. Take pity on me. From your kindness yesterday as we took shelter from the rain, I know that you are a truehearted man, and so I ask that I may devote the rest of my life to serving you. If you do not dismiss me in disgust, let us initiate, with this cup, a vow of one thousand years." Since in his agitated longing for her he had hoped for exactly this, Toyoo felt his heart leap with joy, like a bird soaring from its roost, but then he recalled that he was not yet on his own and did not have permission from his father and brother. Now joyous, now afraid, he could not find words with which to reply right away. Seeing his hesitation, Manago looked forlorn and said, "I am ashamed at having spoken, from a woman's shallow heart, foolish words that I cannot take back. Miserable creature that I am, it was wrong for me to trouble you instead of sinking beneath the waves. Although I did not speak flippantly, please take my words as a drunken jest and cast them into the sea." Toyoo said, "From the first, I thought that you were a high-ranking lady from the capital, and I was right. How often can someone who has grown up on this whale-haunted shore expect to hear such joyful words? I did not answer straight away because I still serve my father and my brother and have nothing to call my own but my nails and hair. I can only lament my lack of fortune, for I have no betrothal gift with which to welcome you as my bride. If you are willing to put up with all adversity, then I will do anything to stand by you, forgetting filial obedience and my status for the sake of the mountain of love, where even Confucius stumbled."[13] "What joyful words I hear," she said. "In that case, do please come and stay from time to time. Here is a sword that my late husband cherished as his greatest treasure. Wear it always at your waist." She handed it to him. Decorated with gold and silver, it was a wonderfully tempered antique. To refuse a gift at the start of their relationship would be inauspicious, he thought, and so he accepted it. "Stay here tonight," she said, eager to detain

---

l. 22 "stand by you": that is, become your husband.

l. 25 "stay from time to time": in Heian court society, it was customary for the husband and wife to live separately and for the husband to spend the night at his wife's residence from time to time.

him, but he replied, "My father would punish me if I slept away from home without his leave. I shall make some clever excuse tomorrow night and come." He departed. That night, too, he lay awake until dawn.

Tarō rose early to assemble the net boys.[14] Glancing into the bedroom through a gap in the door, he saw Toyoo in bed and, beside the pillow, a sword glittering in the lingering lamplight. "Strange, where did he get that?" Suspicious, he opened the door roughly, and Toyoo awoke to the sound. Seeing Tarō there, he said, "Do you need me for something?" Tarō said, "What is that glittery thing beside your pillow? Valuables have no place in a fisherman's house. How Father would scold you if he saw it." Toyoo said, "I did not spend money to buy it. Someone gave it to me yesterday, and I have placed it here." Tarō said, "Who in these parts would give you such a treasure? If you ask me, even these bothersome Chinese writings that you collect are a terrible waste of money, but I have held my tongue until now because Father has said nothing about it. I suppose you plan to wear that sword in the procession at the Great Shrine Festival.[15] Have you lost your mind?" He spoke so loudly that his father heard him. "What has that useless boy done? Bring him here, Tarō," he called. Tarō replied, "Where could he have gotten it? Buying a glittery thing such as a general should wear—it is not right. Please call him to you and ask him about it. As for me, the net boys are probably loafing." With this he went out. The mother summoned Toyoo: "Why did you buy such a thing? Both rice and cash belong to Tarō. What can you call your own? We have always let you do as you please, but if Tarō were to turn against you over something like this, where in the world would you live? How can one who studies the wisdom of the past fail to understand a matter as simple as this?" Toyoo said, "Truly, I did not buy it. Someone gave it to me for a good reason, but Brother was suspicious when he saw it and said what he said." The father shouted, "And what have you done to deserve such a gift? I am even more suspicious now. Tell us the whole story this moment." Toyoo said, "I am too embarrassed. I shall explain through someone else." His father said roughly, "To whom can you speak if not to your parents and brother?" Tarō's wife, the mistress of the house, was seated to one side. She said, "Inadequate though I am, I shall listen to his story. Come with me." Thus making peace among them, she stood and led Toyoo out of the room. "I had planned to tell you secretly, even if Brother had not seen the sword and questioned me, but I was scolded before I could. A certain man's wife,[16] now left defenseless, asked me to care for her and gave me the sword. For me to proceed without permission, when I am not on my own, could bring the heavy penalty of disinheritance, and so I regret all the more what I have done. Please, Sister, take pity on me." The mistress of the house smiled: "For some time, I have felt sorry that you sleep alone. This is very good news. Inadequate though I am, I shall put in a good word for you." That night she explained the situation to Tarō. "Do you not think it very fortunate?" she said. "Please speak with Father and work things out." Tarō knitted his brows: "Strange. I have never heard of an assistant to the governor named Agata. Since our family is the village head, we could hardly have failed to hear of the death of such a person. Anyway, bring the sword here." She returned immediately with the sword, and Tarō examined it closely. Heaving a great sigh, he said, "This is terrible. Recently a court minister presented a great many treasures to the avatar when his prayer was fulfilled,[17] but the sacred objects quickly vanished from the shrine treasury, whereupon the head priest appealed to the provincial governor. In order to find the thief, the governor sent the vice governor, Fun'ya no Hiroyuki, to the head priest's mansion; and I have heard that he is now devoting all his attention to this matter. However you look at it, this is not a sword that a mere provincial official would have worn. I shall show it to Father." Taking it to him, he explained the dreadful circumstances. "What should we do?" he asked. His father blanched.

"This is a wretched business indeed. What retribution from a former life could have aroused such evil thoughts in a boy who, until now, never stole so much as a hair? If this matter is exposed by someone else, our family could be wiped out. For the sake of our ancestors and descendents, I shall harbor no regrets over one unfilial child. Turn him in tomorrow morning," he said. Tarō waited for dawn and then went to the head priest's mansion, where he explained matters and displayed the sword. Astonished, the head priest said, "This sword was indeed an offering from the minister." The vice governor heard and said, "We must find the other missing objects. Arrest him." Ten soldiers set out with Tarō in the lead. Toyoo knew nothing of this and was reading when the soldiers rushed in and arrested him. "What is my crime?" he asked, but they paid no attention and tied him up. Now that it had come to this, father, mother, Tarō, and his wife all were lost in grief. "A summons from the government office! Hurry up!" the soldiers cried as they surrounded Toyoo and pushed him along to the mansion. The vice governor glared at him: "Your theft of sacred treasures is an unprecedented crime against the state. Where have you hidden the various other treasures? Tell me everything." Finally understanding, Toyoo began to weep and said, "I have stolen nothing. For this and that reason, the wife of a certain Agata gave the sword to me, saying that her late husband had worn it. Please summon this woman, right away, and you will understand my innocence." "We have never had an assistant named Agata. Such lies will only make your crimes greater." "Why would I lie, when I have already been arrested like this? I beg of you, please find that woman and question her." The vice governor turned to the soldiers and said, "Where is the house of Agata no Manago? Take him with you, arrest her, and bring them back here."

The soldiers bowed respectfully and, pushing Toyoo along once more, went to the house. The posts of the imposing gate were rotting, and most of the roof tiles had fallen off and shattered; ferns had taken root and were trailing from the eaves.[18] The place did not appear to be occupied. Toyoo was dumbfounded. Soldiers went around and assembled the neighbors. Old woodcutters, rice huskers, and the like knelt in terror. A soldier said to them, "Who lived in this house? Is it true that the wife of a man named Agata lives here?" An elderly blacksmith came forward and said, "I have never heard of a person by that name. Until three years ago, a man named Suguri lived here, and a lively, prosperous place it was, but then he sailed for Tsukushi with a load of merchandise and the ship was lost.[19] After that, the remaining people scattered, and no one has lived here since; but the old lacquer maker here says that he was surprised to see this boy go inside yesterday and then leave a little while later." "Let us take a good look, in any case, and report to our lord," said the soldiers. They pushed open the gates and went in. The house was even more dilapidated than the exterior. They moved farther inside. In the spacious landscape garden, the pond had dried up, and even the water weeds had withered. A giant pine, blown over in the wind, lay ominously in the drooping thicket on the wild moor. When they opened the shutters of the guest hall, a reeking gust of air came at them, and everyone fell back in terror. Toyoo was speechless with fear and sorrow.

Among the soldiers was a bold one named Kose no Kumagashi. "Follow me," he said as he went in, stomping roughly on the floorboards. An inch of dust had piled up. Amid the rat droppings, beside an old curtain stand, sat a blossom-like woman. Addressing her, Kumagashi said, "The governor summons you. Come quickly." When she did not reply, he approached and tried to grasp her. Suddenly there was a clap of thunder as violent as though the ground itself were splitting open. They had no time to escape; everyone toppled over. When they finally looked up, the woman had vanished without a trace. Something glittered on the floor. Creeping forward, they found Korean brocades,

Chinese damasks, *shizuri* weavings, *katori* weavings, shields, halberds, quivers, hoes, and the like—the lost sacred treasures.[20] Gathering up these objects and carrying them back, the soldiers recounted the strange events in detail. The vice governor and the head priest, recognizing the work of an evil spirit, relaxed their investigation of Toyoo. Nevertheless, he could not escape his obvious offense. He was sent to the governor's mansion and confined in jail. The Ōya family made large payments in an attempt to redeem him and were able to obtain a pardon after about a hundred days. Toyoo said, "Under the circumstances, I would be ashamed to mingle in society. I would like to visit my sister in Yamato and live there for a while." His family replied, "Truly, one is likely to fall gravely ill after such a dreadful experience. Go and spend some months there." They sent him off with attendants.

Toyoo's elder sister, the Ōyas' second child, lived in a place called Tsubaichi with her husband, a merchant named Tanabe no Kanetada. They were delighted to have Toyoo visit them and, taking pity on him for the events of the past few months, consoled him warmly, saying, "Stay here just as long as you like." Tsubaichi was near the temple at Hatsuse. Among the many buddhas, that of Hatsuse in particular was known as far away as China for its wonderful effectiveness and so drew many pilgrims from the capital and from the countryside, especially in the spring. Since the pilgrims always stayed here, travelers' lodgings lined the streets. The Tanabe family dealt in lamp wicks and other goods for the sacred flames. Into the crowd of customers came a beautiful, aristocratic lady with a servant girl, apparently on an incognito pilgrimage from the capital, asking for incense. Seeing Toyoo, the servant girl said, "The master is here!" Startled, he looked up—it was Manago and Maroya. Crying out in terror, he fled to the back. "What is going on?" asked Kanetada and his wife. "That demon has followed me here. Do not go

---

l. 7 "obvious offense": possession of a stolen sword.

near it," said Toyoo, desperately looking for a place to hide. "Where? Where?" cried the other customers. Manago went among them and said, "Do not be startled, people. My husband, do not be afraid. In my sorrow at having incriminated you through my own imprudence, I wanted to seek out your home, explain the circumstances, and put your heart at rest. I am overjoyed that I could find this place and meet with you again. Shopmaster, please listen carefully and decide for yourself. If I were some kind of monster, could I appear among this crowd of people and, moreover, at noon on such a tranquil day as this? My robes have seams; when I face the sun, I cast a shadow. Please consider the truth of what I say and throw off your doubts." Feeling more like himself again, Toyoo said, "It is clear that you are not human, for when I was arrested and went with the soldiers, we found the place in a shambles, utterly unlike its condition of the day before, and there, in a house befitting a demon, you sat alone; and when the soldiers tried to capture you, you caused a clear sky suddenly to shake with thunder, and then you disappeared without a trace. All of this I saw with my own eyes. Why have you come chasing after me again? Go away at once." Weeping, Manago said, "Truly, it is no wonder that you think this way, but listen now a little longer to my words. Hearing that you had been taken to the government office, I approached the old man next door, to whom I had shown some kindness in the past, and persuaded him to transform the place quickly into a house in the wilderness. Maroya contrived to have thunder sound when they tried to arrest me. After that, we hired a boat and fled to Naniwa.[21] In my desire to learn what had become of you, I prayed to the Buddha here. It is through his great compassion that, with the sacred sign of the twin cedars,[22] we have flowed

---

l. 11   "My robes . . . a shadow": a popular belief held that ghosts cast no shadows, nor did their clothing have seams, however cunningly they might disguise themselves as humans.

again together on the rapids of joy.[23] How could a woman have stolen those many sacred treasures? That was the doing of my late husband's wicked heart. Please consider carefully and try to grasp even a dewdrop of the love I feel." The tears streamed down her face. Now suspicious, now sympathetic, Toyoo could find nothing more to say. Kanetada and his wife, seeing Manago's reasonableness and feminine demeanor, no longer harbored the slightest doubt: "We were terrified by Toyoo's account, but surely such things could not occur in this day and age. We are deeply moved by the feeling you have shown in your long search and shall let you stay here, even if Toyoo does not agree." They showed her to a room. Ingratiating herself to them during the next day or two, she entreated them, and they, moved by the depth of her determination, prevailed on Toyoo and finally arranged a wedding ceremony. Toyoo's heart melted day by day; he had always rejoiced in her beauty, and as he exchanged thousand-year vows with her, clouds rose by night on Mount Takama of Kazuraki, and the rains subsided at dawn with the bell of the temple at Hatsuse.[24] Toyoo regretted only that their reunion had been so long delayed.

The Third Month came. Kanetada said to Toyoo and his wife, "Of course, it does not compare with the capital, but it surpasses Kii: Yoshino, fair of name, is a lovely place in spring.[25] Mount Mifune, Natsumi River—one would never tire of the views even if one saw them every day, and how fascinating they will be right now. Let us set off." Manago smiled and said, "People of the capital, too, say that they regret not seeing the place that good people consider good,[26] but since childhood I have suffered from an ailment that causes blood to rush to my head when I go among a crowd or walk a long distance, and so, to my deep regret, I cannot go with you. I eagerly await the souvenir that you will surely bring me from the mountains." Kanetada and his wife encouraged her, saying, "Yes, walking would no doubt be painful. We do not have a carriage, but one way or another we shall not let your feet touch the ground. Think how worried Toyoo would be if you stayed behind." Toyoo said, "Since they have spoken so reassuringly, you cannot refuse to go, even if you collapse on the way." And so, reluctantly, she went. Everyone dressed gaily, but none could compare with Manago's beauty and elegance. They stopped at a certain temple with which they had long been on friendly terms. The head priest welcomed them: "You have come late this spring. Half the blossoms have fallen, and the warbler's song has grown a bit wild, but I shall show you where to find the good spots that remain." He served them a beautifully simple and refreshing evening meal. The sky at dawn was thick with haze, but as it cleared they looked out from the temple's high vantage point and could clearly see monks' residences here and there below. Mountain birds were chirping everywhere; trees and grasses blossomed in a profusion of color. Although it was a mountain village like any other, they felt as though their eyes had been opened anew. Thinking that the falls offered the most for a first-time visitor, they employed a guide familiar with that area and set out. They wound their way down the valley. At the site of the ancient detached palace, the rapids crashing along the boulders and the tiny sweetfish struggling against the current delighted their eyes.[27] They spread out their cypress boxes and reveled in the outing as they dined.

Someone approached them, stepping from boulder to boulder. It was an old man with hair like a bundle of hemp threads, but with sturdy-looking limbs. He came alongside the falls. Seeing the group, he eyed them suspiciously, whereupon Manago and Maroya turned their backs and pretended not to see him. Glaring at them, the old man muttered, "Disgraceful. Demons. Why do you go on deceiving people? Do you think that you can get away with this before my very eyes?" Hearing him, the two sprang to their feet and plunged into the falls. Water boiled up into the sky, and they vanished from sight. Just then, as though the clouds had overturned a pot of ink, rain began to fall so hard that it might have crushed dwarf bamboo. The old man calmed the panicky group and led them down to the village, where they cringed together under the eaves of a shabby house, feeling more dead than alive. The old man said to Toyoo, "Looking closely at your face, I see that you are tormented by that demon. If I do not help you, you will surely lose your life. Be very careful from now on." Pressing his forehead to the ground, Toyoo related the affair from the beginning. "Please help me keep my life," he pleaded fearfully and respectfully. The old man said, "It was just as I expected. That demon is a giant snake and very old. Having a lascivious nature, it is said to bear unicorns when it couples with a bull, and dragon-steeds when it couples with a stallion. It appears that out of lust, inspired by your beauty, it has attached itself to you and led you astray. If you do not take special care with one so tenacious as this, you will surely lose your life." When the old man had finished, they were more terrified than ever and began to pay reverence to him as though he were a god in human form. The old man smiled: "I am not a god. I am an old man named Tagima no Kibito who serves at the Yamato Shrine. I shall see you on your way. Let us go." He started out, and they followed him until they reached home.[28]

The next day, Toyoo went to the village of Yamato, thanked the old man, and gave him three bolts of Mino silk and twenty pounds of Tsukushi cotton.[29] "Please perform a purification rite to protect me from the monster," he asked respectfully. The old man accepted the gifts and divided them among the priests under him, keeping not a single measure for himself. Then he turned to Toyoo: "The beast has attached itself to you out of lust for your beauty. You, for your part, have been bewitched by the shape it took and have lost your manly spirit. If henceforth you summon your courage and calm your restless heart, you will not need to borrow an old man's powers to repel these demons. You must quiet your heart." Feeling as though he had awakened from a dream, Toyoo thanked the old man profusely and returned. To Kanetada he said,

"It is because of the unrighteousness of my heart that I have been deceived by the beast these years and months. There is no reason for me to presume on your family, neglecting my duty to my parents and elder brother. I am deeply grateful for your kindness, and I shall come again." So saying, he returned to the province of Kii.

When they heard of these dreadful events, Toyoo's parents, Tarō, and Tarō's wife felt even greater pity for him in his blamelessness and also feared the demon's tenacity. "It is because he is single," they said, and discussed finding a wife for him. In the village of Shiba lived a man known as the steward of Shiba.[30] He had sent his daughter into service

"The two sprang to
their feet and plunged
into the falls."

at the sovereign's palace, but his request that she be relieved
had been granted, and, thinking that Toyoo would make a
fine son-in-law, he approached the Ōya family through a go-
between. The talks went well, and in no time the two were
engaged. An escort was sent to the capital for her, and so
the palace lady, whose name was Tomiko, happily came back
home. Having grown accustomed to her years in service
at the palace, she surpassed other women in the beauty of
her manners and appearance. When Toyoo was received in
Shiba, he saw that Tomiko was a great beauty. Satisfied in
every respect, he could barely remember the giant snake that
had been in love with him. Nothing unusual occurred the

first night, and so I shall not write about it.[31] The second night, Toyoo was feeling pleasantly tipsy. "Considering your years of living in the palace, I suppose you have grown to dislike us rustics. I wonder which captains and councillors you slept with there. It is too late now, but I am quite provoked with you," he said playfully. Tomiko looked up quickly: "And I am all the more provoked with you, who have forgotten your old vows and bestowed your favors on this undistinguished person."[32] The voice was unmistakably Manago's, though her form had changed. Appalled, Toyoo felt his hair stand on end and was speechless with horror. The woman smiled: "Do not be startled, my husband. Even though you have quickly

"Master, why do you
fret so? This is such
an auspicious match."

forgotten our vows of the sea and of the mountains,[33] a bond
from a former life ensured that I would meet you again. But
if you believe what others say and try to avoid me, I shall hate
you and take revenge. However tall the mountains of Kii may
be, I shall pour your blood from the peaks into the valleys.
Do not throw away your precious life." He trembled with fear
and felt faint, thinking that he was about to be taken. Someone emerged from behind a folding screen, saying, "Master,
why do you fret so? This is such an auspicious match." It
was Maroya. Aghast, Toyoo shut his eyes and fell face down.
Manago and Maroya spoke to him by turns, now soothing,
now threatening, but he remained unconscious until dawn.

Then Toyoo slipped out of the bedroom, went to the steward, and described to him these frightening events. "How can I escape? Please help me find an answer," he said, keeping his voice low in case someone was listening behind him. The steward and his wife blanched at the news and were grief-stricken: "What shall we do? There is a monk from Kurama Temple in the capital who goes on a pilgrimage to Kumano every year.[34] Yesterday he took up lodgings at a temple atop the hill across the way. He is a wonderfully efficacious dharma master, revered by everyone in the village for his skill in exorcising plagues, evil spirits, and locusts. Let us call on him for help." They sent for him quickly and, when he finally came, explained the situation. With his nose in the air, the monk said, "It should not be difficult to capture these fiends. You need not worry." He spoke as though nothing could be easier, and everyone felt relieved. First he asked for some orpiment, which he mixed with water and poured into a small flask. Then he turned toward the bedroom. When everyone ran to hide, the monk said with a sneer, "All of you stay there, young and old. I shall capture this giant snake now and show it to you." He advanced toward the bedroom. The moment he opened the door, a giant snake thrust out its head and confronted him. And what a head this was! Filling the door frame, gleaming whiter than a pile of snow, its eyes like mirrors, its horns like leafless trees, its gaping mouth three feet across with a crimson tongue protruding, it seemed about to swallow him in a single furious gulp. He screamed and threw down the flask. Since his legs would not support him, he rolled about and then crawled and stumbled away, barely making his escape. To the others he said, "Terrible! It is a calamitous deity; how can a monk like me exorcise it? Were it not for these hands and feet, I would have lost my life." Even as he spoke, he lost consciousness. They held him up, but his face and skin looked as though they had been dyed black and red, and he was so hot that touching him was like holding one's hand to a fire. He appeared to have been struck by poisonous vapors, for after he came to himself he could move only his eyes, and, although he seemed to want to speak, he could not produce a sound. They poured water over him, but finally he died. Seeing this, they felt as though their spirits had fled their bodies, and they could only weep in terror.

Composing himself, Toyoo said, "Since it pursues me so tenaciously and cannot be exorcised by even such an efficacious monk, it will track me down and catch me as long as I am here between the heavens and the earth. It is false hearted of me to let others suffer for the sake of my own life. I shall not ask for help any longer. Please set your minds at ease." He started toward the bedroom. The steward and his wife cried, "Have you lost your senses?" but he paid no attention and kept going. When he opened the door gently, all inside was calm and quiet. The two were seated facing each other. Tomiko turned to Toyoo: "What enmity has led you to enlist another to capture me? If you continue to treat me like an enemy, I shall not only take your life, but also torment the people of this village. Be glad that I am faithful to you; forget your fickle thoughts." As she spoke, she put on coquettish airs, moving him to disgust. Toyoo replied, "It is as the proverb says: 'Though a man means no harm to the tiger, the tiger will hurt the man.'[35] Your unhuman feelings have led you to pursue me, and even to torment me time and time again, and, what is more, you answer my playful words by speaking of a horrible revenge. You terrify me. Nevertheless, your love for me is, in the end, no different from the love that humans feel. It is cruel for me to stay here and cause these people to grieve. If only you will spare Tomiko's life, you may take me anywhere you wish." She nodded joyfully in agreement.

Toyoo went again to the steward and said, "Since I have been possessed by this wretched demon, it would be wrong

l. 10 "between the heavens and the earth": that is, as long as I live.

for me to stay on here and torment everyone. If I may have your permission to depart right now, I am sure that your daughter's life will be spared." The steward refused, saying, "I know one end of the bow from the other, and the Ōyas' view of such an unavailing notion would put me to shame. Let us think some more. There is a priest named Hōkai at the Dōjōji in Komatsubara, a venerable prayer master.[36] He is very old now, and I have heard that he does not leave his room, but surely he will not reject an appeal from me." He galloped off on horseback. Since the way was long, he reached the temple at midnight. The old priest crept out of his bedroom and listened to the story. "Indeed, you must be perplexed. Having grown so old and foolish, I doubt that I will be of any use, but I cannot ignore a calamity in your family.[37] You go ahead; I shall follow soon." He took out a stole scented with the smoke of poppy seeds and gave it to the steward.[38] "Trick the monster into coming close, throw this over its head, and press down with all your might. If you falter, it will probably escape. Pray well and do your best," the priest instructed him carefully. Rejoicing, the steward galloped back.

He quietly summoned Toyoo, exhorted him to carry out the priest's instructions carefully, and handed him the stole. Toyoo hid it inside his robes and returned to the bedroom. "The steward has just given me permission to go. Let us be on our way." She was delighted. Pulling out the stole, he quickly threw it over her and pressed down with all his strength. "Oh! You're hurting me! How can you be so heartless? Take your hands off me!" she cried, but he pressed down ever harder. Priest Hōkai's palanquin arrived right away. Helped inside by the steward's people, he mumbled incantations as he pushed Toyoo away and lifted the stole. Tomiko was lying prone, unconscious, and on top of her a white serpent, more than three feet long, lay coiled, perfectly motionless. The old

l. 4   "I know one end of the bow from the other": in other words, "I have some knowledge of the martial arts" or "I am a samurai."

priest picked it up and placed it in an iron bowl that one of his disciples held up to him. As he renewed his incantations, a little snake, about one foot long, came slithering out from behind the folding screen. He took it up, placed it in the bowl, covered the bowl tightly with the stole, and entered his palanquin with it. The people of the household, tears streaming down their faces, held their hands together and paid reverence to him. Returning to the temple, he had a deep hole dug in front of the main hall, had the bowl buried there with all its contents, and forbade them ever to appear in this world again. It is said that a Serpent Mound stands there to this day.[39] The steward's daughter eventually fell ill and died. Toyoo's life was spared. So the story has been handed down.[40]

NOTES

1. Murasaki Shikibu, *The Tale of Genji*, trans. Edward G. Seidensticker (New York: Knopf, 1976), pp. 394–400.

2. Donald L. Philippi, trans., *Kojiki* (Princeton, N.J.: Princeton University Press, 1969), pp. 178, n. 4, 415, additional n. 21.

3. Diana Yu, trans., "Eternal Prisoner Under the Thunder Peak Pagoda," in Y. W. Ma and Joseph S. M. Lau, eds., *Traditional Chinese Stories: Themes and Variations* (New York: Columbia University Press, 1978), pp. 355–378.

4. Murasaki Shikibu, *Genji monogatari*, ed. Yamagishi Tokuhei, Nihon koten bungaku taikei, vol. 14 (Tokyo: Iwanami, 1958), p. 178.

5. Murasaki Shikibu, *Genji monogatari*, NKBT, vol. 14, p. 196.

6. Joanne R. Bernardi, *Writing in Light: The Silent Scenario and the Japanese Pure Film Movement* (Detroit: Wayne State University Press, 2001), pp. 300–304.

7. "what era was it?" (*itsu no tokiyo nariken*): this opening formula echoes the openings of earlier tales, such as *The Tale of Genji*—"In which reign was it?" (*izure no oontoki ni ka*)—and thus gives the reader an early hint that the story is probably set in the Heian period.

8. Yamato Province corresponds to the modern Nara Prefecture, north of Shingū and south of Kyoto.

9. Toyoo is showing off his learning. This poem, by Naga Okimaro, appears in the *Man'yōshū*, no. 265. Sano Crossing was southwest of Cape Miwa, now in the city of Shingū.

10. Nachi refers to the various sacred sites of the Nachi area, including the Kumano Nachi Shrine and Seiganto Temple, in Katsuura, south of Shingū.

11. In former times, mats (*tatami*) were placed on a polished wooden floor as needed for guests. The curtain stand (*kichō*), decorated cabinet (*mizushi*), and draperies (*kabeshiro*) were all characteristic furnishings of aristocratic houses in the Heian period. The cabinet would have been decorated with lacquer; the draperies, often painted or embroidered silk, were used to separate one living space from another.

12. That is, "If I died without saying anything, some god would be blamed unfairly for my death, and so I shall tell you." Manago's speech tends to be flowery and decorated with poetic allusions. In this case, the allusion is to a poem by Ariwara no Narihira:

> If I died of love unknown to others, pointlessly,
> which god would carry the unfounded blame? (*Tales of Ise*, sec.
>   89; *Shinzokukokinshū*, no. 1157)

13. The origin of the proverb "Confucius stumbled on the mountain of love" is unclear. It appears in the "Kochō" (Butterflies) chapter of *The Tale of Genji*, in reference to Higekuro (Murasaki Shikibu, *Tale of Genji*, p. 424).

14. An allusion to a poem by Naga Okimaro:

> Even in the palace it can be heard—
> the cry of a fisherman assembling the net boys to pull in the
>   nets. (*Man'yōshū*, no. 238)

15. Great Shrine (Shingū Hayatama Jinja): the festival was held on the fifteenth and sixteenth days of the Ninth Month.

16. "certain man's wife": here and later, the text uses stock expressions to indicate, without repeating them, that all the details are being provided.

17. "avatar": in the blend of Buddhism and Shinto that was characteristic of premodern Japan, the Shinto deity enshrined at Shingū was considered an avatar (*gongen*) of a Buddhist figure.

18. This description of the house and grounds echoes that of the residence of the lady of the "evening faces," in the "Yūgao" (Evening Faces) chapter of *The Tale of Genji* (Murasaki Shikibu, *Tale of Genji*, pp. 68–69).

19. Tsukushi is the island of Kyushu.
20. "*shizuri*": cloth woven from various fabrics and used principally for sashes in ancient times.

    "*katori*" (literally, "tight weave"): a thin but tightly woven silk fabric.

    "hoes" (*kuwa*, here perhaps "plows"): symbolic of agriculture, are often found among a shrine's treasures.
21. Naniwa is the present-day city of Osaka.
22. Twin cedars standing on the banks of the Hatsuse River and associated with the sun goddess, Amaterasu, were celebrated in poetry as a sign of meeting or reuniting. In the "Tamakazura" (The Jeweled Chaplet) chapter of *The Tale of Genji*, Ukon, overjoyed to find Tamakazura at Hasedera, recites:

    > Had I not come to the spot where twin cedars stand
    > would I have met you on this ancient riverbank?
    > (Murasaki Shikibu, *Genji monogatari*, NKBT, vol. 15, p. 354)

23. After reciting her waka, Ukon adds, "on the rapids of joy" (*ureshiki se ni mo*), in which *se* (rapids) also denotes an occasion or opportunity and echoes the "se" in Hatsuse (Murasaki Shikibu, *Genji monogatari*, NKBT, vol. 15, p. 354).
24. Mount Takama is the highest peak in the Katsuragi (formerly, Kazuraki) Range, southwest of Hatsuse. The passage recalls a poem by Retired Emperor Go-Daigo:

    > Clouds on Kazuraki's Mount Takama:
    > even from a distance it is clear that evening showers fall.
    > (*Shinshūishū*, no. 289)

    The image of clouds rising at night and producing rain, which then abates at dawn, suggests lovemaking. There is perhaps an echo here of the legend of King Xiang of Chu, who dreams that he has slept with a woman at Shaman Hill who turns out to have been a rain cloud (Sun Yü, "The Kao T'ang Fu," in *The Temple and Other Poems*, trans. Arthur Waley [New York: Knopf, 1923], pp. 65–72).

    The bell at Hatsuse Temple anticipates that of Dōjōji, the temple that figures in the ending of the story.
25. There is a strong association between *yayoi*, the third month of spring in the Japanese lunar calendar, and cherry blossoms.

    "fair of name" (*naguwashi*): a pillow-word for Yoshino.

26. Manago alludes to a poem by Emperor Tenmu: "On the occasion of a visit to the Yoshino palace":

> Yoshino, which good people could well see was good, and said
>   is good—
> look well, good people, look well. (*Man'yōshū*, no. 27)

The poet puns on "good" (*yoshi*), "well" (*yoku*), and Yoshino (good field).

27. The place described is Miyataki (Palace Falls), on the Natsumi River. Royal visits to the villa that used to stand there are mentioned frequently in the *Man'yōshū*.

28. The Yamato Shrine, now called Ōyamato Jinja, is in the present-day city of Tenri, about three miles north of Tsubaichi. The old man would have passed through Tsubaichi on his way back to the shrine, in any case.

29. Mino Province (Gifu Prefecture) produced high-quality silk used by aristocrats.

30. Uzuki Hiroshi convincingly identifies Shiba with the present Kurisu-gawa area of Nakaheji-chō (formerly, Shiba-mura), Nishimuro-gun, Wakayama Prefecture, about twenty miles west of Shingū (*Ugetsu monogatari hyōshaku*, Nihon koten hyōshaku zenchūshaku sōsho [Tokyo: Kadokawa, 1969], pp. 538–539).

    "steward" (*shōji*): originally designated one who managed a manor (*shōen*) on behalf of its aristocratic owner, but later came to be applied also to village heads and wealthy families of a region.

31. "I shall not write about it": Akinari uses a narrative device often found in Heian *monogatari*, such as *The Tale of Genji*.

32. Tomiko echoes the spirit that possesses the lady in the "Evening Faces" chapter of *The Tale of Genji*: "Though I admire you so much, you do not think of visiting me, but instead keep company with this undistinguished person and bestow your favors on her. I am mortified and hurt" (Murasaki Shikibu, *Genji monogatari*, NKBT, vol. 14, p. 146).

33. "vows of the sea and of the mountains": in addition to reminding the reader of the cliché that vows are "deeper than the seas and higher than the mountains," this phrase refers to the seas around Kii Province and the mountains in Yamato Province.

34. Kurama Temple is on Mount Kurama, in the north of Kyoto. Its mention here is probably due to two literary precedents. First, a popular tradition holds that Murasaki Shikibu was thinking of Mount Kurama when she had Genji, seeking a cure for his illness, visit a sage in the

northern hills in the "Wakamurasaki" (Lavender) chapter of *The Tale of Genji*. Second, the monk Anchin of the Dōjōji legend was from Kurama.

35. The biography of Guo Wen in the *Jin shu* (*The Book of Jin*, seventh century) contains the lines "If a man has no wish to harm the beast, the beast will not hurt the man." In "Eternal Prisoner Under the Thunder Peak Pagoda," this saying becomes "Though a man means no harm to the tiger, the tiger will hurt the man."

36. Dōjōji is about twenty-five miles from Shiba.

37. Hōkai resembles the sage in the "Lavender" chapter of *The Tale of Genji*, who "was old and bent and unable to leave his cave." When Genji goes to him to be cured of malaria, the sage says, "My mind has left the world, and I have so neglected the ritual that it has quite gone out of my head. I fear that your journey has been in vain" (Murasaki Shikibu, *Tale of Genji*, pp. 84–85).

38. Poppy seeds were burned in exorcism rituals of esoteric Buddhism. A vestment imbued with their smell, having been exposed to many such rituals, was deemed to possess special powers. In the "Aoi" (Heartvine) chapter of *The Tale of Genji*, the Rokujō lady is appalled to discover the scent in her own clothing. It is there because, against her will, her jealous spirit has possessed Genji's wife (Murasaki Shikibu, *Tale of Genji*, p. 169).

39. A monument before the main hall of Dōjōji is said to mark the site of the bell in which Anchin died. A "serpent mound" (*jazuka*) stands outside the temple grounds, in what used to be an inlet, marking the spot where Kiyohime is said to have plunged into the water.

40. The story ends, as it began, with a conventional formula (*to nan kataritsutaekeru*). Some chapters of *The Tale of Genji* conclude with an abbreviated form (*to nan*, *to zo*, or *to ya*), and most of the stories in the late-Heian setsuwa collection *Konjaku monogatari shū* (*Tales of Times Now Past*, ca. 1120) end with *to nan kataritsutaetaru to ya*.

BOOK FIVE

THE BLUE HOOD

TITLE

The title, "Aozukin," refers to the dark-blue cowl that Kaian
transfers from his own head to the head of the mad abbot of
Daichūji.

CHARACTERS

After the large cast of "A Serpent's Lust," the number of characters shrinks in "The Blue Hood." Kaian, or Myōkei (1422–
1493), was a priest of the Sōtō school of Zen Buddhism,
while the abbot of Daichūji is a fictional character.

PLACES

"The Blue Hood" takes place at and near the Buddhist
monastery Daichūji, on the lower slopes of Mount Ōhira in
Nishiyamada, village of Ōhira, Tsuga County, Tochigi Prefecture (formerly, Shimotsuke Province). A large establishment,

Daichūji contains a number of buildings on about eighty wooded acres.

Like "Shiramine" and "The Owl of the Three Jewels," "The Blue Hood" includes a michiyuki, though it is a very brief one:

> Ryōtaiji: temple of the Sōtō school of Zen Buddhism, in the city of Seki, Gifu Prefecture (formerly, Mino Province).
> Ōu: area around Echigo Province (Niigata Prefecture).
> Shimotsuke: Tochigi Prefecture.
> Tonda: now called Tomita, part of the village of Ōhira, Shimotsuga County, Tochigi Prefecture. It used to be a station on a post road.

TIME

Autumn of 1471 and winter of 1472.

BACKGROUND

In 1489, seventeen years after the probable setting of "The Blue Hood," the locally powerful Oyama clan asked Kaian to reestablish Daichūji—which had been founded in 1154 as a monastery of the Shingon sect—as a monastery of the Sōtō school of Zen Buddhism. Shingon and Zen are clearly distinguished in the story. Kaian is explicitly identified as a Zen master, while the abbot of Daichūji is referred to as an *ajari*, a title that designates a high clerical rank in Shingon. Shingon is the esoteric sect established by Kūkai (Kōbō Daishi), who figures in "The Owl of the Three Jewels." Zen (meditation [Skt. *dhyāna*]) Buddhism was introduced to China in 520 by the Indian monk Bodhidharma (Ch. Da Mo, J. Daruma), who is regarded as the first Zen patriarch. Zen emphasizes "extralingual transmission" (*kyōgai* or *kyōge*, short for *kyōge-betsuden*), the nonverbal conveyance of Buddhist truths from master to disciple, in preference to a reliance on the verbal teachings of the Buddha as recorded in the sutras. This is true of both the Sōtō school of Zen (Kaian's affiliation) and the Rinzai school, which is more familiar in the West.

Like "The Chrysanthemum Vow," "The Blue Hood" alludes to a sexual relationship between two males. Sexual relations between monks and acolytes were common in premodern Japan, and the sexual nature of the relationship in this story would have gone without saying.[1] No stigma is attached to wakashudō (sexual relations between a man and a boy) per se. The abbot's mistake is "failing to control his mind" and allowing himself to become attached to something ephemeral, which deters him from progress toward enlightenment. Attachment to a woman would have been just as undesirable for a monk in the society of the time. As Kamo no Chōmei wrote in *Hōjōki* (*An Account of a Ten-Foot-Square Hut*, 1212), "The essence of the Buddha's teachings is that we should cling to nothing."

AFFINITIES

"The Blue Hood" seems not to have been adapted from any particular Chinese or Japanese source. It recalls a number of Chinese and Japanese stories that deal with mad monks or cannibalism (or both), and some details were inspired by scenes in chapters 5 and 6 of Shi Nai'an and Luo Guanzhong's *Shuihu zhuan* (*Water Margin*, fourteenth century).

OTHER OBSERVATIONS

A confident, dependable man (Kaian)—a type established in "The Chrysanthemum Vow"—is contrasted with an unstable man (the abbot), repeating a pattern seen in "Shiramine" and "The Owl of the Three Jewels." Kaian's maxim—"He who fails to control his mind becomes a demon; he who governs his mind attains to buddhahood"—applies equally well to Sutoku, in "Shiramine"; Hidetsugu, in "The Owl of the Three Jewels"; and the abbot, in "The Blue Hood." To a lesser extent, it could also be applied to Katsushirō, in "The Reed-Choked House"; Shōtarō, in "The Kibitsu Cauldron"; and Toyoo, in "A Serpent's Lust." Although the maxim has the look of a quotation, no source has been identified. "Hankai," the last story in Akinari's *Harusame monogatari* (*Tales of the Spring Rain*, 1808–1809), concludes with the same sentiment.

The structure of "The Blue Hood" roughly follows that outlined by Robert Ford Campany in his discussion of Chinese Buddhist tales: "A seed of religious instruction or pious habit is planted in the protagonist. . . . The protagonist does something that is 'marked' . . . in the field of specific Buddhist values or precepts. . . . There occurs an anomalous—often strikingly contranatural—response to the protagonist's act. . . . Others react with amazement to the response. . . . These events in turn stimulate . . . positively marked Buddhist acts by others."[2]

"The Blue Hood" has apparently been translated into English more often than any other story in the collection—at least ten English versions exist, including this one.[3] No doubt the taut, economical narrative, references to Zen Buddhism, and intrinsic drama of the story have appealed to translators.

*L*ong ago, there was an eminent priest of great virtue called Zen Master Kaian. From the time he came of age, he understood the spirit of extralingual transmission and surrendered his body to the clouds and waters.¹ One year, having completed the summer retreat at Ryōtai Temple, in Mino Province, he set out on a journey, having decided to spend that autumn in the Ōu region.⁴ Traveling on and on, he entered the province of Shimotsuke.

The sun set as he reached a village called Tonda.⁵ When he approached a large, prosperous-looking house to ask for a night's lodging, men who had just returned from the paddies and fields seemed to be struck with fear at the sight of a monk standing in the dim twilight. "The mountain demon is here! Everyone come out," they shouted. An uproar began inside the house, with women and children screaming, thrashing about, and hiding in shadows and nooks. The master of the house took up a cowl-staff and rushed outside, where he found an old monk, close to fifty years of age, standing with a dark-blue hood on his head, a tattered black robe on his body, and a bundle on his back. Raising his walking staff, the monk beckoned to him: "Dānapati, why do you take such precautions? I am an itinerant monk, waiting here for someone to receive me as I seek lodgings for one night. To be met with such distrust is not what I expected. This haggard monk is not about to rob you. Please do not be suspicious of me." The master of the house dropped his cowl-staff, clapped his hands, and laughed: "Thanks to those fellows' undiscerning eyes, we have startled you, a venerable traveling monk. Let me compensate for our crime by offering you lodging here tonight." With all signs of respect, he escorted the monk inside and cheerfully invited him to dine.

The master of the house gave this account: "There is a reason why those fellows panicked when they saw Your

l. 1 "clouds and waters": that is, he traveled as an itinerant, mendicant monk, constantly on the move and without any particular destination, like clouds and water. *Unsui* (cloud-water) is a common word for an itinerant monk.

l. 18 "Dānapati" (J. *dan'otsu*): the Sanskrit word for a lay believer who supports the monastic community with donations.

Reverence and cried 'The demon is here.' I have a most
unusual story to tell you. Please pass it on to others, though
it is a strange, wild tale. There is a monastery on a mountain
above this village.[6] Originally, it was the family temple of the
Oyama clan, and many priests of great virtue have resided
there over the generations. The current ajari, the nephew of
a certain lord, was famous for his learning and asceticism,
and the people of the province were devoted to him, making
frequent offerings of flowers and incense. He often visited
my house, too, and spoke without reserve; but then came
the spring of last year. He was invited to Koshi to adminis-
ter the vows at an initiation ceremony and stayed for more
than one hundred days.[7] He brought back with him a servant
boy in his twelfth or thirteenth year, whom he made his constant attendant. I noticed that he began to neglect his longtime practices, entranced as he was by the boy's elegance
and beauty. Then, around the Fourth Month of this year, the
boy took to his bed with some slight illness, and as the days
passed his condition grew more serious. The abbot, greatly
distressed and saddened, even called in the official physician
from the provincial capital, but their ministrations had no
effect and the boy finally passed away. Feeling that the jewel
of his breast had been snatched from him, that the blossom
adorning his crown had been stripped away by a storm, the
abbot had no tears to weep, no voice with which to cry out,
and in the extremity of his grief he neither cremated the boy
nor buried him, but pressed his face to the boy's and held his
hand, until, as the days went by, he lost his mind and began to
play with the boy just as he had when the boy was alive, and,
finally, lamenting the decomposition of the flesh, he ate the
flesh and licked the bones until nothing was left. The other
people of the temple fled in a panic, saying that their abbot

l. 16 "practices": ascetic, religious practices designed to facilitate enlighten-
     ment.
l. 24 "storm": the storm of evanescence, a common Buddhist metaphor.

had turned into a demon. Since then, he has come down the mountain every night, terrifying the villagers or digging up graves and eating fresh corpses. I had heard of demons from old tales, but now I have truly seen one with my own eyes. How can we put a stop to this? Every family now locks its doors tightly at dusk, and word has spread throughout the province, so that no one comes here any more. This is why you were mistaken for a demon."

After hearing this tale, Kaian said, "Yes, strange things happen in this world. Among those who have been born as humans but end their days in foolishness and perversity, because they know not the greatness of the teachings of the

"He has come down
the mountain every
night, terrifying the
villagers."

buddhas and bodhisattvas, there are countless examples,
from the past down to the present, of those who, led astray
by the karmic obstacles of lust and wrong thoughts, reveal
their original forms and give vent to their resentments, or
turn into demons or serpents to take retribution. There have
also been people who turned into demons while they were
still alive.[8] A lady-in-waiting to the king of Chu turned into

l. 3   "karmic obstacles": actions (including mental activity) that obscure
one's understanding of Buddhist teachings and impede progress toward
enlightenment.

l. 4   "original forms": one's form, such as an animal, in a previous life.

a snake;[9] Wang Han's mother became an ogre; Wu Sheng's
wife became a moth.[10] Also, long ago, when a certain traveling monk was staying over in a poor house, the night brought
heavy rain and wind, so that the monk, lonely without even
a lamp, could not sleep. As the night deepened, he heard the
bleating of a sheep, and soon thereafter something sniffed at
him intently, to see if he was asleep. Suspicious, the monk
picked up his Zen staff, which lay by his pillow, and struck
out forcefully, whereupon the thing fell over with a scream.
Hearing the noise, the old woman who was the head of the
household lit a lamp and brought it in, and by its light they
saw a girl lying there. The old woman pleaded tearfully for
the girl's life. What could he do? Leaving things as they were,
the monk departed; but later, when he had occasion to pass
through the village again, he found many people gathered
together in a rice paddy, looking at something. Approaching
them, he asked what it was. A villager told him, 'We captured
a girl who has turned into a demon, and now we are burying
her.' But these stories are all of women; I have never heard
one of a man. It is, after all, because of their perverse nature
that women turn into shameless demons. Now, as for men,
there was a minister of Emperor Yang of Sui named Ma
Shumou, who fancied the flesh of small children, whom he
would kidnap from the people, steam, and devour;[11] but this
was shameless barbarity, quite different from the case you
have described. Nevertheless, your monk's turning into a
demon must be the result of his actions in a former life. The
virtue he accumulated through his earlier ascetic practices
is due to his utter sincerity in serving the Buddha, and he
would surely have become a splendid priest had he not taken
in that boy. It was probably his single-minded nature that
caused him to turn into a demon when, once having entered
the maze of lust, he was burned by the karmic flames of
unenlightenment. He who fails to control his mind becomes
a demon; he who governs his mind attains to buddhahood.
Your priest is a good example of this. If I, an old monk, can

instruct the demon and lead him back to his original mind,
I shall also be repaying your hospitality tonight." Thus he
set a noble aim. The master of the house pressed his head to
the floor mat. "If you can accomplish this, Your Reverence, it
will be as though the people of the province had been reborn
in the Pure Land," he said, weeping tears of joy. Lodging in
this mountain village, they heard no sound of conch or bell;
but they knew that the night was late, because the last-quar-
ter moon had risen, spilling its light through a crack in the
old door.[12] "Well, then, have a good rest," the master said,
and retired to his bedroom.

Since the mountain temple was almost deserted, bram-
bles clung to the two-story gate and moss grew on the
neglected sutra pavilion. Spiders had spun webs that bound
the Buddhist statues together; sparrow droppings covered
the goma dais; the abbot's residence, the covered walkways,
and the monks' quarters were all in terrible disrepair.[13] As
the sun declined toward the southwest, Zen Master Kaian
entered the temple grounds and struck his ringing-staff
against the ground. "Please provide lodgings for a traveling
monk tonight," he called, again and again, but there was no
response. Finally, from the sleeping quarters, a withered
monk emerged, came slowly toward him with uncertain
steps, and spoke in a dry, hoarse voice: "Where are you going
that would lead you here? For certain reasons, this temple
has gone to ruin, as you see, and turned into a wilderness.
There is no food, nor am I prepared to offer you lodging. Go
quickly to the village." The Zen Master said, "I have come

l. 6   Pure Land (Jōdo): a Buddhist paradise in the west, presided over by the
Buddha Amitābha (J. Amida).

l. 7   "no sound of conch or bell": that is, there was no active Buddhist temple
nearby, where a conch or bell might be used to mark the hour, among
other functions.

l. 19   "ringing-staff" (shaku[jō]): wooden staff with brass heads, decorated with
metal loops that ring when moved. Originally used by itinerant holy
men in India to frighten off snakes, it evolved into a ceremonial staff
carried by priests.

from the province of Mino and am traveling to Michinoku.[14] When I passed through the village below, I was drawn by the beauty of this mountain and the streams and came here on an impulse. As the sun is setting, the road to the village would be long and dangerous. Please let me stay for just one night." The abbot said, "Bad things happen in a wilderness like this. I cannot encourage you to stay, nor will I order you to leave. Do as you please." He said nothing more. Without another word, Kaian sat near the abbot. Soon the sun went down, and in the darkness of the night he could not make out his surroundings, for no lamps were lit; he could hear only the ripple of a brook nearby. The abbot returned to the sleeping quarters and made no sound thereafter.

The night deepened and the moon rose, its brilliant light reaching every corner. Shortly after midnight, the abbot reemerged from the sleeping quarters and rushed about, looking for something. Unable to find it, he cried, "Where's that damn monk hiding? He ought to be right here." He ran past the Zen master several times, but could not see him at all. He appeared to hurry off toward the main hall, but then danced crazily around the courtyard until finally he collapsed, face down, in exhaustion. Dawn came, and the morning sun began to shine. Looking like a man recovering from too much wine, he seemed dumbfounded when he saw the Zen master sitting right where he had been sitting before. Leaning silently against a column, the abbot heaved a great sigh but said nothing. Drawing near him, the Zen master said, "Abbot, why are you grieving? If you are hungry, fill your belly with my flesh."[15] The abbot said, "Were you there all night?" The Zen master said, "I was here and did not sleep." The abbot said, "Shamefully, I have a fondness for human flesh, but I have never tasted the flesh of a living buddha. You truly are a buddha. It is no surprise that, with the dark eyes of a fiend, I could not see the coming of a living

l. 32 "living buddha": one who has achieved enlightenment in this life.

buddha, try as I might.[16] This is more than I deserve." Bowing his head, he fell silent.

The Zen master said, "Villagers tell me that, once your mind had been distracted by lust, you quickly sank to the level of a fiend. This is an almost unprecedented result of bad karma, and neither 'shameful' nor 'sad' can describe it. Because you go to the village night after night and hurt people, no one in the villages nearby can rest easy. I could not ignore this when I heard of it. I have come here especially to instruct you and lead you back to your original mind. Will you listen?" The abbot said, "Truly, you are a buddha. Teach me, please, how I can quickly put these shameful actions out of my mind." The Zen master said, "If you will listen to me, then, come with me." Having the abbot sit on a flat stone in front of the veranda, he removed the dark-blue hood from his own head, placed it on the head of the abbot, and taught him two lines from the *Song of Enlightenment*:[17]

The moon glows on the river, wind rustles the pines.
Long night, clear evening—what are they for?

Kaian instructed him kindly: "Seek quietly the meaning of these lines without leaving this spot. When you have worked out the meaning, you will probably, without trying, encounter your original buddha-nature." Then he went down the mountain. Although the villagers escaped great harm thereafter, they did not know whether the abbot was alive or dead, and so, in their uncertainty and fear, they forbade anyone to go up the mountain.

One year passed quickly. In the winter of the following year, early in the Tenth Month, Priest of Great Virtue Kaian traveled this way again on his return from the north, stopped at the house of the man who had lodged him for a night, and

l. 23 "buddha-nature": the potential for perfect enlightenment, inherent in every person.

inquired about the abbot. The master of the house welcomed him joyfully: "Thanks to Your Reverence's great virtue, the demon has not come down the mountain again, and all the people feel as though they had been reborn in the Pure Land. They are, however, terrified of going to the mountain, and so not a single person has climbed it. Therefore, I do not know what has happened to him. But how could he still be alive? While you rest here tonight, may you pray that his spirit achieve buddhahood. All of us will follow you in doing so." The Zen master said, "If he has passed on as a consequence of his good actions, then he is my teacher, preceding me on the Way. If he is still alive, then he is one of my disciples. In either case, I must see what has become of him." Going up the mountain again, he could hardly believe that this was the same path he had taken last year, for indeed it appeared that all traffic had ceased. Entering the temple grounds, he found plumed grasses growing thickly, taller than a man; the dew fell on him like a cold autumn shower; and he could not even make out the three paths. The doors of the main hall and the sutra pavilion had toppled to the right and left, and moss grew on rain-dampened cracks in the rotted wood of a walkway that connected the abbot's residence with the kitchen.

When he sought out the place near the veranda where he had told the abbot to sit, he found a shadowy man with hair and beard so tangled that one could not tell if he were monk or layman. Weeds coiled about him and plumed grasses swayed above him, and he murmured something almost inaudible in a wispy voice, no louder than the hum of a mosquito:

l. 12 "the Way": the way to Buddhist enlightenment.

l. 19 "three paths": the proverbial paths in a hermit's garden: to the gate, to the well, and to the toilet. This section echoes a passage in the "Yomo-giu" (The Wormwood Patch) chapter of *The Tale of Genji*: "The gates were coming unhinged and leaning precariously. . . . Even the 'three paths' had disappeared in the undergrowth" (Murasaki Shikibu, *The Tale of Genji*, trans. Edward G. Seidensticker [New York: Knopf, 1976], p. 296).

"The moon glows on the river, wind rustles the pines.
Long night, clear evening—what are they for?"

Seeing this, the Zen master immediately took a firm hold
on his Zen staff, cried "*Samosan*, what are they for?" and
struck him on the head. Instantly, the figure began to fade,
like ice meeting the morning sun, until only the blue hood
and some bones remained on the leaves of grass. No doubt
his long obsession vanished at this moment. Herein lies a
venerable truth.

In this way, the great virtue of the Zen master came to
be known under the clouds and beyond the seas, and people celebrated him, saying "The flesh of the First Patriarch
has not dried up." Gathering together, the villagers cleared
the temple grounds, repaired the buildings, and chose the
Zen master to live at the temple as abbot, whereupon he
changed it from its original, esoteric, sect and established
a revered Sōtō site. It is said that the venerable temple still
flourishes today.

l. 4   "*Samosan*": originally a slang expression in Song-era Chinese, used in
the Zen sect to mean something like "Well, how about it?"
l. 9   "venerable truth": the truth of Buddhist teachings.
l. 11   "under the clouds": that is, in distant lands.
l. 13   "has not dried up": that is, the spirit or teachings of Bodhidharma lived
on in Kaian.

NOTES

1. On this subject, see, for example, Bernard Faure, *The Red Thread: Buddhist Approaches to Sexuality* (Princeton, N.J.: Princeton University Press, 1998).

2. Robert Ford Campany, *Strange Writing: Anomaly Accounts in Early Medieval China*, SUNY Series in Chinese Philosophy and Culture (Albany: State University of New York Press, 1996), pp. 324–328.

3. Hiroshi Chatani, trans., "The Pot at Kibitsu" and "The Blue Hood" (available at: http://www.kcc.zaq.ne.jp/dfeea307/); Kengi Hamada, trans., "Demon," in *Tales of Moonlight and Rain: Japanese Gothic Tales* (Tokyo: University of Tokyo Press, 1971; New York: Columbia University Press, 1972), pp. 123–135; Alf Hansey, trans., "The Blue Hood," *The Young East* 2, no. 9 (1927): 314–319; Donald Richie, "The Ghoul-Priest: A Commentary," in *Zen Inklings: Some Stories, Fables, Parables, Sermons, and Prints* (New York: Weatherhill, 1982), pp. 79–90; Takamasa Sasaki, trans., *Ueda Akinari's Tales of a Rain'd Moon* (Tokyo: Hokuseido, 1981); Dale Saunders, trans., "*Ugetsu Monogatari*, or Tales of Moonlight and Rain," *Monumenta Nipponica* 21, nos. 1–2 (1966): 196–202; William F. Sibley, trans., "The Blue Cowl," in Stephen D. Miller, ed., *Partings at Dawn: An Anthology of Japanese Gay Literature* (San Francisco: Gay Sunshine Press, 1996), pp. 125–133; Makoto Ueda, trans., "A Blue Hood," *San Francisco Review* 1, no. 4 (1960): 42–47; Leon M. Zolbrod, trans. and ed., *Ugetsu Monogatari: Tales of Moonlight and Rain: A Complete English Version of the Eighteenth-Century Japanese Collection of Tales of the Supernatural* (Vancouver: University of British Columbia Press, 1974), pp. 185–194.

4. "summer retreat": Buddhist monks traditionally stay inside their monasteries for three months during the rainy season. In Japan, the period of confinement was from the sixteenth day of the Fourth Month to the fifteenth day of the Seventh Month of the old calendar, in which the Fourth, Fifth, and Sixth Months were summer.

5. The situation that follows—a village householder conversing with a traveling monk who ultimately saves the day—was apparently inspired by chapter 5 of Shi Nai'an and Luo Guanzhong, *Water Margin*.

6. The temple is Daichūji.

7. Koshi refers to the former provinces of Echigo, Sado, Etchū, Kaga, Noto, Echizen, and Wakasa (prefectures of Niigata, Toyama, Ishikawa, and Fukui), on the coast of the Sea of Japan.

8. The examples that follow are drawn, with some garbling, from book 5 of Xie Zhaozhe, *Wuzazu* (*Five Miscellanies*, 1618).

9. King Zhuang (r. 613–591 B.C.E.) ruled the ancient Chinese state of Chu.

10. Nothing is known of Wang Han or Wu Sheng.

11. Emperor Yang succeeded to the throne of Sui in 605 by murdering his father and reigned until his own assassination in 618. Ma Shu-mou is said to have progressed from lamb meat, which he began eating to treat a rare illness, to human flesh.

12. In the lunar calendar, the moon reaches its last quarter on the twenty-first day of the month and rises at about midnight.

13. The description suggests a fairly large monastic complex and seems to have been inspired by the first part of chapter 6 of Shi and Luo, *Water Margin*.

    "sutra pavilion": a repository for sacred texts.

    The Buddhist statues would be in the main hall of the temple.

    "goma dais": characteristic of Shingon temples, is used in the goma ritual, in which a priest chants spells and incantations while burning poppy seeds and slips of wood on a dais, to symbolize the flames of wisdom extinguishing bad karma.

14. Michinoku was a province in northeastern Honshū, corresponding to the modern prefectures of Aomori, Iwate, Miyagi, and Fukushima.

15. There is a precedent for Kaian's offer in story 5:7 in the late-Heian setsuwa collection *Konjaku monogatari shū* (*Tales of Times Now Past*, ca. 1120), which tells of the Buddha's giving his own flesh to save a starving couple.

16. "dark eyes of a fiend" (*kichiku*, literally, "hungry-ghost beast"): in Japanese Buddhism, hungry ghosts (*gaki*), whose bad karma condemned them always to be famished, and beasts (*chikushō*) occupied two of the Six Realms (*rokudō*) into which humans were reborn. Their eyes are "dark" because they cannot discern the truth of the Buddha's teachings.

17. The *Song of Enlightenment* (*Zhengdaoge*), by Yongjia Xuanjue (665–713), a disciple of the founder of the Sōtō school of Zen, expresses essential Zen teachings in 166 lines of poetry. Quoted here are lines 103 and 104.

ON POVERTY AND WEALTH

TITLE

The title, "Hinpukuron," refers to the discussion, in the story, between a wealthy samurai and the spirit of gold.

CHARACTERS

There are only two characters in "On Poverty and Wealth": Oka, or Okano, Sanai (late sixteenth century), a samurai in the service of the Gamō and Uesugi clans, and the spirit of gold.

PLACE

"On Poverty and Wealth" is set at the home of Oka Sanai, in Mutsu, which refers to the northeastern part of the island of Honshū. Sanai's master, Gamō Ujisato, was based in Aizu Province (Fukushima Prefecture).

TIME

An autumn night in 1593, 1594, or 1595 (after the birth of Toyotomi Hideyori and before the death of Gamō Ujisato), during the hegemony of Toyotomi Hideyoshi.

BACKGROUND

Sanai's master, Gamō Ujisato (1556–1595), was a warlord in the service of Oda Nobunaga (1534–1582) and Hideyoshi (for more on Hideyoshi, see the introduction to "The Owl of the Three Jewels").

Many samurai of the time pursued elegant hobbies such as tea ceremony, incense sampling, and nō drama. Several sources confirm Sanai's interest in money, a remarkable preoccupation for members of his class, since samurai ideals disdained moneymaking.

The late-sixteenth-century warlords Nobunaga, Takeda Shingen, Uesugi Kenshin, and Hideyoshi, as well as Hideyoshi's baby son Hideyori (1593–1615), are mentioned toward the end of "On Poverty and Wealth." They contrast with Tokugawa Ieyasu (1542–1616), the founder of the shogunate that followed Hideyoshi's hegemony and under whose rule Akinari lived.

AFFINITIES

"On Poverty and Wealth" draws from or alludes to several Chinese works: the *Lun yü* (*Analects*, fifth century B.C.E.?) of Confucius; *Zhong yong* (*The Doctrine of the Mean*, fifth century B.C.E.?), one of the classics of the Confucian canon; the *Mengzi* (*Mencius*, third century B.C.E.?); Xie Zhaozhe's *Wuzazu* (*Five Miscellanies*, 1618); "Biographies of the Money-makers," part of Sima Qian's *Shiji* (*Records of the Grand*

Historian, early second–late first centuries B.C.E.); and Qu You's *Jiandeng xinhua* (*New Tales After Trimming the Lamp,* 1378). It is also indebted to Japanese historical sources that mention Sanai.

*I*n Mutsu lived a samurai named Oka Sanai, in the service of Gamō Ujisato. Highly paid and much honored for his martial prowess, he was known for his bravery everywhere east of the barrier. Sanai was a most eccentric warrior. His desire for riches and honor far exceeded that of the ordinary samurai. Because he ruled his house on the principle of frugality, his wealth increased as the years piled up. Furthermore, when he rested from military training, he would take pleasure not in savoring tea or playing with incense, but in lining up a great many gold coins on the floor of a room—a pastime he savored even more than others might enjoy the moon and the blossoms.[1] Everyone considered Sanai's behavior strange and dismissed him contemptuously as a miserly boor.

Hearing that a groom, long employed in his household, secretly carried a gold piece with him, Sanai summoned the man and said, "Even a disk of jade from the Kunlun Mountains is, in troubled times, no better than a tile or a pebble. One who has been born into this age and wields a bow and arrow prizes, above all, a sword from Tangxi or Moyang and, next, prizes wealth. Even with the best sword, however, one

---

l. 8   "east of the barrier": that is, east of the Hakone Barrier, referring to what is now the Tokyo region and the northeast.

l. 21   Kunlun Mountains: in western China, noted as a source of precious stones.

l. 23   "wields a bow and arrow": is a samurai.

l. 24   Tangxi and Moyang: noted in ancient China for the production of excellent swords.

cannot fight off a thousand enemies; but the virtue of gold will sway all the people of the world. A samurai must not use it recklessly. He should store it away carefully. It is wonderfully rash of you to have gained wealth beyond your lowly status. I must reward you." He gave the man ten *ryō* in gold, allowed him to wear a sword, and took him into his service.[2] When people heard about this, they heaped praise on Sanai, saying, "Sanai does not accumulate gold out of insatiable greed. He is simply the most eccentric samurai of the day."

That night, Sanai heard the sound of someone at his pillow. When he opened his eyes, he saw a tiny old man, smiling as he sat near the lamp stand. Sanai raised his head from the pillow and said, "Who are you? If you were here to borrow provisions, you would have brought some brawny fellows with you. Taking the form of a dotard like you and coming to wake me up must be the prank of some fox or raccoon-dog.[3] What tricks do you know? Show me a little something, to drive away the sleepiness on this autumn night." He showed no sign of being agitated. The old man said, "This is neither a goblin nor a man who has come to you tonight. I am the spirit of the gold that you care for so well. In my joy at having being warmly received all these years, I have presumed to come for a nighttime chat. Deeply moved by the way you rewarded your servant today, I felt that I could not rest until I told you what is in my heart, and so I have appeared temporarily in this form. What I have to say is only idle talk, not worth one part in ten, but if I do not speak, my belly will be overfull.[4] This is why I have come to interrupt your sleep.

"Now, then, wealth without pride is the way of the great sage.[5] We hear insults, such as 'The rich are always perverse' and 'Most rich men are fools,' but these apply only to wild dogs, wolves, snakes, and scorpions like Shi Chong of Jin and Wang Yuanbao of Tang.[6] The rich of ancient times derived their wealth naturally, from measuring heavenly time and closely observing the benefits of the land.[7] When Lü Wang was enfeoffed in Qi, he taught the people how to make a

living, and so others came to his state from the seaside, hoping for profit.[8] Guan Zhong assembled the princes nine times, but, although his status was only that of a minister, his wealth was greater than that of the lords of all the states.[9] Fan Li, Zigong, and Bo Gui profited from selling produce and accumulated vast amounts of gold.[10] Since Sima Qian included these men in his 'Biographies of the Money-makers,'[11] later scholars vied with one another to condemn his views as vulgar, but theirs were the words of men who lacked deep understanding. 'Without a constant livelihood, there will be no constant heart.'[12] Farmers work to produce grain, artisans work to assist them, and merchants work to dis-

"Sanai raised his
head from the
pillow and said,
'Who are you?'"

tribute their production: each manages his own livelihood,
enriches his family, venerates his ancestors, and plans for
his posterity—what else is there for a person to do? As the
proverbs say, 'A millionaire's son will not die in the city,' and
'The wealthy man's pleasures are the same as the king's.'[13]
If the pool is deep, the fish will swim freely; if the mountains are vast, the animals will grow up strong—truly, this
principle follows the natural course of heaven.[14] 'Poor and
yet happy'[15]—these words have been a source of confusion
for men who study letters and search for rhymes; and for-

l. 10 "men who study letters and search for rhymes": scholars and writers.

getting that wealth is the foundation of the state, even warriors, with their bows and arrows, train in senseless tactics,
smash things, kill people, lose their own virtue, and let their
progeny die out—all because, in their confusion, they belittle
wealth and prize fame. If you think about it, the desire is
the same, whether for fame or for wealth. When people get
caught up in words and belittle the virtue of gold, they pro-
claim themselves immaculate and say that a man is wise who
wields a spade and abandons society. Such a man may be
wise, but such behavior is not wise. Gold is first among the
Seven Rarities. When buried in the earth, gold causes magi-
cal springs to spill forth, eliminates filth, and harbors a mysterious sound. Can it be that a thing of such purity gathers
only in the homes of the foolish, ignorant, greedy, and cruel?
It cannot be. I am overjoyed that tonight I have been able to
vent my resentment and dispel the gloom of many years."

Sanai moved forward, intrigued: "You have said that the
way of wealth is noble, and this does not differ in the slightest from what I have always thought. Although my question
is foolish, I hope that you will give me a detailed answer.
The principle you have just elucidated is that one makes a
terrible mistake to underestimate the virtue of gold and to
be unaware that wealth is a great endeavor; and yet what the
bookworms say is not without reason. Eight of ten rich men
in the world today are greedy and cruel. Although they are
satisfied with their own stipends, they do nothing to help
the poor, including even brothers, relatives, and people who
have served their families for generations; when their longtime neighbors lose their strength, have nowhere to turn for
help, and decline in the world, the rich will beat down the
price of the neighbors' paddies and fields and take the land
as their own; even when they have risen to the esteemed
position of village head, they will not return the things they

l. 11 Seven Rarities: the Seven Rarities of Buddhist texts are gold, silver, lapis
lazuli, crystal, coral, agate, and clamshell.

have borrowed in the past;[16] if a courteous man yields his seat to them, they will despise him as though he were a servant; if an old friend calls to offer greetings of the season, they will suspect him of coming to borrow something and let it be known that they are not at home. I have seen many of this sort. There are also people who are utterly loyal to their lords and are known for the purity of their devotion to their parents, who respect their superiors and aid the wretched; and yet they struggle through the three months of winter with only a single woolen garment, and the heat of summer with no chance to wash their single linen robe, and even in a bountiful year they fill their stomachs, morning and evening, with a single bowl of gruel; such people, of course, are never visited by their friends and are shut out by their relatives; but they have no way to express their sadness at being cut off from others, and they live out their lives in drudgery.[17] Is this because they neglect their livelihoods? Rising early, retiring late, they devote all their energy to their work and have no time to pause as they rush frantically east and west—these people are not stupid, but it is rare that the application of their talents leads to success. They do not even know the taste of Master Yan's single gourd.[18] A Buddhist will explain this outcome in terms of actions in former lives; a Confucian will tell you about the Will of Heaven. If there is a future, then hidden virtues and meritorious actions hold promise for the next life, and, in anticipation of this, people will suspend their anger for a time.[19] Can we say, then, that only Buddhism fully accounts for the nature of the Way of wealth, and that Confucian teachings on the subject are incoherent? You seem to adhere to Buddhist teachings. If I am mistaken, please explain your thoughts to me in detail."

The old man said, "The point of your question has been discussed since ancient times, but has never been resolved. If we listen to Buddhist teachings, we hear that wealth and poverty result from good and bad actions in former lives. This is nothing more than wishful thinking. When a man who, in a former life, has cultivated himself, striven to be compassionate, and dealt kindheartedly even with strangers is, as a result, reborn into a rich family, struts before strangers on the strength of his fortune, abuses others with outrageous nonsense, and reveals the base heart of a barbarian—then we have to ask what kind of result it is when the compassionate heart of a former life falls so low in this life.[20] I have heard that the buddhas and bodhisattvas abhor fame and greed; why, then, are they so obsessed with poverty and wealth? The explanation that wealth comes as the result of good actions in a former life, and poverty as the result of badness, is pseudo-Buddhism propagated for the deception of ignorant old wives and girls. A man might not benefit himself who concentrates on doing good deeds without regard for poverty and wealth, but his descendants will surely be favored with good fortune. 'His ancestral temple received these; his descendants preserved these' subtly expresses this truth.[21] It is not a sincere heart that does good and then waits to be rewarded for it. I have my own view regarding covetous men who do bad things and not only grow rich, but also live long, fulfilling lives. Please listen to a little more of what I have to say.

"I have taken this temporary form to speak with you, but I am neither a god nor a buddha: I have no feelings, and so my thinking is different from that of humans. The rich of ancient times became wealthy by managing their affairs in conformance with heavenly time and their observations of the benefits of the land. Since this strategy followed the natural course of heaven, it also followed the natural course of heaven that wealth gathered around these people. Also, when a base, stingy, cruel man, seeing gold and silver, treats us as warmly as he treats his own parents, stops eating what he should eat, stops wearing what he should wear, and even

---

l. 9   "obsessed with poverty and wealth": in other words, "Why do they spend so much time and effort trying to explain poverty and wealth?"

risks his precious life as he thinks of gold and silver constantly, whether awake or asleep, then it is perfectly obvious that gold and silver will gather around him. I am neither a god nor a buddha, simply a thing without feelings. As such, I have no reason to weigh the good and bad in people and act accordingly. It is heaven, the gods, and the buddhas who praise goodness and punish badness. These three provide Ways. We are no match for them. Nevertheless, you must understand that we will gather around a man when he fawns over us. In this respect, gold differs from the human heart, even though it has a spirit. Further, a man may grow rich and sow the seeds of good karma, but if he is generous for no reason, or lends money to someone without perceiving that he is dishonorable, then his fortune will surely dissipate despite his good deeds. This is because a man like that treats gold lightly, knowing how to use it but not knowing its virtue. Also, a man who suffers in narrow circumstances, even though he conducts himself well and is sincere to others, will never attain wealth in his lifetime, no matter how much he taxes his spirit, because he was born with few of the blessings of nature. It is precisely for this reason that a wise man of old escaped from society to the wooded hills, where he lived out his years in peace just as he wanted to do, seeking wealth when the search was fruitful, and not seeking when the search was not fruitful.[22] It makes one envious to think how clean and fresh his heart must have been.[23] Nonetheless, the Way of wealth is an art—the skillful will accumulate much; the foolish will crumble more easily than tiles. Furthermore, we follow men's livelihoods and depend on no master in particular.[24] No sooner have we gathered here than we might run over there, depending on the master's actions.

l. 7   "These three provide Ways": heaven (*ten*) refers to the Chinese cosmology adapted by Japan, especially as expressed in Confucianism; gods (kami), to Shinto; and the buddhas (*hotoke*), to Buddhism.

l. 8   Ways (dō, michi): teachings, values, and principles marking a path that people should follow through life.

We are like water flowing to the lowest spot. Day and night, we come and go with no time to rest. An idle man with no livelihood, however, will finally deplete even a Mount Tai of food and drink up the rivers and oceans. As I said before, the unrighteous man's accumulation of wealth has nothing to do with virtue or its lack; and the case of the upright man need not be discussed.[25] If a man who is blessed by the trends of the times will exercise frugality, curtail expenses, and work hard, his house will naturally grow rich and others will surely bow to him. I know nothing of the Buddhists' karma in a former life, nor do I concern myself with the Confucianists' Mandate of Heaven.[26] I roam freely in a different realm."

Sanai was more and more intrigued: "Your theory is marvelous. My long-held doubts have been dispelled tonight. Let me try asking you one more thing. The powerful winds of the Toyotomi have forced all within the four seas into submission, and the five home provinces and seven highways seem finally to be calm;[27] but samurai loyal to vanquished domains are plotting to achieve their long-cherished desires, lurking here and there in hiding, or serving masters of great domains for the time being as they await upheavals in the world.[28] The people, too, being people of a country at war, drop their plows, exchange them for halberds, and neglect their crops. Samurai cannot sleep on high pillows. In this situation, surely the regime cannot last much longer. Who will unite the country and bring respite to the people? And with whom will you ally yourself?" The old man said, "Since this, too, is of the world of men, I do not know. But speaking from the perspective of wealth: Shingen's schemes were on target every time, and yet during his life he wielded power in only

---

l. 3   Mount Tai: in eastern China, used here as a metaphor for a vast amount.

l. 25   "sleep on high pillows": that is, sleeping without any worries. The expression appears in Sima Qian, *Records of the Grand Historian*.

three domains.[29] Moreover, he was universally praised as a masterful commander. They say that his last words were, 'Of all the generals today, Nobunaga's karmic rewards are unsurpassed. Underestimating him for all these years, I failed to bring him down, and now I have taken ill. No doubt my posterity will soon be destroyed by him.' Kenshin was a brave commander.[30] There was no one to rival him after Shingen died. Unfortunately, he died early. Nobunaga surpassed the others in his capacities, but in wisdom was no match for Shingen, and in courage was inferior to Kenshin. Nevertheless, he acquired wealth and was entrusted with control of the whole country.[31] Since he lost his life for humiliating a vassal, however, he cannot be said to have combined both letters and the martial arts.[32] Although Hideyoshi's ambitions are great, they did not encompass the world at first. We know this from the way he crafted the name 'Hashiba,' out of envy for the wealth of Shibata and Niwa.[33] Now he has turned into a dragon, rising to the skies; but has he not forgotten what life was like in the pond? Hideyoshi may have turned into a dragon, but in fact he is no more than a water snake.[34] It is said that a water snake that turns into a dragon lives for only three years.[35] Hideyoshi's descendants will not last long, will they?[36] The world has never seen a realm endure that was governed with arrogance and extravagance.[37] What people must cherish is frugality, but those who carry it too far degenerate into meanness. One must strive, therefore, carefully to maintain the distinction between frugality and meanness. The rule of the Toyotomi may not last much longer, but the time cannot be far off when the people will prosper in peace, and every house will sing *Music of a Thousand Autumns*.[38] In answer to your question, let me offer this." He intoned an eight-character verse:

---

l. 18 "but has he not forgotten what life was like in the pond": that is, in his present ascendancy, he has forgotten his humble origins.

"The ming-grass of Yao will grow, the sun will shine high in
  the sky;
and the one hundred families will return to the house."[39]

As they reached the end of their diverting conversation,
the bell of a distant temple signaled the fifth watch. "The
night is coming to an end. I must take my leave. I fear that
my long tale has disturbed your rest tonight." The old man
seemed about to stand and depart, when suddenly he vanished without a trace.

Sanai thought back on what had occurred during the
night and considered the verse. When he grasped the sense
of the phrase "the one hundred families will return to the
house," he came firmly to believe in what the old man had
said. Truly, these were auspicious words for an age of auspicious grasses.[40]

l. 5   "fifth watch": the time between sunset and sunrise was divided into five
equal watches of about two hours each. The fifth watch corresponded
roughly to the period from 4:00 A.M. until daybreak.

NOTES

1. The moon stands for the natural beauty of autumn, and blossoms for the beauty of spring and, by extension, poetry, painting, and other arts.

2. In the 1590s, ten ryō would buy from three to six *koku* (150 to 300 bushels) of rice. By allowing the man to wear a sword, Sanai raised him to the status of samurai.

3. Foxes and raccoon-dogs (tanuki) were thought to have the power to assume human form and play tricks on people.

4. "if I do not speak, my belly will be overfull": apparently a proverb, but its provenance has not been identified.

5. The "great sage" is Confucius. The spirit is referring to *Analects* 1:15: "Tsze-kung said, 'What do you pronounce concerning the poor man who yet does not flatter, and the rich man who is not proud?' The Master replied, 'They will do; but they are not equal to him, who though poor, is yet cheerful, and to him, who, though rich, loves the rules of propriety'" (James Legge, trans., *The Four Books: Confucian Analects, The Great Learning, The Doctrine of the Mean, and The Works of Mencius* [1879, 1923; reprint, New York: Paragon, 1966], pp. 10–11).

6. "wild dogs . . . and Wang Yuanbao of Tang": emblems of greed and cruelty, from book 5 of Xie Zhaozhe, *Five Miscellanies*. Much in the following section was probably drawn from this source. Shi Chong (d. 300) was a famously rich man during the Jin dynasty (265–419), and Wang Yuanbao of the Tang dynasty (618–906) was said to have constructed walls of his house by piling up gold and silver. Toyotomi Hideyoshi, who built a teahouse of gold, might be an implied target of the spirit's criticism.

7. "heavenly time": refers to climate, the seasons, day and night, and other cyclical phenomena.

   "benefits of the land": refers to topography, soil conditions, and other terrestrial phenomena.

   The phrases come from *Mencius*: "Heavenly time is less important than the benefits of the land, and the benefits of the land are less important than harmony among men" (2.2.1).

8. Lü Wang refers to Grand Duke Wang Lüshang, the first ruler of Qi in the early Zhou dynasty (eleventh century–770 B.C.E.). This account was derived from the *Shiji* (Ssu-ma Ch'ien [Sima Qian], *Records of the Grand Historian of China*, trans. Burton Watson [New York: Columbia University Press, 1961], vol. 2, p. 478).

9. Guan Zhong was prime minister under Duke Huan (685–643 B.C.E.) of Qi. Akinari apparently misread the *Shiji*: "assembled . . . nine times" should be simply "assembled" (Ssu-ma Ch'ien, *Records of the Grand Historian*, vol. 2, pp. 478–479). According to Confucius, "That Duke Huan was able to convene the rulers of all the States without resorting to the use of his war-chariots was due to Kuan Chung" (*The Analects*, trans. Arthur Waley [London: George Allen & Unwin, 1938], 14:17, p. 185).

10. Fan Li, a minister in the state of Chu (Spring and Autumn period, 722–481 B.C.E.), made several fortunes as he traveled from state to state; Zigong was one of the favorite disciples of Confucius; and Bo Gui was a merchant at the time of Marquis Wen of Wei (Zhou dynasty, 424–387 B.C.E.).

11. "Biographies of the Money-makers" is a section in Sima Qian, *Records of the Grand Historian*.

12. The spirit is quoting from *Mencius* 1.1.

13. Both proverbs are from "Biographies of the Money-makers" in Sima Qian, *Records of the Grand Historian*.

    "die in the city": in ancient China, a euphemism for being executed and having one's corpse displayed in the city.

14. These aphorisms, too, are from "Biographies of the Money-makers."

    "follows the natural course of heaven": that is, is in accordance with the laws of nature.

15. The spirit is referring to Confucius, *Analects* 1:15 (see note 5).

16. "longtime neighbors . . . borrowed in the past": examples from a story in Qu You, *New Tales After Trimming the Lamp*.

17. "a single woolen garment . . . drudgery": a sentence adapted from the same story in *New Tales After Trimming the Lamp*.

18. Master Yan was Confucius's favorite disciple, Yan Hui or Yan Yuan. Sanai is alluding to Confucius, *Analects* 6:9: "The Master said, 'Admirable indeed was the virtue of Hui! With a single bamboo dish of rice, a single gourd dish of drink, and living in his mean narrow lane, while others could not have endured the distress, he did not allow his joy to be affected by it. Admirable indeed was the virtue of Hui!'" (Legge, trans., *Four Books*, p. 69).

19. In Buddhism, actions in previous lives have consequences in this life, and actions in this life will affect the next. The idea here is that virtue and good behavior in this life will be rewarded in the next.

    "hidden virtues": good qualities that are unknown to others. It was considered tasteful to keep quiet about one's virtues and good deeds. See, for example, Confucius, *Analects* 5:25: "Yan Yuan said, 'I should like not to boast of my excellence, nor to make a display of my meritorious deeds'" (Legge, trans., *Four Books*, pp. 61–62).

20. Underlying this question is the Buddhist principle of cause and effect, or action (karma) and result (*phala*). The spirit questions the principle by raising the example of a man whose goodness results in wealth and baseness in the next life.

21. The spirit is quoting from chapter 17 of *The Doctrine of the Mean*: "How greatly filial was Shun! His virtue was that of a sage; his dignity was the throne; his riches were all within the four seas. *His ancestral temple received these; his descendants preserved these.* Therefore having such great virtue, it could not but be that he should obtain the throne, that he should obtain those riches, that he should obtain his fame, that he should attain to his long life" (Legge, trans., *Four Books*, pp. 372–373; italicized sentence, my translation, adapted from Legge). Shun was one of the legendary sage-kings of ancient China. The idea is that Shun's ancestors and descendants benefited from his virtue: his ancestors, from receiving the filial king's veneration; and his descendants, from preserving his throne, riches, fame, and longevity.

22. The spirit is alluding to Confucius, *Analects* 7:11: "The Master said, 'If the search for riches is sure to be successful, though I should become a groom with whip in hand to get them, I will do so. As the search may not be successful, I will follow after that which I love'" (Legge, trans., *Four Books*, p. 83).

23. An allusion to a poem by Fujiwara Kintō (966–1041), sent to a friend who had taken Buddhist vows and gone to live in Ōmi:

> Ripples in the breeze on Shiga Bay—
> how clean and fresh your heart must be. (*Shūishū*, no. 1336)

24. "Nonetheless . . . particular": paraphrases from "Biographies of the Money-makers" (Ssu-ma Ch'ien, *Records of the Grand Historian*, vol. 2, p. 499).

25. The original sentence, the most obscure in the book, has been variously interpreted. The thrust of the second part could be that (a) the case of an upright man who has accumulated wealth is so different from that of the unrighteous man that it should not be discussed in the same context; (b) there is nothing to discuss, since an upright man does only good; or (c) an upright man should not discuss such things.

26. It was the Confucian philosopher Mencius who most clearly enunciated the concept that the people have the right to depose a ruler whose corruption has caused him to lose the Mandate of Heaven.

27. The Toyotomi refers to Toyotomi Hideyoshi and his son Hideyori. Hideyoshi completed the unification of Japan in 1590.

    "within the four seas" (a phrase from the *Analects*) and "five home provinces and seven highways": that is, all of Japan. The five home provinces were those of the capital and the surrounding region (Yamashiro, Yamato, Kawachi, Izumi, and Settsu, corresponding to all or part of the prefectures of Kyoto, Nara, Osaka, and Hyōgo), and the seven highways linked the capital with the rest of the country.

28. The cherished desire of the loyal samurai was to reinstate their masters, who had been vanquished by Oda Nobunaga and Hideyoshi.

29. Takeda Shingen (1521–1573), who controlled the three domains of Kai, Shinano, and Echigo (prefectures of Yamanashi, Nagano, and Niigata), died of illness while laying siege to Nobunaga's forces.

30. Uesugi Kenshin (1530–1578), a warlord based in Echigo (Niigata Prefecture), was a rival of Shigen and Nobunaga.

31. That is, his hegemony over the country was recognized by the emperor.

32. The vassal was Akechi Mitsuhide (1528–1582), who turned on Nobunaga and forced him to commit suicide. The mastery of both letters and martial arts was a samurai ideal.

33. In 1572, Hideyoshi, whose surname had been Kinoshita, took the name Hashiba, which consists of one character each from the surnames of Niwa Nagahide (1535–1585) and Shibata Katsuie (1522–1583). Both Niwa and Shibata were vassals of Nobunaga. Hideyoshi later defeated Shibata in battle and took Niwa as a vassal.

34. "water snake" (*kōshin* or *mizuchi*): a mythical, water-dwelling creature thought to have horns and four legs and to emit poisonous breath.

35. This is reported in book 9 of Xie Zhaozhe, *Five Miscellanies*.

36. The Toyotomi clan came to an end in 1615 with the death of Hideyori.

37. This echoes the famous lines in the opening of *Heike monogatari* (*The Tale of the Heike*, mid-thirteenth century): "The arrogant do not endure; they are like a dream of a night in spring."

38. *Music of a Thousand Autumns* (*Senshūraku*) is a piece of ancient court music (*gagaku*) originally intended as a wish for a long reign. Here the idea is that the people would sing it in celebration of their new-found peace and prosperity.

39. The lines of the poem are in Chinese.

"ming-grass": auspicious ming-grass was said to grow during the reign of the legendary sage-king Yao (with Shun, one of the rulers held up as ideals by Confucius). According to legend, ming-grass put out a new leaf each day for the first fifteen days of each month, and then lost one leaf a day for the rest of the month.

"one hundred families" (*hyakusei*): that is, all the people, especially the farmers.

"return" (*ki* or *kaeru*): suggests "allegiance" (*kifuku*).

"house" (*ie*): alludes to Tokugawa Ieyasu.

The verse, then, is both the spirit's prediction that Ieyasu would prevail when Hideyoshi's rule ended and, in the context of Akinari's times, a paean to the Tokugawa regime and an expression of allegiance to it.

40. "auspicious grasses": refers to the auspicious ming-grass of the spirit's verse. The implication is that the Tokugawa rulers were as sage and upright as Yao of ancient China.

BIBLIOGRAPHY

TEXTS AND COMMENTARIES

Nakamura Yukihiko, ed. *Ueda Akinari shū.* Nihon koten bungaku taikei, vol. 56. Tokyo: Iwanami, 1968.

Nakamura Yukihiko, Takada Mamoru, and Nakamura Hiroyasu, eds. *Hanabusa sōshi, Nishiyama monogatari, Ugetsu monogatari, Harusame monogatari.* Nihon koten bungaku zenshū, vol. 48. Tokyo: Shōgakukan, 1973.

Suzuki Tanjirō. *Ugetsu monogatari honbun oyobi sōsakuin.* Tokyo: Musashino Shoin, 1990.

Uzuki Hiroshi. *Ugetsu monogatari hyōshaku.* Nihon koten hyōshaku zenchūshaku sōsho. Tokyo: Kadokawa, 1969.

SECONDARY MATERIALS IN JAPANESE

Bandō Takeo. *Ueda Akinari "Ugetsu monogatari" ron.* Osaka: Izumi Shoin, 1999.

Inoue Yasushi. *Ugetsu monogatari ron—gensen to shudai.* Tokyo: Kasama Shoin, 1999.

Konoe Noriko, ed. *Akinari kenkyū shiryō shūsei.* 12 vols. Tokyo: Kuresu Shuppan, 2003.

Matsuda Osamu. "'Kikka no chigiri' no ron: *Ugetsu monogatari* no saihyōka (2)." *Bungei to shisō* 28 (February 1963).

Mishima Yukio. "*Ugetsu monogatari* ni tsuite." In *Mishima Yukio zenshū*, vol. 25, pp. 270–274. Tokyo: Shinchōsha, 1975.

Morita Kirō. *Ueda Akinari bungei no kenkyū*. Osaka: Izumi Shoin, 2003.

Murasaki Shikibu. *Genji monogatari*. Edited by Yamagishi Tokuhei. Nihon koten bungaku taikei, vols. 14–18. Tokyo: Iwanami, 1958–1963.

Nihon Bungaku Kenkyū Shiryō Hankōkai, ed. *Akinari*. Tokyo: Yūseidō, 1972.

Ōwa Yasuhiro. *Ueda Akinari: Sono ikikata to bungaku*. Tokyo: Shunjūsha, 1982.

Tanizaki Jun'ichirō. *Bunshō tokuhon*. In *Tanizaki Jun'ichirō zenshū*, vol. 21, pp. 87–246. Tokyo: Chūō Kōronsha, 1974.

SECONDARY MATERIALS IN ENGLISH

Addiss, Stephen, ed. *Japanese Ghosts and Demons: Art of the Supernatural*. New York: Braziller, in association with the Spencer Museum of Art, University of Kansas, 1985.

Araki, James T. "A Critical Approach to the *Ugetsu Monogatari*." *Monumenta Nipponica* 22, nos. 1–2 (1967): 49–64.

Asai Ryōi. *The Peony Lantern: "Botan no tōrō" from Otogi bōko (1666)*. Translated by Maryellen Toman Mori. An Episodic Festschrift for Howard Hibbett, vol. 3. Hollywood, Calif.: Highmoonoon, 2000.

Aston, W. G., trans. *Nihongi: Chronicles of Japan from the Earliest Times to A.D. 697*. 1896. Reprint, Rutland, Vt.: Tuttle, 1972.

Bishop, John Lyman, trans. "Fan Chü-ch'ing's Eternal Friendship." In *The Colloquial Short Story in China: A Study of the San-Yen Collections*, pp. 88–102. Cambridge, Mass.: Harvard University Press, 1956. [An English translation of the Chinese story from which "The Chrysanthemum Vow" was adapted]

Brooke-Rose, Christine. *A Rhetoric of the Unreal: Studies in Narrative and Structure, Especially of the Fantastic*. Cambridge: Cambridge University Press, 1981.

Brower, Robert H., and Earl Miner. *Japanese Court Poetry*. Stanford, Calif.: Stanford University Press, 1961.

Campany, Robert Ford. *Strange Writing: Anomaly Accounts in Early Medieval China*. SUNY Series in Chinese Philosophy and Culture. Albany: State University of New York Press, 1996.

Cheung, Dominic. "With You a Part of Me: A Study of *New Tales of the Trimmed Lamp*, *Tales of Moonlight and Rain*, *New Tales of the Golden Carp*, and the 'Ghost-Wife' Theme in China, Japan, and Korea." In Makoto Ueda, ed., *Explorations: Essays in Comparative Literature*, pp. 148–173. Lanham, Md.: University Press of America, 1986.

Confucius. *The Analects*. Translated by Arthur Waley. London: George Allen & Unwin, 1938.

Confucius. *The Analects*. Translated by D. C. Lau. London: Penguin, 1979.

Faure, Bernard. *The Red Thread: Buddhist Approaches to Sexuality*. Princeton, N.J.: Princeton University Press, 1998.

Feng Meng-Lung, ed. *Stories from a Ming Collection: Translations of Chinese Short Stories Published in the Seventeenth Century*. Translated by Cyril Birch. New York: Grove, 1958.

Fessler, Susanna. "The Nature of the Kami: Ueda Akinari and *Tandai Shōshin Roku*." *Monumenta Nipponica* 51, no. 1 (1996): 1–15.

Gerstle, C. Andrew, ed. *18th Century Japan: Culture and Society*. Sydney: Allen & Unwin, 1989.

Graham, Patricia J. *Tea of the Sages: The Art of Sencha*. Honolulu: University of Hawai'i Press, 1998.

Hanan, Patrick. *The Chinese Vernacular Story*. Cambridge, Mass.: Harvard University Press, 1981.

Huntington, Rania. *Alien Kind: Foxes and Late Imperial Chinese Narrative*. Cambridge, Mass.: Harvard University Asia Center, 2003.

Kamo no Chōmei. "An Account of a Ten-Foot-Square Hut." Translated by Anthony Chambers. In David L. Pike, Sabry Hafez, Haruo Shirane, and Pauline Yu, eds., *The Longman Anthology of World Literature*. Volume B, *The Medieval Era*, pp. 335–344. New York: Pearson Longman, 2004.

Kamo no Chōmei. "An Account of a Ten-Foot-Square Hut." Translated by Anthony Chambers. In Haruo Shirane, ed., *Traditional Japanese Literature: An Anthology: Beginnings to 1600*, pp. 623–635. New York: Columbia University Press, 2007.

Kao, Karl S. Y., ed. *Classical Chinese Tales of the Supernatural and the Fantastic: Selections from the Third to the Tenth Century*. Bloomington: Indiana University Press, 1985.

Keene, Donald. *World Within Walls: Japanese Literature of the Pre-Modern Era, 1600–1867*. New York: Holt, 1976. [Chapter 16 is on Akinari]

Keikai [Kyōkai]. *Miraculous Stories from the Japanese Buddhist Tradition: The "Nihon ryōiki" of the Monk Kyōkai.* Translated by Kyoko Motomochi Nakamura. Cambridge, Mass.: Harvard University Press, 1973.

LaFleur, William R. *Awesome Nightfall: The Life, Times, and Poetry of Saigyō.* Boston: Wisdom, 2003.

LaFleur, William R. *The Karma of Words: Buddhism and the Literary Arts in Medieval Japan.* Berkeley: University of California Press, 1983.

Legge, James, trans. *The Four Books: Confucian Analects, The Great Learning, The Doctrine of the Mean, and The Works of Mencius.* 1879. 1923. "An unaltered and unabridged reprint of the Shanghai 1923 Edition," New York: Paragon, 1966.

Leupp, Gary. *Male Colors: The Construction of Homosexuality in Tokugawa Japan.* Berkeley: University of California Press, 1996.

Lin Yutang. "The Man Who Became a Fish." In *Famous Chinese Short Stories*, pp. 273–278. New York: Day, 1948.

Marceau, Lawrence E. *Takebe Ayatari: A* Bunjin *Bohemian in Early Modern Japan.* Ann Arbor: Center for Japanese Studies, University of Michigan, 2004.

McCarthy, Paul. "*Ugetsu Monogatari*, from Page to Screen: An Interpretive Essay." *Asiatica Venetiana* 6–7 (2001–2002): 139–148.

McCullough, Helen Craig, trans. *Tales of Ise: Lyrical Episodes from Tenth-Century Japan.* Stanford, Calif.: Stanford University Press, 1968.

McCullough, William H., and Helen Craig McCullough, trans. *A Tale of Flowering Fortunes: Annals of Japanese Aristocratic Life in the Heian Period.* 2 vols. Stanford, Calif.: Stanford University Press, 1980.

Mencius. *Mencius.* Translated by D. C. Lau. Harmondsworth: Penguin, 1970.

Miner, Earl, Hiroko Odagiri, and Robert E. Morrell. *The Princeton Companion to Classical Japanese Literature.* Princeton, N.J.: Princeton University Press, 1985.

Moore, Jean. "*Senjūshō:* Buddhist Tales of Renunciation." *Monumenta Nipponica* 41, no. 2 (1986): 127–174. [Includes "7 Shiramine in Sanuki Province," pp. 158–160]

Morris, Mark. "Buson and Shiki: Part One." *Harvard Journal of Asiatic Studies* 44, no. 2 (1984): 381–425.

Morris, Mark. "Group Portrait with Artist: Yosa Buson and His Patrons." In C. Andrew Gerstle, ed., *18th Century Japan: Culture and Society*, pp. 87–105. Sydney: Allen & Unwin, 1989.

Murasaki Shikibu. *The Tale of Genji: A Novel in Six Parts*. Translated by Arthur Waley. Boston: Houghton Mifflin, 1935.

Murasaki Shikibu. *The Tale of Genji*. Translated by Edward G. Seidensticker. New York: Knopf, 1976.

Murasaki Shikibu. *The Tale of Genji*. 2 vols. Translated by Royall Tyler. New York: Viking, 2001.

Najita, Tetsuo. *Visions of Virtue in Tokugawa Japan: The Kaitokudō, Merchant Academy of Osaka*. Chicago: University of Chicago Press, 1987.

Nakano Mitsutoshi. "The Role of Traditional Aesthetics." Translated by Maria Flutsch. In C. Andrew Gerstle, ed., *18th Century Japan: Culture and Society*, pp. 124–131. Sydney: Allen & Unwin, 1989.

Nosco, Peter. *Remembering Paradise: Nativism and Nostalgia in Eighteenth-Century Japan*. Harvard Yenching Monograph Series, no. 31. Cambridge, Mass.: Harvard University, Council on East Asian Studies, 1990.

Okada, H. Richard. *Figures of Resistance: Language, Poetry, and Narrating in The Tale of Genji and Other Mid-Heian Texts*. Durham, N.C.: Duke University Press, 1991.

Po Chü-I. *Selected Poems*. Translated by Burton Watson. New York: Columbia University Press, 2000.

Pollack, David. *The Fracture of Meaning: Japan's Synthesis of China from the Eighth Through the Eighteenth Centuries*. Princeton, N.J.: Princeton University Press, 1986.

Reider, Noriko T. *Tales of the Supernatural in Early Modern Japan: Kaidan, Akinari, Ugetsu Monogatari*. Japanese Studies, vol. 16. Lewiston, N.Y.: Mellen, 2002.

Reischauer, Edwin O., and Joseph K. Yamagiwa, eds. and trans. *Translations from Early Japanese Literature*. Cambridge, Mass.: Harvard University Press, 1951. [Includes Reischauer's partial translation of *Heiji monogatari*]

Rimer, J. Thomas. *Modern Japanese Fiction and Its Traditions: An Introduction*. Princeton N.J.: Princeton University Press, 1978. [Chapter 7 is on Akinari]

Saigyō. *Poems of a Mountain Home*. Translated by Burton Watson. New York: Columbia University Press, 1991.

Sansom, George. *A History of Japan*. Vol. 1, *To 1334*. Stanford, Calif.: Stanford University Press, 1958.

Sansom, George. *A History of Japan*. Vol. 2, *1334–1615*. Stanford, Calif.: Stanford University Press, 1961.

Sansom, George. *A History of Japan*. Vol. 3, *1615–1867*. Stanford, Calif.: Stanford University Press, 1963.

Schulte, Rainer, and John Biguenet, eds. *Theories of Translation: An Anthology of Essays from Dryden to Derrida*. Chicago: University of Chicago Press, 1992.

Screech, Timon. *Sex and the Floating World: Erotic Images in Japan, 1700–1820*. Honolulu: University of Hawai'i Press, 1999.

Shi Nai'an and Luo Guanzhong. *The Broken Seals: Part One of "The Marshes of Mount Liang," a New Translation of the "Shuihu Zhuan" or "Water Margin."* Translated by John Dent-Young and Alex Dent-Young. Hong Kong: Chinese University Press, 1994.

Shirane, Haruo. *The Bridge of Dreams: A Poetics of The Tale of Genji*. Stanford, Calif.: Stanford University Press, 1987.

Shirane, Haruo, ed. *Early Modern Japanese Literature: An Anthology, 1600–1900*. New York: Columbia University Press, 2002.

Shirane, Haruo, ed. *Traditional Japanese Literature: An Anthology, Beginnings to 1600*. New York: Columbia University Press, 2007.

Ssu-ma Ch'ien [Sima Qian]. *Records of the Grand Historian of China*. 2 vols. Translated by Burton Watson. New York: Columbia University Press, 1961.

Statler, Oliver. *Japanese Pilgrimage*. New York: Morrow, 1983. [Statler deftly summarizes the stories of Saigyō, Sutoku, and the Hōgen Insurrection, and describes his own visit to Shiramine]

Takata [Takada] Mamoru. "*Ugetsu Monogatari*: A Critical Interpretation." In Kengi Hamada, trans., *Tales of Moonlight and Rain: Japanese Gothic Tales*, pp. xxi–xxix. Tokyo: University of Tokyo Press, 1971; New York: Columbia University Press, 1972.

Takebe Ayatari. "A Tale of the Western Hills: Takebe Ayatari's *Nishiyama Monogatari*." Translated by Blake Morgan Young. *Monumenta Nipponica* 37, no. 1 (1982): 77–121.

Todorov, Tzvetan. *The Fantastic: A Structural Approach to a Literary Genre*. Translated by Richard Howard. Cleveland: Press of Case Western Reserve University, 1973.

Totman, Conrad. *Early Modern Japan*. Berkeley: University of California Press, 1993.

Waley, Arthur, ed. and trans. *The Book of Songs.* 1937. Reprint, New York: Grove Press, 1960.

Washburn, Dennis. "Ghostwriters and Literary Haunts: Subordinating Ethics to Art in *Ugetsu Monogatari.*" *Monumenta Nipponica* 45, no. 1 (1990): 39–74.

Watson, Burton, trans. *Chuang Tzu: Basic Writings.* New York: Columbia University Press, 1964.

Watson, Burton, trans. *The Lotus Sutra.* New York: Columbia University Press, 1993.

Wilson, William R., trans. *Hōgen Monogatari: Tale of the Disorder in Hōgen.* Cornell East Asia Series, no. 99. Ithaca, N.Y.: East Asia Program, Cornell University, 2001. [Includes a translation of the *Senjūshō* (*Selected Stories*) tale "The Grave of the Shin-in at Shiramine," from which Akinari drew material for "Shiramine"]

Yoshida Kenkō. *Essays in Idleness: The "Tsurezuregusa" of Kenkō.* Translated by Donald Keene. New York: Columbia University Press, 1967.

Young, Blake Morgan. *Ueda Akinari.* Vancouver: University of British Columbia Press, 1982.

Zeitlin, Judith T. *Historian of the Strange: Pu Songling and the Chinese Classical Tale.* Stanford, Calif.: Stanford University Press, 1993.

PREVIOUS ENGLISH TRANSLATIONS OF AKINARI

Allen, Lewis, trans. "'The Chrysanthemum Vow,' from the *Ugetsu Monogatari* (1776) by Ueda Akinari." *Durham University Journal,* n.s., 28, no. 2 (1967): 108–116.

Blacker, Carmen, and W. E. Skillend, trans. "Muo no rigyo (The Dream Carp)." In F. T. Daniels, ed., *Selections from Japanese Literature (12th to 19th Centuries),* pp. 91–103, 164–171. London: Lund Humphries, 1959.

Chambers, Anthony, trans. "The Chrysanthemum Vow," "The Reed-Choked House," and "A Serpent's Lust." In Haruo Shirane, ed., *Early Modern Japanese Literature: An Anthology, 1600–1900,* pp. 567–598. New York: Columbia University Press, 2002. [Earlier versions of my translations of these three stories]

Chambers, Anthony, trans. "Hankai: A Translation from *Harusame monogatari.*" *Monumenta Nipponica* 25, no. 3 (1970): 371–406.

Chatani, Hiroshi, trans. "The Pot at Kibitsu" and "The Blue Hood." Available at: http://www.kcc.zaq.ne.jp/dfeea307/.

Hamada, Kengi, trans. *Tales of Moonlight and Rain: Japanese Gothic Tales.* Tokyo: University of Tokyo Press, 1971; New York: Columbia University Press, 1972.

Hansey, Alf, trans. "The Blue Hood." *The Young East* 2, no. 9 (1927): 314–319.

Hearn, Lafcadio, trans. "Of a Promise Kept" (Kikka no chigiri) and "The Story of Kogi" (Muō no rigyō). In *The Writings of Lafcadio Hearn*, pp. 193–198, 230–237. Boston: Houghton Mifflin, 1922.

Jackman, Barry, trans. *Tales of the Spring Rain.* Tokyo: University of Tokyo Press, 1975; New York: Columbia University Press, 1979.

Richie, Donald. "The Ghoul-Priest: A Commentary." In *Zen Inklings: Some Stories, Fables, Parables, Sermons, and Prints*, pp. 79–90. New York: Weatherhill, 1982. [On "The Blue Hood"]

Sasaki, Takamasa, trans. *Ueda Akinari's Tales of a Rain'd Moon.* Tokyo: Hokuseido, 1981.

Saunders, Dale, trans. "*Ugetsu Monogatari*, or Tales of Moonlight and Rain." *Monumenta Nipponica* 21, nos. 1–2 (1966): 171–202. [Includes "Author's Preface," "The Chrysanthemum Tryst," "Buppōsō," and "The Blue Hood"]

Seitz, Don C., ed. "The Carp in a Dream." In *Monogatari: Tales from Old and New Japan*, pp. 106–112. New York: Putnam, 1924.

Sibley, William F., trans. "The Blue Cowl." In Stephen D. Miller, ed., *Partings at Dawn: An Anthology of Japanese Gay Literature*, pp. 125–133. San Francisco: Gay Sunshine Press, 1996.

Ueda, Makoto, trans. "A Blue Hood." *San Francisco Review* 1, no. 4 (1960): 42–47.

Whitehouse, Wilfrid, trans. "'Shiramine': A Translation with Comments." *Monumenta Nipponica* 1, no. 1 (1938): 242–258.

Whitehouse, Wilfrid, trans. "*Ugetsu Monogatari*: Tales of a Clouded Moon." *Monumenta Nipponica* 1, no. 2 (1938): 549–567. [Includes "Asajigayado (The Cottage in the Wilderness)" and "Binfukuron (An Argument on Wealth)"]

Whitehouse, Wilfrid, trans. "*Ugetsu Monogatari*: Tales of a Clouded Moon." *Monumenta Nipponica* 4, no. 1 (1941): 166–191. [Includes "Jasei no In (The Passion of a Snake)" and "Kibitsu no Kama (The Kibitsu Cauldron)"]

Zolbrod, Leon M., trans. and ed. *Ugetsu Monogatari: Tales of Moonlight and Rain: A Complete English Version of the Eighteenth-Century Japanese Collection of Tales of the Supernatural.* Vancouver: University of British Columbia Press, 1974.

Translations from the Asian Classics

Major Plays of Chikamatsu, tr. Donald Keene 1961

Four Major Plays of Chikamatsu, tr. Donald Keene. Paperback ed. only. 1961; rev. ed. 1997

Records of the Grand Historian of China, translated from the Shih chi of Ssu-ma Ch'ien, tr. Burton Watson, 2 vols. 1961

Instructions for Practical Living and Other Neo-Confucian Writings by Wang Yang-ming, tr. Wing-tsit Chan 1963

Hsün Tzu: Basic Writings, tr. Burton Watson, paperback ed. only. 1963; rev. ed. 1996

Chuang Tzu: Basic Writings, tr. Burton Watson, paperback ed. only. 1964; rev. ed. 1996

The Mahābhārata, tr. Chakravarthi V. Narasimhan. Also in paperback ed. 1965; rev. ed. 1997

The Manyōshū, Nippon Gakujutsu Shinkōkai edition 1965

Su Tung-p'o: Selections from a Sung Dynasty Poet, tr. Burton Watson. Also in paperback ed. 1965

Bhartrihari: Poems, tr. Barbara Stoler Miller. Also in paperback ed. 1967

Basic Writings of Mo Tzu, Hsün Tzu, and Han Fei Tzu, tr. Burton Watson. Also in separate paperback eds. 1967

The Awakening of Faith, Attributed to Aśvaghosha, tr. Yoshito S. Hakeda. Also in paperback ed. 1967

Reflections on Things at Hand: The Neo-Confucian Anthology, comp. Chu Hsi and Lü Tsu-ch'ien, tr. Wing-tsit Chan 1967

The Platform Sutra of the Sixth Patriarch, tr. Philip B. Yampolsky. Also in paperback ed. 1967

Original Tao: Inward Training (Nei-yeh) *and the Foundations of Taoist Mysticism*, by Harold D. Roth 1999

Lao Tzu's Tao Te Ching: *A Translation of the Startling New Documents Found at Guodian*, by Robert G. Henricks 2000

The Shorter Columbia Anthology of Traditional Chinese Literature, ed. Victor H. Mair 2000

Mistress and Maid (Jiaohongji), by Meng Chengshun, tr. Cyril Birch 2001

Chikamatsu: Five Late Plays, tr. and ed. C. Andrew Gerstle 2001

The Essential Lotus: Selections from the Lotus Sutra, tr. Burton Watson 2002

Early Modern Japanese Literature: An Anthology, 1600–1900, ed. Haruo Shirane 2002

The Sound of the Kiss, or The Story That Must Never Be Told: Pingali Suranna's Kalapurnodayamu, tr. Vecheru Narayana Rao and David Shulman 2003

The Selected Poems of Du Fu, tr. Burton Watson 2003

Far Beyond the Field: Haiku by Japanese Women, tr. Makoto Ueda 2003

Just Living: Poems and Prose by the Japanese Monk Tonna, ed. and tr. Steven D. Carter 2003

Han Feizi: Basic Writings, tr. Burton Watson 2003

Mozi: Basic Writings, tr. Burton Watson 2003

Xunzi: Basic Writings, tr. Burton Watson 2003

Zhuangzi: Basic Writings, tr. Burton Watson 2003

The Awakening of Faith, Attributed to Aśvaghosha, tr. Yoshito S. Hakeda, introduction by Ryuichi Abe 2005

The Tales of the Heike, tr. Burton Watson, ed. Haruo Shirane 2006

Modern Asian Literature

Modern Japanese Drama: An Anthology, ed. and tr. Ted. Takaya. Also in paperback ed. 1979

Mask and Sword: Two Plays for the Contemporary Japanese Theater, by Yamazaki Masakazu, tr. J. Thomas Rimer 1980

Yokomitsu Riichi, Modernist, by Dennis Keene 1980

Nepali Visions, Nepali Dreams: The Poetry of Laxmiprasad Devkota, tr. David Rubin 1980

Literature of the Hundred Flowers, vol. 1: *Criticism and Polemics*, ed. Hualing Nieh 1981

Literature of the Hundred Flowers, vol. 2: *Poetry and Fiction*, ed. Hualing Nieh 1981

Modern Chinese Stories and Novellas, 1919–1949, ed. Joseph S. M. Lau, C. T. Hsia, and Leo Ou-fan Lee. Also in paperback ed. 1984

A View by the Sea, by Yasuoka Shōtarō, tr. Kären Wigen Lewis 1984

Other Worlds: Arishima Takeo and the Bounds of Modern Japanese Fiction, by Paul Anderer 1984

Selected Poems of Sŏ Chŏngju, tr. with introduction by David R. McCann 1989

The Sting of Life: Four Contemporary Japanese Novelists, by Van C. Gessel 1989

Stories of Osaka Life, by Oda Sakunosuke, tr. Burton Watson 1990

The Bodhisattva, or Samantabhadra, by Ishikawa Jun, tr. with introduction by William Jefferson Tyler 1990

The Travels of Lao Ts'an, by Liu T'ieh-yün, tr. Harold Shadick. Morningside ed. 1990

Three Plays by Kōbō Abe, tr. with introduction by Donald Keene 1993

The Columbia Anthology of Modern Chinese Literature, ed. Joseph S. M. Lau and Howard Goldblatt 1995

Modern Japanese Tanka, ed. and tr. Makoto Ueda 1996

Masaoka Shiki: Selected Poems, ed. and tr. Burton Watson 1997

Writing Women in Modern China: An Anthology of Women's Literature from the Early Twentieth Century, ed. and tr. Amy D. Dooling and Kristina M. Torgeson 1998

American Stories, by Nagai Kafū, tr. Mitsuko Iriye 2000

The Paper Door and Other Stories, by Shiga Naoya, tr. Lane Dunlop 2001

Grass for My Pillow, by Saiichi Maruya, tr. Dennis Keene 2002

For All My Walking: Free-Verse Haiku of Taneda Santōka, with Excerpts from His Diaries, tr. Burton Watson 2003

The Columbia Anthology of Modern Japanese Literature, vol 1: *From Restoration to Occupation, 1868–1945*, ed. J. Thomas Rimer and Van C. Gessel 2005

Studies in Asian Culture

The Ōnin War: History of Its Origins and Background, with a Selective Translation of the Chronicle of Ōnin, by H. Paul Varley 1967

Chinese Government in Ming Times: Seven Studies, ed. Charles O. Hucker 1969

The Actors' Analects (Yakusha Rongo), ed. and tr. Charles J. Dunn and Bungō Torigoe 1969

Self and Society in Ming Thought, by Wm. Theodore de Bary and the Conference on Ming Thought. Also in paperback ed. 1970

A History of Islamic Philosophy, by Majid Fakhry, 2d ed. 1983

Phantasies of a Love Thief: The Caurapañcāśikā Attributed to Bilhaṇa, by Barbara Stoler Miller 1971

Iqbal: Poet-Philosopher of Pakistan, ed. Hafeez Malik 1971

The Golden Tradition: An Anthology of Urdu Poetry, ed. and tr. Ahmed Ali. Also in paperback ed. 1973

Conquerors and Confucians: Aspects of Political Change in Late Yüan China, by John W. Dardess 1973

The Unfolding of Neo-Confucianism, by Wm. Theodore de Bary and the Conference on Seventeenth-Century Chinese Thought. Also in paperback ed. 1975

To Acquire Wisdom: The Way of Wang Yang-ming, by Julia Ching 1976

Gods, Priests, and Warriors: The Bhrgus of the Mahābhārata, by Robert P. Goldman 1977

Mei Yao-ch'en and the Development of Early Sung Poetry, by Jonathan Chaves 1976

The Legend of Semimaru, Blind Musician of Japan, by Susan Matisoff 1977

Sir Sayyid Ahmad Khan and Muslim Modernization in India and Pakistan, by Hafeez Malik 1980

The Khilafat Movement: Religious Symbolism and Political Mobilization in India, by Gail Minault 1982

The World of K'ung Shang-jen: A Man of Letters in Early Ch'ing China, by Richard Strassberg 1983

The Lotus Boat: The Origins of Chinese Tz'u Poetry in T'ang Popular Culture, by Marsha L. Wagner 1984

Expressions of Self in Chinese Literature, ed. Robert E. Hegel and Richard C. Hessney 1985

Songs for the Bride: Women's Voices and Wedding Rites of Rural India, by W. G. Archer; ed. Barbara Stoler Miller and Mildred Archer 1986

The Confucian Kingship in Korea: Yŏngjo and the Politics of Sagacity, by JaHyun Kim Haboush 1988

Companions to Asian Studies

Approaches to the Oriental Classics, ed. Wm. Theodore de Bary 1959

Early Chinese Literature, by Burton Watson. Also in paperback ed. 1962

Approaches to Asian Civilizations, ed. Wm. Theodore de Bary and Ainslie T. Embree 1964

The Classic Chinese Novel: A Critical Introduction, by C. T. Hsia. Also in paperback ed. 1968

Chinese Lyricism: Shih Poetry from the Second to the Twelfth Century, tr. Burton Watson. Also in paperback ed. 1971

A Syllabus of Indian Civilization, by Leonard A. Gordon and Barbara Stoler Miller 1971

Twentieth-Century Chinese Stories, ed. C. T. Hsia and Joseph S. M. Lau. Also in paperback ed. 1971

A Syllabus of Chinese Civilization, by J. Mason Gentzler, 2d ed. 1972

A Syllabus of Japanese Civilization, by H. Paul Varley, 2d ed. 1972

An Introduction to Chinese Civilization, ed. John Meskill, with the assistance of J. Mason Gentzler 1973

An Introduction to Japanese Civilization, ed. Arthur E. Tiedemann 1974

Ukifune: Love in the Tale of Genji, ed. Andrew Pekarik 1982

The Pleasures of Japanese Literature, by Donald Keene 1988

A Guide to Oriental Classics, ed. Wm. Theodore de Bary and Ainslie T. Embree; 3d edition ed. Amy Vladeck Heinrich, 2 vols. 1989

Introduction to Asian Civilizations

WM. THEODORE DE BARY, GENERAL EDITOR

Sources of Japanese Tradition, 1958; paperback ed., 2 vols., 1964. 2d ed., vol. 1, 2001, compiled by Wm. Theodore de Bary, Donald Keene, George Tanabe,

Neo-Confucian Studies